A PRIVATE WALTZ

Harriet sought refuge in polite conversation. "It was a very nice ball. The Hatterlees seemed pleased with their turnout."

"Yes." Marcus nodded equally polite agreement.

"The music was exceptional. I think I might have danced the night away."

Marcus set his glass down and rose, extending his hand. "Come, Harriet, dance with me now."

Laughing nervously, she allowed him to pull her to her feet. "But, Marcus, we have no music."

"We shall make our own music." He took her in his arms and began to hum. "Come," he encouraged her. "Join me."

She added her low voice to his in nonsense syllables of the piece to which they had danced earlier. She had no idea how long they danced about the room in tight but graceful little steps. She was lost in the sheer presence of this man. Had she really dreamed of this moment her whole life? Their feet slowed and finally stopped.

"Harriet?" he whispered. He put a finger under her chin to lift her face to his. His mouth settled on hers in a kiss that was exquisitely sweet. . . .

Books by Wilma Counts

WILLED TO WED

MY LADY GOVERNESS

THE WILLFUL MISS WINTHROP

THE WAGERED WIFE

THE TROUBLE WITH HARRIET

Published by Zebra Books

THE TROUBLE WITH HARRIET

Wilma Counts

ZEBRA BOOKS
Kensington Publishing Corp.
http://www.zebrabooks.com

ZEBRA BOOKS are published by

Kensington Publishing Corp.
850 Third Avenue
New York, NY 10022

All Kensington titles, imprints, and distributed lines are available at special quantity discounts for bulk purchases for sales
promotion, premiums, fund-raising, educational or institutional
use.

Special book excerpts or customized printings can also be created to fit specific needs. For details, write or phone the office
of the Kensington Special Sales Manager: Kensington Publishing Corp., 850 Third Avenue, New York, NY 10022. Attn. Special Sales Department. Phone: 1-800-221-2647.

Zebra and the Z logo Reg. U.S. Pat. & TM Off.

First Printing: July 2001
10 9 8 7 6 5 4 3 2 1

Printed in the United States of America

Prologue

Autumn, 1802

Miss Harriet Glasser tucked an errant curl behind her ear and took a last look at herself in the cheval glass. Peach-colored sarcenet draped loosely around her underdeveloped figure.

"What do you think?" she asked her sister, Charlotte, who had flung herself across Harriet's bed to watch with envy the "great preparations."

"It is a very pretty gown," Charlotte said tentatively.

"But . . . ? You do not like it?"

"The color is too bland for you. I am sure it suited Mama when the gown was new."

Trust Chal to say exactly what she thought, Harriet mused. Aloud, she said, "Well—beggars cannot be choosers. What if I add this green sash and a green ribbon in my hair?"

"That would help," Charlotte agreed. Then her face puckered into the pout she had worn off and on for a week. "I still do not see why Papa and Mama are allowing *you* to go to the Wyndham ball but will not condone my going."

"You know very well—because I am the older." It came out more smug than she intended.

Charlotte sniffed. "Three years!"

"Three years can seem a long time from your

eleven to my fourteen," Harriet said more gently. "And even so, were this not a country affair, I doubt I should be allowed to go. The rules are more relaxed so far from London."

Charlotte returned to her scrutiny of the gown. "Perhaps if you stuffed handkerchiefs in the bosom, it would help."

"Certainly not! Mama would have the vapors."

"Then be sure to remember to keep your shoulders back."

"I just hope someone asks me to dance."

"They will." Charlotte was reassuring. "The twins are home, and they brought Jason with them again— Melanie told me even before we saw them all at church."

Harriet did not say anything. It was not the twins, Trevor and Terrence, who dominated her day-dreams—despite their being of an age with her—and devastatingly handsome as well. Nor was it their friend Jason. No. It was one of the twins' older brothers with whom Harriet yearned to dance.

Marcus. Marcus, whose mere presence on the street in the village would send her heart racing. Marcus, who had caught her fancy some five years before, when he had rescued her kitten from a tree. Marcus, who at seventeen had been young manhood in perfection and now seemed to have gone beyond perfection.

Now that she was all grown up, surely Marcus would notice her. Surely he would sense the fateful tie that pulled them together. He would take her by the hand and lead her out to the terrace. He would tell her she was beautiful and then kiss her in a most tender and romantic way and ask if he might speak with her father. . . .

"She is at it again," Charlotte announced with disgust to the maid, Maggie, who was tying the ribbon in

Harriet's hair. "Cinderella is dreaming of her prince again."

"And what prince would that be, Miss Know-All?" Harriet wondered if Charlotte did know. Somehow her younger sister always seemed to know far more than anyone wanted her to know.

"Jason Garriton, of course. I saw you acting the mooncalf over him on Sunday last."

Harriet shrugged and smiled inwardly. For once nosy Charlotte had been fooled. Jason had been standing right next to Marcus.

Charlotte climbed down from the bed. "Please do not wake me when you come in. I can wait until morning to hear all about a ball I am not allowed to attend. But—mind you, do not forget any of the details!" With that, she flounced out of the room.

Harriet could hardly contain her excitement in the carriage as she and her parents journeyed the short distance to Timberly, the most majestic dwelling in all the district. Timberly, principal seat of the powerful Earl of Wyndham, had been a well-fortified castle in former times. Even now it conjured romantic notions of knights and fair ladies, Harriet thought. As she and her parents entered the Great Hall, where musicians already played softly, she was struck by the grandeur.

The room was huge. Rising two stories to its beamed ceiling, it had a gallery at the level of the first story that ran the length of one long wall and was supported by large Greek-style pillars. Two large chandeliers of brass and crystal shed light to glitter from several mirrors, windows, and pieces of metal armor around the room. Tapestries dominated either end.

The centerpiece of the hall was a huge painting that hung above the fireplace on the wall opposite the gallery. It was a portrait of the present earl and his family made some years earlier. Each of the figures in the painting was life-sized. Harriet's attention was immediately drawn to the image of the second son—Marcus.

Then she caught sight of the earl, his wife, and two elder sons in a receiving line formed strategically beneath the portrait. Harriet wondered if the countess had planned it that way. There stood Marcus, tall and handsome. Her heart did a flip-flop, and she caught her breath.

As the line of guests inched forward, she was aware of only one being in the whole room. Him. Then she was right before him and actually being presented to *him*. She raised her gaze to his blue-gray eyes as he took her hand ever so briefly and nodded politely. Did he, too, feel that lightning-like shock as their hands touched? She quickly lowered her gaze, and then she was rudely moved on by the person behind her as *he* greeted the next guest.

Her father joined a cluster of gentlemen. Harriet and her mother took places with a group of women and young girls along the sidelines. Harriet noted that mothers and daughters alike seemed intent on being noticed while seeking to appear as though they had no interest in being noticed.

When the receiving line broke up, the musicians swung into a stately dance and the earl led his countess to the floor. Soon other couples joined them to make up the figures of the dance. Harriet watched enviously as several young ladies somewhat older than she were asked to join the growing number of dancers.

She continued to watch enviously through two more sets. Still, no one asked *her* to dance. She found it increasingly difficult to appear interested in the conversations around her—forced conversations on "made-up," innocuous topics. She tried to keep a smile pasted on her face, though she felt it slip from time to time, especially when she saw Marcus Jeffries lead other women to the floor. She pretended to be watching—and enjoying watching—all the dancers, but she really saw only one of them.

She was miserable and wanted more than anything to be back at home, where she could freely sob out her misery into her pillow. She watched stoically as the fourth set was forming, then she felt a movement at her elbow.

"Miss Glasser? May I have this dance?" That voice. *His* voice. Unable to quell the joy she knew must show in her eyes, she kept her gaze lowered as she extended her hand. "With your mother's permission, of course," he added.

Harriet felt rather than heard her mother's acquiescence, and Marcus guided her onto the dance floor. None of the sparkling wit with which she had imagined herself capturing his attention and affection materialized. Her brain refused to function—though other parts of her anatomy seemed to have accelerated at his closeness.

"Have you enjoyed the Harvest Festival this year, Miss Glasser?" His tone sounded surprisingly ordinary to her ears.

"What? Oh. I beg your pardon. Yes. Yes, I have— very much, Mr. Jeffries." She groped for a more suitable response—or for another topic. Ah. His studies. "I—I understand you have been studying law, sir."

"Yes, I have. For nearly two years now. I shall finish soon."

"So you plan to be a barrister or a solicitor?"

"Probably neither. I am inclined toward the diplomatic corps."

"Oh, I see," she said vaguely as the steps of the dance separated them. The diplomatic corps? What did she know of the diplomatic corps? Ah, yes. Travel. "Does that mean you would travel abroad?" She glanced at him only briefly as they came together again.

"Possibly. I should hope to travel at any rate."

Both were silent for a few turns, then Marcus asked, "Do you still have that kitten I helped you rescue? Though it must be a full-grown cat now."

"Yes. I still have Petruchio."

"Petruchio? That is your *cat's* name?"

"Well . . . yes. He is so very saucy and arrogant, you see."

He laughed aloud, and suddenly it was over. He returned her to her mother and bowed.

"Thank you, Miss Glasser."

"I enjoyed the dance," she said, looking at him directly, and quickly away.

Then he was gone. Oh! But *he* had remembered her!

Later in the evening she was returning from the ladies' withdrawing room. As she paused behind one of the pillars supporting the gallery, she was aware that Marcus and his older brother, Gerald, stood on the other side of it. She lingered, savoring the bliss of being even this near him.

"Noticed you out there with Sefton's chit," Gerald was saying. "Doing the pretty with the wallflowers, were you?"

Harriet drew in a breath, awaiting Marcus's response.

"Not exactly" was his terse reply.

Gerald sniffed. "You *do* know, of course, that the Viscount Sefton hasn't a feather to fly with?"

Behind the pillar Harriet blushed with embarrassment at this bald assessment of her family's finances.

"And what might that have to do with my having danced once with his daughter?"

"Perhaps nothing," Gerald sad airily. "But you *are* aware that as our father's *second* son, you will eventually have to hang out for an heiress?"

"Oh, for—"

Gerald interrupted with a mirthless laugh. "Unless you are looking for a bit of dalliance during your holiday. But in that case, you should not run the risk of trifling with someone of our own class who is so decidedly unsuitable."

"You allow your imagination to roam too freely, dear brother." Marcus's voice had an edge to it that even the eavesdropping Harriet recognized. "I merely danced with the young lady. Had I dalliance—or marriage—in mind, I would not be looking to a schoolroom miss for such."

"You always were one for picking up strays." Gerald's sneering tone was apparently meant to hurt.

"There are worse things to be." Marcus turned on his heel and left.

Soon Gerald strolled off too, and Harriet remained seething behind the pillar.

"Schoolroom miss," indeed! Here she was—practically a woman grown, and the man to whom she had thought to bestow her heart merely felt sorry for a "stray." What an amazing display of insufferable arrogance! How she regretted now all those months—even years—of dreaming of a grand passion with one Marcus Jeffries!

I shall certainly contrive to forget *you*, Mr. High-and-Mighty!

One

October, 1816

Marcus Quentin Jeffries, Earl of Wyndham, frowned at the sound of a knock on his library door. Had he not given strict instructions he was not to be disturbed until he had dealt with the papers piling up inexorably on his desk?

"Come." He forced a neutral tone.

Heston, the butler who had served both previous earls—Marcus's father and brother—stood in the doorway. "My lord, I apologize, but there is a woman—a lady—and her . . . her charge—urgently requesting audience with you."

"Who is she? And what does she want?"

"A Mrs. Hepplewhite. She says the girl with her is your ward."

"My *what*?"

"Your ward, sir."

"Heston, do you know anything of a ward?" Marcus had, in the last few months, often found it necessary to have servants and retainers fill him in on his new responsibilities as earl.

Heston shook his head. "No, my lord."

Marcus laid down his pen and sighed inwardly. "All right. Show them in."

A few minutes later Marcus stood at the entrance

of the library as a middle-aged woman and a young girl were shown in. The woman was dressed soberly in a brown traveling outfit that was definitely not the first stare of fashion. The girl was young—fourteen or fifteen, Marcus surmised. Her hair was the color of rich honey, and she, too, was attired in rather unfashionable apparel.

"Mrs. Winston Hepplewhite and Miss Annabelle Richardson, my lord," Heston intoned.

"Mrs. Hepplewhite. Miss Richardson." Marcus gestured to two chairs in front of the desk and reseated himself behind it. He hoped to make short work of this interruption. "How may I help you?"

Mrs. Hepplewhite cleared her throat. "I have come to deliver your charge back to you, my lord."

The girl sat rigidly with a defiant air, refusing to meet his gaze when he looked at her.

"I fear there has been some mistake," Marcus began. "I have no ward."

"It was an Earl of Wyndham who delivered Miss Richardson to us, and it is the Earl of Wyndham to whom she is being returned." The woman's tone was clipped, adamant.

"We?" Marcus lifted one brow in what he hoped was an imperious manner.

"I am headmistress of the Lady Adelaide Chesterton-Jones School for Young Ladies."

"I see." Marcus glanced toward the girl again. "I assume Miss Richardson is a pupil in your school?"

"Was."

He lifted the eyebrow again.

"She *was* a pupil in our school. But her deportment is such that we no longer may tolerate her deleterious effect on the other girls, especially the younger ones." Mrs. Hepplewhite emphasized this little speech by subtly but visibly distancing herself from the girl in the chair next to her.

Miss Richardson rolled her eyes heavenward and shrugged.

"I fail to see what this has to do with me," Marcus began. "Surely her parents—" He caught himself and turned his attention full on the girl. "I beg your pardon, Miss Richardson. It is rude of us to be discussing you in such a callous manner."

He saw Mrs. Hepplewhite color up at this, but the girl turned a surprised pair of brown eyes on him, then dipped him a regal little bow of the head but said nothing.

"Miss Richardson's parents are both deceased, my lord. They were unfortunately killed when their ship was attacked by a French warship on their return from the West Indies."

"And how long ago did this mishap occur?"

Marcus had addressed the question to the young Miss Richardson, but it was Mrs. Hepplewhite who responded. "Three years ago. Annabelle was brought to London by a governess, who left her in the care of . . . your father, I believe."

"Why? Are we somehow related?" Marcus asked the girl.

"Answer his lordship," the older woman said sharply.

"I do not know, sir." The response was on the nether side of civility.

"Mrs. Hepplewhite?"

"Our records show only that she was in our care under the auspices of the Earl of Wyndham. And we are terminating the arrangement for cause. It is all here. You may see for yourself." She pulled out a sheaf of papers and stood to place them on the desk. "Now, if you will excuse me, I must be going."

Marcus had risen when Mrs. Hepplewhite stood and now watched in astonishment as the woman made to leave.

"What—? Now, see here, madam, you cannot just leave her here like—like some foundling!"

"You *are* the Earl of Wyndham?"

"Yes, but—"

"Then she is your responsibility. We at the Chesterton-Jones school have had quite enough of dealing with an incorrigible." She marched out of the room with Marcus on her heels.

"Wait," he called, and took fleeting notice of several articles of luggage piled in the entrance way.

"Good day, my lord." Mrs. Hepplewhite waved airily and was out the door that the surprised butler had hurriedly opened for her.

"Oh, good grief," Marcus muttered. "Heston, get Mrs. Benson in here immediately." He gestured toward the library, which—until a few moments before—he had considered a sanctuary of sorts.

As he reentered the room, leaving the door ajar, he thought he saw Miss Richardson dab a handkerchief at her face and sit straighter. She glanced at him, then away. He took a seat behind the desk, picked up his pen, dipped it, and began a hasty note.

"You cannot force me to stay here." The voice was quiet but tinged with rebellion and uncertainty.

"Nor would I wish to do so," he said, not bothering to hide his irony. "However, neither can I turn a young person such as you out on the street." He thought she seemed to relax a bit at this.

There was a soft rap at the open door. "My lord? You wished to see me?" his housekeeper asked.

"Yes." He stood and gestured toward the girl. "Mrs. Benson, this is Miss Richardson. She will be a guest at Wyndham House. Will you see to her accommodation, please?"

"Very good, my lord." The housekeeper's lips tightened in obvious disapproval of this female addition to a bachelor household.

Marcus grinned at the housekeeper and addressed

her with easy familiarity, for Mrs. Benson, too, had served both previous earls and had watched Marcus and his siblings grow up. "And before you allow your sensibilities to become too ruffled, please send a footman to Lady Hermiston with this note." He stood and handed her the paper. "You will need to see a room prepared for her as well. Oh. And send in some tea, please."

"Very good, my lord." The response came this time with an approving smile.

Marcus picked up the papers Mrs. Hepplewhite had left, but instead of resuming his seat behind the desk, he directed his guest to one of two wing chairs next to a marble-topped table in another part of the room.

"Now, Miss Richardson, suppose you tell me as much as you know of the circumstances that brought you here." He spoke in a conversational tone that had once invited confidences from diplomats.

She chewed at her lower lip. "Truly, my lord, it was not I who was at fault this time."

"*This* time?"

"I admitted to trading the sugar for salt at the headmistress's table. And it *was* I who put the snake on Miss Manson's bed. But it was only a harmless grass snake, and it was *dead*, you see, but no one else would touch it, so I was the one to do it."

Marcus felt his lips twitching and looked down at the papers in his hand. "Hmm. Secret meetings after lights were extinguished? Unsuitable reading materials?"

She seemed to squirm a bit at this. "Well, you see, Letty and I had a larger room than the others—she being a duke's daughter, you know—so naturally the others came to our room."

"The others?" Marcus prompted.

"Our special friends. There were six of us, but when Catherine squealed just as the evil count was about to grab the fair maiden, it woke that horrid Belinda in the next room and she snitched on us—I mean, she *informed* on us—and I am sure she did so because none of us could tolerate her superior airs. That is when Mrs. Hepplewhite discovered it."

"It?"

"The book." She looked at him impatiently. "The novel."

"You brought a novel into the school?"

"No. Letty did. But as her mother would positively have the vapors over such, we allowed Mrs. Hepplewhite to believe I had done it—for I've no family to care, you see." She said this very matter-of-factly.

"So you lied?"

The squirming was more pronounced. "Not precisely. She just assumed it was I and not the duke's daughter because I was the one reading aloud when she came in."

"Hmm," Marcus mumbled, trying to sort this out as the girl babbled on.

"Oh, it was so good! All about this count who turned into a monster during a full moon and—"

Just then a footman came in bearing a tea tray, which he set on the table between them.

"Ooh. Apricot tarts. My favorites," Miss Richardson said, and then seemed to recall her training as a young lady. She sat back and folded her hands.

Marcus smiled and gestured to the servant to pour the tea. "Help yourself, Miss Richardson. I am partial to apricot tarts myself."

They sat in comfortable silence for a moment, Marcus savoring the tea as he glanced through more of the papers. He looked up when he realized the girl was talking again.

"—we were not even allowed to finish the story," she lamented.

"Yes. Well. It would appear that the novel—while iniquitous enough in the eyes of Mrs. Hepplewhite—was not your worst offense."

"Wha-what do you mean, my lord?"

"According to this," he said, reading, "you also 'introduced wantonly salacious material including both drawings and text that were shockingly unsuitable for any young lady at the Chesterton-Jones school.' Can you explain that?"

"Oh." It was a little squeak. She carefully replaced the tart she had been about to bite into. "Oh, dear."

He waited, letting the silence do far more than words could.

"That—that must refer to the pamphlet found under my mattress."

"Pamphlet," he prodded.

She blushed and looked away. "I . . . uh . . . It—"

Suddenly, he knew. The same sort of reading matter fascinated adolescent boys, if memory served. He was somewhat surprised to find a young girl with access to such, though. He cleared his throat. "A pamphlet dealing with the most intimate matters between men and women, I gather?"

Her blush deepened. "Yes, sir."

"Where did *you* obtain such literature?"

"Letty found it behind the armoire when she moved into her sister's room after Lady Pamela was married."

"Letty again. Letty sounds a remarkably cowardly sort to lay the blame on you all the time."

"No! She is not." Miss Richardson defended her friend vehemently. "It was just that—well, you see, Letty is Lady Letitia Atkinson. Her father is the Duke of Turlington, and he is very strict, and Letty is so very afraid of him. Letty said even Mrs. Hepplewhite seemed afraid of the duke. Truly, we did not think it would come to expulsion—and heaven knows the school could not inform *my* father, so . . ." Her voice trailed off, and she sat with a worried look. "You . . . you will not inform the duke, will you?"

"What? No. No, of course not."

They sat silently—she seemingly nervous and apprehensive, he thoughtful. He finished his tea and set the cup down deliberately.

"Well, Miss Richardson, you have presented me with quite a dilemma."

"I *am* sorry, my lord."

"I shall have it sorted out in due time," he said with far more confidence than he felt. "In the meantime, you will be a guest here."

"H-here?"

He recognized her trepidation. "Yes. Here. You will be taken care of properly. My aunt, Lady Hermiston, will arrive shortly to lend propriety to your being at Wyndham House."

She sat with greater ease at this. "Thank you, my lord."

"I shall have someone show you to your room." He rose, tugged on a bellpull, and added, "I assume you can entertain yourself until dinner?"

"Oh, yes, my lord."

"You will find much that is soberly edifying in this collection," he said, making a sweeping gesture of the ample library and keeping his expression bland. "There is even a novel or two, I believe."

She blushed, then grinned impishly. "Thank you, my lord."

A maid arrived to lead her above stairs.

An hour later Marcus sat in front of a desk piled high with paperwork. Looks as though my misery has found good company, he said to himself. Aloud, he said to Mr. Dickinson, his solicitor, "I apologize for barging in on you with no notice."

"Not at all, my lord." The balding, portly man had just reseated himself after greeting the man Marcus knew—with no pretension of false modesty—to be the lawyer's most important client.

Marcus explained the purpose of the visit and related the events of the morning.

"Yes." Dickinson shifted in his chair. "I remember very well the earl's part in dealing with the Richardson offspring. However, I believe there was another party—it was to be a joint guardianship. Allow me to check the records." He gave a short jerk on a bellpull behind the desk. Almost immediately a young clerk poked his head in the door.

"Yes, sir?"

"Go into the vault and bring me the file on the Richardson guardianship—in the cabinet containing the Wyndham papers."

Presently the young man returned and laid a thick folder before his employer. "Here you are, sir."

Dickinson leafed through the folder. "Ah-hah. Here it is." Peering over his glasses, he handed some papers to Marcus. "As you can see, my lord, the guardianship was shared between your father and a Mr. Raymond Knightly. Apparently the earl and Mr. Knightly were longtime friends of Miss Richardson's father."

"Knightly? I do not recall either that name or Richardson's."

"They were school-fellows. I doubt your father had even seen Richardson in twenty years when that governess and her charge appeared on his doorstep. Richardson had amassed quite a fortune, and his will stipulated that it be held in trust for his daughter and supervised jointly by Wyndham and Knightly."

"So, she is an heiress." Marcus made a cursory examination of the papers that confirmed what Dickinson had outlined.

The solicitor held out another paper. "Here is a memorandum from Mr. Knightly approving your father's plan to put the child in a boarding school." Dickinson coughed politely. "Actually, I believe that plan was your mother's and had Lord Gerald's concurrence, for your father was quite ill at the time."

Marcus noted the dates. As a diplomat with the Foreign Office, he himself had been out of the country at the time. "It sounds the sort of solution they would seek." He kept his voice neutral, but his thoughts were bitter. Gerald and his mother had rid themselves of a nuisance with no thought of the child's loss. And what of this Knightly? He posed this question to the solicitor, who leafed through some more papers.

"Hmm. Nothing here," Dickinson said. "Only that memorandum with his approval." He turned over some more sheets. "Oh, this is interesting . . ."

"What?"

"A letter from Carton and James, Mr. Knightly's solicitors. It appears that Mr. Knightly died in 1814. He was in his late fifties and in poor health the last year or so. He left his widow in full control of everything."

"His domestic household, you mean."

"No, sir. Everything. The businesses, the country estate, a London town house, some charitable interests—everything! Most unusual for a woman to have such control."

"Or such expertise," Marcus said.

Dickinson nodded. "What that means—as I am sure you know, my lord—is that Mrs. Knightly must agree to any decision made on behalf of Miss Richardson."

Two

Despite its being well into the afternoon, Marcus was intent on meeting with Mrs. Knightly. Might as well get this over with, he told himself. The direction Dickinson had given him was in the Bloomsbury area, where several rich merchants had established town houses in recent years. The middle-aged widow of some cit would probably not find a call by a titled lord inconvenient, he thought—and then was immediately ashamed of the inherent arrogance of such an idea. Now, *that* was an attitude worthy of his predecessor, the inimitable Gerald.

He hoped the woman would not be one of those nervous, fluttery sorts who could never make a decision. All he really needed was that she agree to allowing *him* to see to Miss Richardson's affairs. He—on behalf of his family, who had ignored her—owed the girl that much. Besides, there was something about young Annabelle that called for protection.

"I shall see if Mrs. Knightly is available, my lord," a very proper butler of indeterminate years said as Marcus handed him a card along with his hat and walking stick. In a few moments the man returned and showed Marcus to a small drawing room on the first floor. As they climbed the stairs, Marcus could hear several voices raised in lively conversation. "Mrs. Knightly will be right with you, my lord."

"Thank you."

He laid his portfolio on a table, took a seat, and waited. It was a small room, tastefully decorated with comfortable furniture. He thought this must be a family drawing room. There were portraits on the walls, along with other paintings, and an opened basket of needlework on the floor near one chair. A number of books lay about with places clearly marked in them. He rose to look more closely at a certain landscape. Yes. It *was* one of Mr. Turner's works.

"That is one of my favorite paintings." It was a pleasant female voice from the doorway. "I am sorry to keep you waiting, Lord Wyn—" Her voice ended on a note of surprise.

He blinked at the vision before him. He had expected a middle-aged matron in black bombazine. Here was a lovely woman—probably midtwenties— with stylishly arranged light brown hair, intelligent hazel eyes, and a very modish deep blue gown that clung to a delectable figure.

The sound of applause and a babble of voices from another room brought him to his senses.

"I—I am sorry to intrude," he said. "And I meant to speak with Mrs. Knightly. Your mother, perhaps?"

She seemed to recover from her surprise and extended her hand with a smile. "I am Mrs. Knightly."

"Mrs. Raymond Knightly?"

"Yes."

He looked at her more closely. Something in the recesses of memory tried to assert itself. Marcus Jeffries, urbane diplomat, rarely forgot a face—and would certainly never have forgotten this one.

"My lord?" she asked curiously as he bent over her hand.

"Mrs. Knightly—I am embarrassed to ask this question of such a lovely woman, but—have we met before?"

Her laugh was a throaty chuckle. "Not in many years." He gave her a questioning look and she continued. "I was Miss Harriet Glasser." As he groped for the connection of the familiar name, she hurriedly rescued him. "My father was William Glasser, Viscount Sefton. He had a holding near Timberly."

"Ah, yes. Of course. And you had a kitten."

"Which you retrieved from a tree for me." She smiled, withdrew her hand, and assumed a business-like tone. "How may I help you, my lord?"

"I expect this to be a mere formality." His tone, too, was now very matter-of-fact. "I simply need you to sign a form releasing your interest in a ward we both seem to have inherited."

"I beg your pardon? I have no idea what you are talking about."

"Are you familiar with Miss Annabelle Richardson?"

"Nooo. I do not recall ever hearing the name."

"It came as a surprise to me as well," he said agreeably. He explained the situation as fully as he knew its legal particulars, omitting information about Annabelle's being expelled from school. No need to noise *that* about. He ended by saying, "And what I need from you, Mrs. Knightly, is merely your signature on this document so that I may properly see to Miss Richardson's affairs." He handed her a paper from the portfolio.

She had a mystified expression as she took the document and perused it silently. She handed it back to him.

"I am sorry, my lord. I cannot sign this. At least not right now."

"I fail to see what prevents your owing do. It is, after all, a mere formality."

"That may be so. But I shall want to consult my solicitor before signing away my responsibilities."

"But you did not even know of Miss Richardson's existence until a few moments ago!"

"That is true, but now that I do, I shall want to know fully what my duties may be to her. I am not in the habit of turning away from my responsibilities, sir."

He tried for a "reasonable" tone. "I had thought to see this matter handled more expeditiously." He picked up his portfolio and prepared to leave. "When may I expect to hear from you?"

"Tomorrow, I should think. Where is the child now?"

"At Wyndham House."

"I should, of course, like to meet her."

"As you wish, madam. We shall expect you tomorrow afternoon, then." He executed a polite bow and turned to leave.

"My lord?"

He turned back.

"Thank you for bringing this to my attention."

He gave her a clipped little nod and made his way down the stairs to retrieve his hat and walking stick.

Back on the street, he hailed a hackney and fumed about contrary women all the way home.

Harriet knew Lord Wyndham was annoyed as he left, but did he really expect that she would, willy-nilly, sign some paper without being fully apprised of what was involved? How like a man—well, most men—to deal thus with a woman.

She had been surprised when Phelps had brought a card from the Earl of Wyndham. Having given the card only a cursory glance, she had been even more surprised to see Marcus Jeffries. Somehow she had missed reading of his ascending to the title. You covered that little *faux pas* smoothly enough, she congratulated herself. But what *was* that little flip of the heart on seeing the true identity of her visitor? Why, one might almost think her still that giddy girl of a bygone day.

"Harriet dear, are you all right?" Agnes, her companion, broke into her reverie. "I do believe our guests are leaving."

"Oh. I shall be right there. Whatever am I to do without you to remind me of such polite niceties? I do hope Mr. Helmsley knows what a treasure he is getting in you."

Agnes blushed. "I think I have managed to fool him as well as you. The question is—have you settled on my replacement yet?"

"No. Not yet. But there is still time—the wedding is ten days off."

"A week."

"A *week!* Well, I must consider this more seriously, I see. But—first things first."

A few moments later she stood at the door of the larger, more formal drawing room to bid farewell to members of the Antiquities Society, which she had hosted this month and whose current interest centered on Greek artifacts.

"Oh, my dear Mrs. Knightly," gushed Lady Travers, a matron of middle years who wore a headdress of outlandish ostrich feathers. "You missed Lord Sayers's announcement."

"The purchase of Lord Elgin's marbles, you mean?"

"Oh, you knew." The woman sounded disappointed.

"Only that it was *possible* the government would buy them," Harriet assured her. "And I agree—it is wonderful news."

Harriet tried not to be too obvious in hurrying the last of the group on their way. Then she penned a quick note to her solicitor, asking Mr. James to call on her the next morning. A small dinner party and a theater excursion filled out the rest of her day.

It was late when she dismissed her maid and climbed into bed. But sleep did not come easily. "He is still the handsomest man of my acquaintance," she said aloud to herself. "Those streaks of silver in his hair merely make him more distinguished. He looks every inch the lord that he is."

And undoubtedly as reactionary as all the rest of that high-and-mighty lot, some ever-cynical imp cautioned.

Marcus had returned home to spend some time reviewing more carefully the documents his solicitor had given him. In the end, he uttered a low whistle at the extent of Annabelle Richardson's financial assets. There was an extensive holding in Kent, managed by an apparently capable steward, as well as investments on the 'change and a plantation in the West Indies— the one her parents had been visiting when they died on their return. The girl was a very wealthy young woman!

Dinner was a pleasant enough affair. His aunt Gertrude had arrived while he was out, and she had made herself known to Annabelle. Marcus thought the two of them seemed comfortable with each other. Conversation was lively. Marcus had always enjoyed his aunt's rather unorthodox opinions, and he was not averse to deliberately taking an opposite view merely to tease her. However, he was surprised—and not at all sure he approved—that a girl as young as Miss Richardson would share those views so thoroughly. He rarely agreed with the positions either female extolled, but he found himself gaining respect for the quality of his ward's mind.

Having refused to sit alone with a bottle of port after dinner, he joined the ladies in the drawing room. He gave them an abbreviated account of his discoveries. "So," he ended, "we are in something of a state of limbo regarding your future, Miss Richardson, until Mrs. Knightly signs off on her late husband's guardianship."

"Is this by any chance *Harriet* Knightly?" Aunt Gertrude asked.

"Yes. Do you know her, then?"

"Somewhat. She is well received but not often seen in the highest circles of the *ton.*" Aunt Gertrude gave a rueful chuckle. "But then, neither am I."

"In your case, at least," he observed, "we both know that is largely by choice."

"I think it is in hers as well. Her husband was a scholarly sort—gentry, of course—who did not go about in society much. And one must remember she was in mourning until fairly recently."

"Knightly cannot have been merely one of those reclusive academic sorts. The man amassed a fortune in shipping." Marcus found himself unusually interested in the sort of man who had caught Harriet Glasser's attention. Given the age discrepancy, she had probably found his fortune the major attraction. This idea came as a rather peculiar disappointment, but, after all, it was of no concern to *him.*

Aunt Gertrude broke into his musings. "I never knew her husband. Her younger sister is now married to a baronet named Berwyn."

"Welsh, I take it?"

"I believe so. Captain Berwyn served in the Peninsula with your brother."

"Is that so?" Marcus asked, but his tone was disinterested. "Well, to our current business. With only fifteen years, Miss Richardson, you can hardly be sent off to fend for yourself—even if your father had not made such careful provision for you."

"Yes, my lord." Despite her apparent meekness, Marcus sensed some stronger fiber in her.

He went on. "But the logical course of action would be for you to return to school."

She lifted her chin. "I will not do that, my lord."

"You will not—?"

"I will not return to that . . . that *prison* with Mrs.

Hepplewhite as the warden. It is too . . . too suffocating. Besides, she hates me."

"I see," he said, not seeing at all. "Another school, then."

"No!" Her voice rose. "I cannot abide the thought of school. And if—if you force me to go to one, I shall . . . I shall run away! I promise you. I shall run away!"

Marcus was taken aback by her emotional outburst, but his mind conjured images of a gently bred girl at the mercy of cutthroats and procuresses on the streets of London.

Aunt Gertrude patted her hand. "There, there, dear. Marcus does not mean to have you mistreated or unhappy. But would you not be more content with young ladies your own age?"

"I have been with young ladies my own age since my parents died." Miss Richardson stifled a sob.

Marcus had a sudden vision of a bereaved child sent off to a boarding school to deal with her grief on her own. He had enough memory of the sterility, the coldness, of such an institution to feel profoundly sorry for the girl before him.

"All right." His voice was calming. "We shall not entertain the notion of a school just yet. Perhaps in a few weeks you will feel different. Meanwhile, we could engage a governess."

"A governess? My lord, I am far too old to be shepherded about by a nursemaid or a governess! I am not a baby, you know."

Marcus was beginning to lose that diplomatic patience for which he was so well known in Paris and Vienna. It was especially annoying that it was a mere slip of a girl who was causing the loss. He schooled his voice to cool neutrality. "Miss Richardson. Your education is far from complete. May I assume that you have considered this point?"

"Yes, I have," she said, sounding defensive. "I had

not—that is, before you gave me some idea of my financial situation. Now it occurs to me that I can well afford to set up my own household and hire a companion and . . . and perhaps have tutors come in occasionally."

"Impossible," he said flatly.

"*Why* is it impossible?"

"It just is not done," Aunt Gertrude said.

Marcus stifled an urge to throttle the girl. "You would require my approval for a venture like that, and I would never condone such a scheme." He was tempted to add that the idea of a girl of fifteen years being so independent was utterly preposterous.

"Perhaps Mrs. Knightly will approve," Miss Richardson said.

"Perhaps she will," he replied. "But that would be of only the slightest consequence, for I assure you that *I* will not." He rose. "Now, if you ladies will excuse me, I have some work I must finish in the library." He gave his aunt a speaking look.

He had been working for perhaps an hour when there was a gentle tap at the door. Aunt Gertrude—tall, white-haired, with dark eyes that missed nothing and an energetic air about her—came in. She waved him to remain seated and immediately took a chair across from his desk.

"I gathered you wanted to speak to me, my dear? Miss Richardson has retired."

"Yes. First of all, thank you for coming to my rescue on such short notice."

"Of course. How could I have refused? But what *are* you going to do about this ward of yours?"

"Can I possibly persuade you to stay on until I have it sorted out?"

"I shall be glad to be of use, my dear. However, you are perfectly right in thinking Miss Richardson's education is a matter of concern."

"And—? I heard more in your voice."

"Well, I am willing to lend my countenance as a chaperone as long as you need me. I quite like Annabelle already. But I am not equipped in either attitude or ability to take on responsibility for teaching her properly."

"I would not impose upon you to that extent." He grinned at her. "Besides, we would not want to drag you away from your efforts to improve society. What is it this week? Chimney sweeps or fallen women?"

"Now, you just never mind your teasing about my projects," she admonished him with a twinkle. "You worry about the girl upstairs. That child has been sadly neglected. She is hurt far more than she lets on, too."

"Yes, I could see that. But I can do nothing until we have Mrs. Knightly out of the picture."

Even as he said this, it occurred to him that under different circumstances he might have welcomed Mrs. Knightly into the picture. He remembered vividly the distress in the eyes of a child of nine as he returned a kitten rescued at no little damage to the dandified apparel of a "man" just down from Oxford. He also remembered a few years later, standing up with a gaminlike waif with large hazel eyes.

But there was nothing waiflike about the determined woman in that drawing room today.

The next day Harriet alighted from her carriage in front of Wyndham House. She dismissed her driver, telling him she would take a hackney home. The Wyndham butler looked with obvious disapproval at her very singular arrival. She knew it was unorthodox for a lady to call at a gentleman's residence, but this was, after all, a business matter, and she had not the heart to drag Agnes away from her Mr. Helmsley. As she removed her bonnet and pelisse, she caught a glimpse of herself in a looking glass hanging in the entryway. She had dressed in a stylish day dress—a russet silk creation that she knew showed her own coloring to good advantage.

"This way, madam. His lordship has been expecting you."

She was shown into a well-stocked library, where Lord Wyndham sat chatting with an older woman and a young girl.

"Lady Hermiston!" Harriet said warmly. "How very nice to see you again."

Lord Wyndham had stood as Harriet entered. "Mrs. Knightly. Since you already know my aunt, may I present Miss Annabelle Richardson?"

Miss Richardson, too, stood and gave a polite curtsy as she murmured an appropriate greeting. As the ladies exchanged pleasantries, Marcus spoke quietly to the butler, then rejoined them.

"You and Mrs. Knightly seem rather well acquainted, Aunt Gertrude. May I correctly assume you share similar interests?"

Harriet thought there was a certain amusement in his tone, and she felt herself bristling at it.

His aunt smiled. "We are both members of a charitable group—and the Antiquities Society."

"We missed you yesterday," Harriet told her.

A footman brought in a tray with refreshments, and Lady Hermiston busied herself in serving. Harriet noted that not only did the girl not hesitate to assist, she seemed perfectly at ease in doing so. Harriet mused that she herself had not been so self-possessed at that age. When they had all settled back again, Lord Wyndham turned to Harriet.

"Well, Mrs. Knightly, have you considered our dilemma?"

"I spoke with my solicitor this morning. He confirmed all that you told me." She saw him give an I-told-you-so sort of nod before she turned to Miss Richardson. "I am sincerely sorry, my dear, that I knew nothing of you until his lordship called yester-day."

"Nor I of you," the girl replied in a polite tone. "I did not know anything of the guardianship until Mrs. Hep—that is, until I arrived here yesterday. Lord Wyndham informed me and Lady Hermiston of the details last night."

Lord Wyndham, who had sat patiently through this exchange, now interjected, "Are you satisfied, Mrs. Knightly, that Miss Richardson is properly provided for? And are you prepared to sign the document I presented yesterday?"

Harriet was offended at his bluntness. Good heavens. The man was supposed to be a diplomat. She forced herself to speak in an amiable tone. "I never doubted the proprieties would be handled with efficiency, my lord. I merely wished to be assured of the extent of my own interest in this matter."

"I assume you have that assurance now," he said.

"Yes, I do."

"And—?"

"And I find I cannot sign away my responsibilities."

His eyes narrowed in speculation and his lips tightened. "Cannot? Or *will* not?"

"It amounts to the same thing, my lord."

Lady Hermiston and Miss Richardson watched this exchange like spectators at a game of lawn tennis.

"And just what do you see your particular responsibilities to be?" he asked her, an edge to his tone.

She willed herself to patience. "Exactly as the guardianship document states. I am to provide oversight of investments made on her behalf and to approve of plans for her education."

"That document, madam, was drawn up with your husband. There seems to have been no question of *his* business acumen."

"Are you suggesting, my lord, that there is a question of *my* ability in that regard?" She noticed Lady

Hermiston's lips twitch at this sally and that Lord Wyndham seemed taken aback.

He gave her a penetrating look. "I am *suggesting* nothing at all, madam. But I would point out that such expertise is most unusual in one of your gender, and I think it not unreasonable to expect some confirmation of such—beyond your late husband's obvious confidence in you, that is."

Harriet wanted to toss her tea at him. Instead, she looked at him over the brim of the cup and said sweetly, "I think you will find Mr. Knightly's confidence was not misplaced."

"I hope not."

Three

Harriet deliberately turned her attention to Miss Richardson. Their conversation revealed that Annabelle had not been to London since she was a small child and had, of course, seen none of the sights.

"Oh! You must allow me to show you around a bit. Perhaps you and Lady Hermiston will accompany me for a drive tomorrow? With his lordship's concurrence, of course?"

Annabelle's eyes lit up in anticipation as she looked toward Lord Wyndham. He nodded his agreement.

But Lady Hermiston demurred. "I have a previous engagement. However, it is an excellent idea and will afford the two of you opportunity to become better acquainted."

"When you return," Marcus said, "perhaps we can discuss more concrete plans for Miss Richardson's continued education."

"As you wish, my lord." Harriet took this as a signal for her departure. There was some polite chitchat as the ladies planned the details of the next day's outing. When Harriet asked that a footman be dispatched to hail a hackney for her, his lordship insisted on sending her home in his own carriage.

"So—he is not totally without sensibilities, you see," she said to Agnes as the two of them awaited dinner that evening.

"He sounds a fine gentleman to me. Did you not say you had known him some years ago?"

"Yes. I did. I was very young and easily impressed in those days."

"Ah, but you *were* impressed. They say the Earl of Wyndham is a very handsome man. And *very* eligible . . ." Agnes's tone was teasingly suggestive.

Harriet laughed. "Agnes, you must stop trying to make a match of it every time an unmarried man speaks to me!"

"It is just that I shall hate to see you alone."

"I am quite content to be alone. My marriage was as good as most and far better than some—but truth to tell, I am reveling in my independence. At first I missed Ray something fierce, but he prepared me well to handle my life now."

Indeed, he had, she thought. Raymond Knightly had guided his young wife's education, never once suggesting any of her enthusiasms was "unladylike" or "not quite the thing." While he himself was not a member of Parliament, many of his friends were. They soon became accustomed to talking freely in the presence of Knightly's young wife. Some were initially surprised at her interest and knowledge but eventually accepted her insight about matters near and dear to their hearts.

"He must have been an extraordinary man," Agnes said. "I wish I had known him."

"He was." Harriet lost herself in the past for a moment. "God alone knows what might have happened to Chal and Mama and me had Raymond Knightly not lived up to his name—rescuing us like a knight in shining armor."

Harriet's viscount father had died when she was fifteen—just the age of Annabelle Richardson, she thought. The estate had been depleted long before her father had inherited it. A stronger, more disciplined man might have made a going concern of such an inheritance. Her father—good-humored, lovable, feckless—was not that man. Years later Harriet had concluded that his having no son to carry on had been at the root of his own negligence.

In any event, when he died, his wife and daughters were left with a very small pittance—what remained of his wife's marriage settlements—definitely not enough for them to live on for more than a few weeks, especially as they would be forced to seek other lodgings. The estate, along with the title, was entailed to a certain George Edward Glasser, a distant cousin whom Harriet had met only when he arrived to attend her father's funeral.

George Glasser had been unctuous in extending his condolences. Harriet remembered with distaste how he had clung overlong to her hand, his own clammy with sweat. A decade younger than her father and rather short in stature, he had very pale, slightly protruding eyes and thinning blond hair. He affected the appearance of a dandy.

Still, he had, upon meeting his predecessor's family, promptly invited the widow and her daughters to stay on for a few months. After all, they were "family," were they not? Surely, there could be no excessive gossip about a bachelor's offering lodging to a mother and her children.

Initially, this offer came as manna from heaven to the impoverished widow and her daughters. So, George Glasser moved in, taking over the master's bedroom, once shared by Harriet's father and mother. Eventually, however, his presence became wearing. He was a nonstop talker, often repeating himself, and rarely offering conversation of any substance.

Even before Harriet had turned sixteen, Cousin George had begun to make her uncomfortable. He would often stand too close to her. His hands would stray, lingering on her arm or shoulder, "accidentally" brushing her breast. He made coy remarks about her youth and beauty. Harriet tried to avoid him, but in a small household this was not possible.

Then late one evening he caught her in the hallway. Having just checked on her mother, who was feeling unwell, she was returning to the room she now shared with Charlotte. Her hair was down and her dressing gown no longer fit her as well as it should. He put out a hand to stop her and leered at her.

"Ah, my oh-so-lovely cousin. What a delectable little piece you are." He quite literally licked his lips.

"I—I beg your pardon, sir?"

He put an arm around her shoulder, hugging her close. She caught a whiff of brandy. He had been sitting all evening in what she still thought of as her father's library, drinking what was left of her father's brandy.

"Come, come, my dear. I am quite fatigued with these games."

"Games?"

"It has been—what?—six? seven months since your father's death?"

"S-seven."

"Your temporary residence here has gone on for some time."

"I am not sure I follow you, sir."

"You cannot suppose that I can allow the three you to stay on here indefinitely without some . . . um . . . 'compensation,' shall we say?"

"C-compensation? But you know we—we have very little money."

"I had something other than money in mind, my dear." His eyes drifted to the open neck of her dressing gown. Before she knew what he was about, he lowered his face to hers. His lips were squishy and wet. He immediately thrust his tongue into her mouth. The taste of stale liquor and smell of stale sweat sent the bile rising in her throat. His hand squeezed her breast hard.

She pushed against him. "Please—"

He ignored her and tried to pull her close again. "I—I have to have you in my bed." His voice was husky.

She jerked away in amazement. "What? You—you want to marry me?"

Reacting as though she had thrown cold water in his face, he pulled away and said in an incredulous tone, "Marriage? Good heavens, no! Of course, I shall have to take a wife some day, but it will be someone with a substantial dowry. I am sorry, dear cousin, but I seriously doubt you will ever qualify."

She felt a blush suffuse her cheeks. She quickly ran into her room and closed and locked the door. She heard his derisive laughter in the hall.

Now, twelve years later, she again heard that awful laughter in memory.

"Harriet? Are you all right?" Agnes's voice brought her back to he present.

"Yes. I am fine. I just had a rather vivid image of what Raymond Knightly saved me from."

They changed the subject, and the rest of the evening passed in pleasurable talk of the upcoming wedding. But that night the rest of the memories came flooding back.

Cousin George had not mentioned the incident in the hallway. Nor had he suggested to her mother that the previous viscount's family was no longer welcome.

Then, one afternoon, he caught Harriet in a secluded area of the garden. He had emerged from behind a mulberry bush right in front of her. He grabbed her and locked her in his arms.

"Surely, you have had sufficient space to consider my offer. It is time you stopped being so coy." He bent his head to put his wet lips to hers again, but she turned her head.

"It was a despicable suggestion, and you are no gentleman for having made it."

"Why, you—" He grabbed her head to hold it rigid and kissed her savagely.

Instinctively, she struggled, finally positioning herself to bring her knee up in a sharp jerk that caught him in a very tender area. He quickly released her and doubled over in pain.

"You . . . will . . . be sorry . . . for this," he gasped.

That evening he had turned his lecherous attentions to thirteen-year-old Charlotte, who had no idea what was going on—merely that she found Cousin George to be "truly repugnant" and she wished he did not live with them.

When Harriet pointed out that *they* now lived with *him,* Charlotte burst into tears.

Harriet knew she had to do something to remove her sister from proximity to the lascivious viscount. Within the week she had persuaded her mother that the three of them should visit one of Mrs. Glasser's girlhood friends.

The widowed Raymond Knightly owned a neighboring estate, and it turned out that he had been a friend to Harriet's father. He was quite taken with Harriet. Later he told her that her concern for her mother and protectiveness toward her sister had quite won him over. Apparently, her mother had been more aware of the new viscount's intentions than Harriet had known, for *someone* had informed Mr. Knightly of the situation.

At the end of their two-month visit, Harriet had accepted Mr. Knightly's gentle proposal of marriage. There were no protestations of undying love, but Knightly pledged to give her—and her mother and sister—a good home and that he would treasure his wife as a valued friend and companion.

And so he had.

He had seen to the rest of her education, filling gaps she had not even known existed. He had indulged his bride in her various interests—actually sharing many of them. He also served as a gentle, calming force when she became overly enthusiastic in advocating women's rights or denouncing slavery. He had happily provided a home for her mother until her death four years after her husband's. He had also willingly ensured her sister's dowry so that Charlotte could marry her soldier-baron.

No, theirs was not a great love match, she thought, but they had got on well together. His lovemaking had been gentle and considerate rather than passionate. But then, she had no real basis for comparison. Her biggest disappointment was that there were no children. In the first years she had wept bitter tears over this, but her husband had been kind about that, too. Eventually, she managed to put the idea into the darkest closets of her mind.

The next day Marcus saw the ladies off—Aunt Gertrude to a meeting of some "improvement" society and Mrs. Knightly and Miss Richardson on a round of sight-seeing.

Mrs. Knightly had arrived dressed in a moss-green outfit trimmed with cream-colored frogging. Marcus considered himself to be quite inadequate in judging women's apparel, but, even to his unpracticed eye, it was clear that Mrs. Knightly had an eye for style and color. Perhaps he should ask her to oversee a wardrobe for Miss Richardson, for the girl had looked a veritable frump next to her companion as they set out.

Determined to learn as much as he could about the woman with whom he shared the guardianship, he spent the day talking with businessmen and bankers. He found nothing of a negative nature. Indeed, the managers of her late husband's shipping business—now hers—had nothing but praise for her. In their view she was knowledgeable and astute. She, like her husband before her, paid good wages and expected top-notch service. Nor was she likely to be overly nice

in her supervision of employees. She hired people for
their expertise and expected them to use good judgment.

There was one thing on which she was absolutely
adamant. She would have nothing to do with the slave
trade.

"I was under the impression that British ships had
not engaged in trading in slaves since Parliament forbade it in 1808," Marcus said with a touch of irony.

"True, my lord. But Mrs. Knightly refuses to allow
our ships even to carry goods produced by slave labor," the shipping manager replied. "Her exact words
were 'We shall not be a party to that abomination in
any way.' "

"That must be somewhat limiting in your business."

" 'Tis at that. So we transport goods—and passengers—mostly to and from Canada and the northern
colonies—former colonies, that is. Also, our business
with France and Italy has improved since Waterloo.
Not so dangerous anymore."

While the bankers were not forthcoming with specifics—nor had he expected them to be—they did inform him that Mrs. Knightly's fortune was substantial.
And that she oversaw all her investments directly.

"Do you not find that to be rather unusual?" Marcus asked.

"In truth, my lord, we did—at first." The banker
chuckled and folded his hands on his ample middle.
"Did not take her long to put us in her places." He
leaned forward and said in a confidential tone, "Some
of us now often follow her lead. If she says something
is a promising venture, believe me, it usually is."

These inquiries put one of his fears at least partially
to rest. There was no reason that Harriet Knightly
should look greedily upon their ward's fortune. He
knew of instances in which a guardian had managed
to deplete a minor's estate.

Still, why had a vibrant young woman chosen to

marry a man so very much her senior if not for his wealth? And having done that, why would she not have similar motivation in other concerns?

In the matter of Annabelle Richardson's fortune, of one thing he was absolutely certain—when Miss Richardson came of age, it would be intact.

Harriet had a marvelous time with Miss Richardson. On the previous day she had thought the girl presentable and acceptable. Today Harriet found her companion possessed a delightful sense of humor and that she shared Harriet's appreciation of the ridiculous. The three-foot-high ostrich feathers in the headdress of one matron they saw in the park had sent both of them into a discreet fit of the giggles.

At the Tower of London the girl showed herself surprisingly knowledgeable about England's history. She wanted to see the rooms where Sir Walter Raleigh and Sir Thomas More had been held. She insisted upon standing on the very spot where Anne Boleyn had lost her head. She reveled in walking along the rampart said to be "Elizabeth's Walk" when the sixteenth-century princess was imprisoned in the tower prior to becoming England's greatest queen.

Her pleasure was so unabashed that Harriet was both amused and charmed. Then a thought occurred to her. This was what it had been like for Raymond when he introduced *her* to so many delightful experiences. She was not only grateful to her young companion for affording her this new perspective on her own life but once again grateful to the man who had enriched that life.

Actually, there was much in Annabelle Richardson that reminded her of her younger self. She felt even more drawn to the girl as a result. She was also determined that Annabelle's spirit of adventure and eagerness to learn would not be quashed in the stifling dictates of what society said was a "proper education" for a young woman—precisely what the Earl of Wyndham undoubtedly had in mind for the ward they shared.

Well, not if Harriet Knightly had any say in the matter! The first thing would be to see the girl was provided a decent wardrobe.

Marcus and Aunt Gertrude, who had returned earlier, were waiting in the drawing room when Mrs. Knightly and Miss Richardson appeared.

"Oh, Lady Hermiston, you will not credit what a fine day I have had." Annabelle's eyes fairly danced with eagerness. Marcus smiled at her exuberance.

Aunt Gertrude also smiled indulgently. "What did you enjoy most, my dear?"

"The Tower, of course." Annabelle responded without hesitation. "Is it not wonderful? The whole history of England—well, much of it, certainly—right there in one easily accessible spot!"

"And I must say we 'accessed' all of it!" Mrs. Knightly said with a laugh.

As Annabelle bubbled on about the sights she had seen, Marcus covertly observed the young girl's companion for the day. Harriet Knightly had clearly enjoyed herself.

Heston brought in a heavily laden tea tray containing sandwiches and tarts as well as the usual biscuits.

"Oh!" Annabelle said in delight. "Apricot tarts again! They are my favorites," she explained to the other two ladies.

Good grief, Marcus thought. *A mere two days—and the chit even has my cook indulging her!*

When they had all partaken of the repast and talk of the day's outing had reached a natural conclusion, Mrs. Knightly turned to Marcus.

"I believe you wished to discuss plans for Miss Richardson's education, my lord?"

"Yes, I do," he said firmly.

"Would you like Miss Richardson and me to leave?" Aunt Gertrude asked, beginning to rise.

Marcus looked at Mrs. Knightly. She gave a small shrug that suggested it was up to him.

"No, I think not," he said. "Your views are always enlightening, dear aunt, and since Miss Richardson has very decided opinions on this matter, we should be well advised to include her."

Miss Richardson blushed in apparent embarrassment at her outburst the previous evening, but she murmured, "Thank you, my lord."

Mrs. Knightly's inquisitive expression prompted Marcus to explain that Annabelle had objected vigorously to being returned to the Chesterton-Jones school.

"Another school, then? My sister attended Miss Sotheby's School and was quite happy there."

Annabelle directed an anguished look at Marcus.

He hurriedly brushed aside that idea. "No. Our Miss Richardson is not disposed to any school." He raised a hand to forestall Mrs. Knightly's next comment. "Nor will she entertain the idea of a governess."

"What, then?" Mrs. Knightly asked their ward.

"Tutors?" Miss Richardson responded in a small voice. Marcus thought she had probably dispensed with the ludicrous notion of an independent household.

"Tutors?" Mrs. Knightly looked from Annabelle to Marcus. "Hmmm. I suppose that would suffice, *if* Lord Wyndham agrees."

"That would entail a good many people coming and going all the time, Marcus," Aunt Gertrude said in a cautionary tone. "It would probably be better if you had one person who could instruct in several areas."

He nodded but said nothing.

Mrs. Knightly looked thoughtful, then said, "I could

contrive to teach her some of the essentials one would learn in a school—"

"Oh, would you—truly?" Annabelle asked in undisguised delight.

"But," Mrs. Knightly continued, "tutors would have to be hired for music and dance. I could help her *practice* French, but it would probably be best if a native speaker actually taught the language."

"I am sure your schedule is far too busy to allow your coming to Wyndham House on a daily basis, Mrs. Knightly," Marcus said. The woman was going far too fast in his opinion.

"You are right," she said with a smile. "So it would be better if Miss Richardson removed to the country with me."

"Removed to—? Now, hold on just a moment."

"Well, you see," Mrs. Knightly explained with a show of infinite patience, "I am losing my companion to the bonds of matrimony, and I have already agreed to a year's lease on my town house. I believe Miss Richardson and I would get on famously together."

Marcus thought, I'll just bet you would, but aloud he said, "I am sorry, but I cannot abrogate my responsibilities to that extent."

"Oh, but the Knightly estate is only just outside London. You might easily visit from time to time."

"No. I cannot approve her removal from my household."

"*Can*not? Or *will* not, my lord?"

He knew she was deliberately throwing his words back at him. So he responded in kind. "It amounts to the same thing, madam. No."

A cloud of anger descended across her face, and all of them sat in uncomfortable silence for a moment. Then Aunt Gertrude said, "Marcus, might I have a word with you?"

Four

Marcus followed Aunt Gertrude into the hall. He was mystified. It was not like her to treat a guest with what bordered on rudeness. They moved away from the door of the drawing room before Aunt Gertrude spoke softly.

"It seems to me, dear, that the perfect solution is to invite Mrs. Knightly *here*."

"What do you mean, *here?*"

"Invite her to stay at Wyndham House to become Miss Richardson's tutor—her governess, if you will, though one had best not use that term in front of Annabelle."

"You want me to invite a young widow into a bachelor household? Good heavens, Aunt Gertrude, she would be ruined socially."

"Not so long as you have me here to ensure propriety."

"Hmmm." He ran a hand over his chin, his thumb rubbing along a small scar on his jawline. It was a characteristic gesture of which he was only vaguely aware.

Aunt Gertrude went on. "Harriet Knightly is a knowledgeable woman. She obviously gets on well with the girl. She shares the guardianship—and she seems as intent on fulfilling her responsibilities as you are."

"You do have a point, but why would she agree to such? And how would it appear?"

"Well, we do not know that she *will* agree. As to

how it will appear—it will appear as exactly what the
very proper Earl of Wyndham—and *I*—say it will."
Aunt Gertrude squared her shoulders proudly.

He grinned at his favorite relative. "Now, now. Do
not get your feathers all ruffled. I am well aware that
you, in your own inimitable fashion, are as much of
an arbiter of society as any of the patronesses of Al-
mack's."

"Well, I would not be so presumptuous as to say
that," she said in what Marcus took to be a tone of
false modesty.

He laughed outright. "All right. We shall ask her. At
the least, it has merit as a temporary measure—until
we can persuade the chit that school is the best course
to pursue."

As they returned to the drawing room, Mrs.
Knightly and Miss Richardson broke off a discussion
of the parade of fashionable people they had seen in
the park earlier.

"Lady Hermiston has come up with what I believe
to be a reasonable solution to our dilemma," he announced. They listened intently as he explained. Miss
Richardson's expression showed growing delight; Mrs.
Knightly shook her head in disapproval.

"I fear that would be impossible, my lord."

"I see." Marcus nodded. "You have commitments
that would not allow this disturbance in your routine."

"No, that is not it at all. Have I not indicated I
would willingly take on certain aspects of the education of *our* ward?" She sounded a bit testy, he thought.
"Indeed, I should consider it not only a duty but a
pleasure."

"And I have an obligation that is equally compelling
to oversee the situation," he said. "As I envision it,
this would be a temporary measure and would pre-
clude either of us making inconvenient trips for con-
sultations. It seems a reasonable compromise." He
ended in a tone that had been effective with Tal-

leyrand and the Prussians. Surely it would persuade one rather reluctant English woman.

"I—I just do not know . . ."

"Perhaps you have family obligations that would prevent your agreeing to this proposal," Aunt Gertrude suggested.

"I—uh—no. No. My sister is my only relative of any significance. She and her family live on the Welsh border."

"Well, then . . . ?" Aunt Gertrude prompted.

"It . . . it would be a rather unorthodox arrangement, would it not?" Mrs. Knightly seemed apprehensive.

Aunt Gertrude nodded and smiled encouragingly. "Unusual, but neither bizarre nor exceptional. I doubt the situation would occasion much comment."

"I should not want to be the cause of scandal that might ruin Miss Richardson's standing before she has even made her come-out."

Marcus cleared his throat and said, "I think we all have Miss Richardson's best interests at heart in this matter."

"Yes, I am sure we do." Mrs. Knightly was quiet for a moment. The other three seemed to hold their breath. Then Marcus knew she was weakening as she turned to his aunt and said, "This was *your* idea, my lady? And . . . you *would* remain in residence?"

"Yes, my dear. It *was* my idea and I shall remain."

"Well . . . if it has *your* sanction, I, too, doubt it would occasion untoward speculation. . . ."

Annabelle clapped her hands gleefully. "Then you will do it? Oh, please—say that you will!"

Mrs. Knightly's voice was somewhat shaky at first, then became more firm. "Yes. Yes, Miss Richardson, I do believe I will."

"Good," Marcus and Aunt Gertrude said in unison.

Annabelle looked from one to another of them, her

eyes bright. "We . . . we shall be almost like a family, shall we not?"

Marcus saw unshed tears spring to the eyes of both Aunt Gertrude and Mrs. Knightly at the poignancy of this innocent remark. His own throat tightened.

"I suppose we shall," Aunt Gertude said gently.

Annabelle hesitated momentarily. "Do . . . do you think you might all call me Annabelle instead of Miss Richardson all the time? I mean—only when we are alone, of course," she added hastily.

He recognized the wistfulness of her tone. "As we shall be living more or less in each other's pockets for the next few weeks, I quite agree. Annabelle it is. Aunt Gertrude? Mrs. Knightly?"

Aunt Gertrude smiled. "I shall not mind being 'aunt' to all three of you."

"I would much prefer to be addressed as Harriet, if you please," Mrs. Knightly said.

"All right, then," he said. "Harriet and Marcus it shall be within our own circle."

"Oh, my lord—" Annabelle murmured.

"In our own circle, Annabelle," he admonished.

Aunt Gertrude added, "It would not do for a young miss to be so forward in company."

"Of course," Annabelle agreed, and Harriet nodded her concurrence.

Marcus looked at the three females before him. Annabelle was clearly delighted. Aunt Gertrude seemed content, composed. And Harriet? He could not quite read her expression. Was she apprehensive? Uncertain?

He was surprised at how important it was to him that she feel at ease with their decision. At the same time, he had a premonition that Harriet Knightly was likely to disturb *his* ease mightily.

My God! What *had* he agreed to? Three days earlier he had been master of a dignified, serene bachelor household. He knew instinctively that his ordered life

was about to be turned topsy-turvy with the introduction—
nay, the invasion—of three strong-willed, opinionated females.

In the few days it took to see Agnes happily married
and prepare her town house for new tenants, Harriet
chastised herself repeatedly. *Why* had she agreed to
such an idiotic scheme?

Informed of her friend's plans, Agnes had been
blunt. "Do you not think this rather a risky move?"

"Risky? Lady Hermiston will be there to lend propriety."

"I was thinking more of political than of social con-
siderations."

"Political? There is nothing *political* about being
guardian to a young girl."

"My dear Harriet, you will be moving the Gadfly
into the midst of the enemy camp!"

"Oh. I had not really thought of that."

"The Earl of Wyndham has always been hand-in-
glove with the Tory government. Surely you were
aware of that." Agnes raised her brows in surprise.

"Yes, that *was* true of the two previous earls. . . ."

"I think it equally true of the current holder of that
title. You cannot suppose that he spent all those years
as a diplomat for a government with which he disagreed!"

"No, of course not." Harriet was thoughtful. "But
there is no real reason to think he will even take notice
of the scribblings of a writer using the Gadfly pseudonym."

"My dear, your modesty allows you to underestimate
the influence of Gadfly's message."

"Only three people know the Gadfly's identity—you
and I and my editor, Mr. Watson."

"You know what that colonist Mr. Franklin, said? 'Three may keep a secret if two them are dead.' "

Harriet smiled. Agnes loved to quote adages. "Are you suggesting you and Mr. Watson are not trustworthy?"

"No. Good heavens! No. Merely that secrets are hard enough to guard without taking them into close proximity to those you would least like to know them."

"Well, my friend," Harriet said, patting her companion's hand, "I shall not worry about *your* revealing my secret up there in Yorkshire. And I am sure Mr. Watson's discretion may be relied upon."

"Nevertheless, *I* shall worry. It would do you no little damage if you were found out, my dear."

Harriet was aware that with the move to Wyndham House she would have to be more circumspect about when and where she actually did her writing. However, her remaining in London would allow her to continue to convey manuscripts to Mr. Watson personally, using their usual meeting places between the shelves in various bookshops. She dismissed the deeper concerns Agnes voiced.

As to the question of *why* she had agreed to the scheme—well, of *course* she had been motivated by concern for her newly discovered ward. Honesty compelled her to admit to herself that she was also curious about her own reaction to Marcus Jeffries. Despite her efforts to be totally rational in dealing with him, her awareness was heightened whenever he was near. But, surely, this was merely a holdover of the childish memories of her youth.

A few days later, having overseen a myriad of details, she removed to Wyndham House. Agnes was on her way to Yorkshire with a doting new husband. Certain members of Harriet's staff had chosen to stay on at the new tenant's request. Her coachman and two grooms were dispatched, along with several others, to augment the staff at her place in the country. Betsy, her maid, would accompany her to Wyndham House.

It was late in the afternoon as the housekeeper showed her to her room. She was struck by the grandeur of the place, with thick Oriental carpets found in hallways and bedrooms as well as the more public rooms. Carved wall panels, stair newels, and handrails had the rich patina of countless polishings.

They passed the master chamber and the adjoining suite for the mistress—"which is not in use now, of course," the housekeeper, Mrs. Benson, explained. She pointed out the rooms occupied by Lady Hermiston and Annabelle. Finally, she opened the door of a large chamber that had a small dressing room off to the side. Besides a large bed, the room contained a small settee, an upholstered chair, a desk with another chair, two small tables—one of which sported a bright bouquet of flowers—a large dresser, and an armoire. The room was decorated in shades of beige and brown. Its overwhelmingly masculine decor was alleviated by a brightly flowered spread on the bed.

The housekeeper seemed apologetic. "This room used to be his lordship's. His brother's wife had not got around to redecorating this one before Lord Marcus succeeded to the title. He thought you would like this chamber, as it has a nice view of the garden." Mrs. Benson opened the drapes to demonstrate.

Harriet murmured an appropriate response, but her mind was occupied by the fact that Marcus himself had been concerned about which room she should have. She was pleased with her accommodations. The desk was placed so that once seated at it one could look through the window to the well-tended garden below. Gadfly should be duly inspired by this scene, she thought.

Harriet's request to see the quarters her maid would

have seemed to come as a mild surprise to the house-keeper. Harriet knew it was unusual for a member of the upper echelons of society to take such interest in a servant's well-being. She was pleased to learn that the Earl of Wyndham did not stint at providing adequate accommodations for his own and visiting staff.

The housekeeper informed her of the time for dinner and left Harriet and Betsy to their unpacking.

Dinner, with all four places set at one end of the vast dining table, was an informal affair. Conversation was rather lively, with Marcus often asking questions or making comments that—judging by an occasional wink or knowing grin—he knew would provoke an outraged response from his aunt or his ward. This relaxed, teasing side of him came as a surprise but not an unwelcome one.

Later Marcus left the ladies to their own devices as he announced a previous engagement at his club. To entertain the other two ladies, Annabelle played the pianoforte with studied skill but showed no ready talent for the instrument. Harriet thought some of the evening's sparkle had departed along with the master of house and then chastised herself severely for such a ridiculous notion.

In the next few days they settled into a routine of sorts. Harriet and Annabelle worked out a schedule for studies. Harriet would see to such matters as art—proficiency in drawing and watercolors was required of any young miss of the *ton*. Harriet would also oversee Annabelle's studies in such things as history, geography, literature, composition, and arithmetic. Tutors were interviewed and hired for other subjects.

Harriet spent much of their time in the first few days assessing Annabelle's background in various topics. Many young girls demonstrated or professed ennui with anything remotely academic. Not Annabelle. She soaked up such matters like a sponge.

"So? How are your studies coming along?" Marcus

directed the question in a conversational tone to Annabelle one afternoon as he joined the ladies for tea.

"Very well, thank you," Annabelle replied.

Marcus looked for confirmation from Harriet who concurred with a fond smile at their ward. "Our Annabelle is an apt pupil."

"In everything but arithmetic," Annabelle said with a rueful laugh. "I *do* dislike working with numbers. They are so cold—and dull."

"But necessary," Harriet affirmed in a prim tone.

"Yes," Aunt Gertrude agreed. "You shall run a household one day and be expected to keep domestic accounts."

"Perhaps . . ." Annabelle did not sound convinced. "I readily agree to a fundamental need, but I *can* add, subtract, divide, and multiply. That should be enough."

Marcus nodded. "That would appear to cover the basics. To what are you objecting?"

"I hate dealing with percentages, and interest rates, and . . . and *equations!*"

"*Hate* is a very strong word, dear," Aunt Gertrude admonished her.

"Well, I just do not see a need for such." Annabelle's youthful stubbornness had a certain charm about it.

"I must admit to some curiosity of my own," Marcus said.

Immediately, Harriet felt defensive, but she directed her explanation to Annabelle. "My dear girl, you will one day come into a substantial fortune. However will you manage it properly if you do not learn the methods and tools for doing so?"

Annabelle gave an airy wave of her hand. "I shall simply have someone else to do that for me."

"Quite right," Marcus said with an approving nod. "You will have a husband to handle such matters."

Harriet tried to quell her annoyance at this glib

assumption, but she could not stifle the irony in her voice. "One is sometimes left without a husband. And—strange as it may seem—some men welcome a wife's interest in the family's financial affairs. And—perhaps even stranger—some men are not above squandering away the wealth of an unsuspecting female."

"Harriet *does* have a point, Marcus," Aunt Gertrude said. "When I lost my dear Clarence in that awful business in the colonies, I knew precious little about our affairs. It was very difficult to deal with all that—and my grief."

The expression on Marcus's face, which had taken on a certain granite quality at Harriet's words, now softened slightly at his aunt's comment.

"I am sure your male relatives were willing to take on that responsibility—as well they should have done," he said.

"Oh, yes." Aunt Gertrude's tone was pointedly ironic. "My husband's cousin—who inherited the title, you know—had robbed me of several hundred pounds before I caught on to what he was doing."

"But you employ a capable man of business now," Marcus said.

"Yes, I do. A very trustworthy fellow he is, too."

"Quite right. And Annabelle, too, shall have such. I shall see that her interests are duly protected and"—he turned to Harriet—"that any future husband will be unable to 'squander' her inheritance."

"Very well," Harriet said firmly. "And *I* shall see that she has the ability to handle her own affairs if need be."

"I still hate—dislike—mathematics," Annabelle muttered. Then she brightened. "But I love literature. We are reading *Twelfth Night*—and it is such fun."

There followed some discussion of Shakespeare's sprightly comedy. Harriet knew Annabelle had deliberately changed the subject to prevent her two guardians from being at cross purposes with each other.

Annabelle, Harriet surmised, wanted no discord in her "family."

Harriet's heart went out to the young girl who was certain to suffer disappointment when this temporary arrangement was dissolved.

Marcus enjoyed the discussion of Shakespeare's play, which led to the observation that Mr. Kean was currently reprising his role of Shylock at the Drury Lane Theatre. Annabelle announced that she had never seen a "real" play outside a schoolroom. The enthusiasm of the ladies was irresistible, and he accepted the task of obtaining tickets for the next performance. Annabelle's excitement was both delightful and contagious, he thought.

The evening ended on an amicable note.

However, he had not forgotten the discussion earlier—and it disturbed him. His sister was the only female with whose education he had truly intimate knowledge, but he certainly did not recall estate management and business finances as part of her course of study. Just what did Harriet Knightly intend by such?

He decided he would take a keener interest in the details of Annabelle's studies. And in her principal teacher.

He admitted privately that his interest in that teacher went beyond the purely academic. He found himself intensely aware of her person whenever they were in the same room. He listened for her voice among the visitors in a crowded drawing room.

The theater outing took place a few days later. In the meantime, Marcus and Harriet had quietly agreed that the latter should oversee obtaining a new wardrobe for Annabelle. Marcus had been on his way out when one of the new garments had been delivered that very afternoon.

Annabelle came bouncing into the library in her new finery, a pale yellow creation with a long darker-yellow sash tied in a bow under the bust. She carried a matching cloak lined with the darker fabric.

"I take it this is the season's 'golden goddess' look," he said, smiling his approval.

She twirled in front of him. "Is it not wonderful? I have never—ever—worn such elegant apparel."

Aunt Gertrude entered on the tail end of Annabelle's remark. "It suits you very well, my dear."

Lady Hermiston wore a lavender gown with a modest turban that matched it. When Harriet came in a few moments later, she was attired in a light gray silk. It occurred to Marcus that these two had probably deliberately—and generously—chosen gowns that would allow Annabelle's to show to best advantage.

At the theater, the Jeffries family box, with Harriet and Annabelle occupying the chairs in front, drew a good deal of attention. Annabelle sat seemingly mesmerized through the first half. During the interval she turned shining eyes to the other three.

"Oh, this such a wonderful treat," she said breathlessly.

"You are fortunate to be initiated with such a fine performance," Harriet said.

Marcus was determined to ensure Annabelle had the full experience of a theater outing. "Come, Annabelle. You and I shall take a turn and bring back some refreshments."

He guided her out to the hallway and to a refreshment counter, where they procured four drinks. He noticed that Annabelle missed very little as she observed the elegant people and plush surroundings.

"Thank you, my lord, for allowing me this—this—oh, for everything!"

"You are very welcome, I am sure." He handed her

two of the glasses, picked up the other two himself, and they started back to the box, when a voice caught his attention.

"Marcus! Darling! It has been sooo long!"

He recognized the voice and cringed inwardly. Cynthia. He turned to face the raven-haired, green-eyed beauty who clung to the arm of a man some twenty years her senior—and having several thousand per annum, Marcus remembered.

"Lady Teasler. Lord Lynwood." He nodded to each in turn. "May I present my ward, Miss Annabelle Richardson."

The others acknowledged the introduction—Annabelle somewhat awkwardly, what with two glasses of liquid in her hands.

"Ah, yes," Cynthia said with a keen look at the young girl. "I had heard that you had opened the nursery at Wyndham House."

Marcus saw Annabelle try to hide a crestfallen look at this.

"Strange," he said coolly, "how gossips always seem to get things slightly twisted. Miss Richardson, her other guardian, and my aunt are my houseguests."

"Oh, to be sure," Cynthia said, but Marcus did not know what to make of that meaningless comment.

"If you will excuse us." He nudged Annabelle gently with his elbow.

"Not until you *promise* to call upon me." Cynthia's voice was plainly flirtatious, and Marcus had the distinct feeling this little scene was being played out for Lynwood's benefit.

"As you wish, my lady." He nodded again to her and her companion, and they murmured polite nothings in return.

"Lady Teasler is very beautiful, is she not?" Annabelle asked.

"Yes, she is." His voice was neutral, but he squirmed inwardly. He wondered how long it would be before innocent Annabelle was apprised of the fact that Cynthia Teasler had, until recently, been his mistress. Thank God he had given her her congé some weeks earlier. At the time the parting had not been amicable, but apparently she wanted now to put a new face on it. Probably for Lynwood's notice, he decided.

He and Annabelle returned to their box to find it crowded with visitors; only two of whom were clearly Aunt Gertrude's elderly friends. The others were three gentlemen and a lady of Harriet's acquaintance. Marcus recognized one of the gentlemen as Dexter Taverner, younger son of an earl whom Marcus knew to be on the lookout for a monied bride.

Now, why on earth should he find that annoying?

The guests departed. He and Annabelle resumed their seats. As he looked around, he saw Cynthia and her companion in a nearby box. She gave him a discreet but enthusiastic wave. Aunt Gertrude saw this little by-play and looked at him questioningly. He merely shrugged.

Harriet's removal to Lord Wyndham's residence had not curtailed either his or her social activities. He was aware that she attended an occasional evening soiree, sometimes in the company of Aunt Gertrude. His own social obligations rarely overlapped with theirs.

Then, one evening, they did.

Having discovered at breakfast that Harriet and his aunt were to attend the Hatterlee ball to which he was also committed, Marcus offered to escort them. Aunt Gertrude accepted eagerly, Harriet politely.

He was waiting for them in the library when Harriet appeared first. She was stunning in a pale green silk creation embroidered with darker-green ivy trim. She wore simple gold jewelry, though he had no doubt she *could* have worn glittering jewels.

"Very nice," he murmured with an elegant little bow, and was pleased to see her blush with apparent pleasure.

"Thank you, my lord."

"Marcus."

"Marcus." She smiled.

He liked hearing his name on her lips. Did he imagine extra warmth in her voice?

He handed Harriet into the carriage, then Aunt Gertrude, who, instead of sitting next to Harriet, deliberately took the opposite seat and spread her skirt out neatly. Marcus smiled inwardly at his aunt's machinations, but he was happy enough to take the seat next to Harriet, aware of the occasional touch of shoulder or knee as the carriage bumped over uneven cobbles on the street. He was also aware of the refreshingly subtle flowery scent she wore. Marcus hated to be in the company of women who drowned themselves in exotic perfumes.

The Hatterlee ball was a modest affair attracting a smattering of people who might lay claim to recognition among the most elite of the *ton*. Marcus took no notice of the extraordinarily warm welcome accorded his aunt, but he was surprised to see Harriet's easy familiarity with a good many of the guests.

Nor was he best pleased to find himself actually competing with other men for a dance with his own houseguest. He smiled triumphantly to find it was a waltz. The biggest jolt of the evening came when he took her in his arms, though. The Honorable Marcus Jeffries, diplomat and man of fashion, had danced with literally dozens and dozens of women. Never had he felt that he had "come home." Yet that was the thought that popped into his mind as he began to waltz Harriet Knightly around the ballroom.

Five

Harriet was gratified by her reception at the Hatterlee ball. She had not appeared in society much since coming out of mourning some months before. Nor had she been a lioness in the social jungle prior to her husband's death. Mr. and Mrs. Knightly had enjoyed quiet acceptance among their friends and enjoyed pursuing their interests in political and cultural circles, though here, too, both had assumed secondary rather than leading roles.

Now she found herself the center of an admiring circle. Among her would-be swains was Dexter Taverner, whom she had known for several years but whose attentions had grown more pronounced in recent months.

"Ah, Mrs. Knightly, I cannot tell you how much you brighten our social horizon," he said with a twinkle in his eye.

"You know very well, Mr. Taverner, that you need not use such blatant flummery with *me.*"

He put his hand over his heart in an exaggerated gesture. "I am wounded. Mortally wounded by your indifference."

"*Mister* Taverner!" she reprimanded.

"And"—he continued in a more normal tone—"it is only *partly* flummery, dear lady."

She felt herself warming to his sincerity. She smiled

at him and readily accepted his invitation to dance. His was the first of many invitations that evening.

At first she had thought Marcus meant to ignore her, but then there he was—signing her card for one of the later dances. A waltz. Oh, how the young Harriet Glasser would have swooned at such a prospect. However, the more mature, sophisticated widow, Mrs. Knightly, must demonstrate far more decorum.

In the event, that demeanor was more difficult to achieve than she had expected. His hand in hers—gloves notwithstanding—and his arm around her waist alerted all her senses. She schooled herself *not* to lean in closer, *not* to press her body against his, *not* to inhale more closely the spicy, masculine scent of him.

He clasped her firmly and guided her expertly. She lost herself in graceful motion and music and his nearness. It struck her that neither of them seemed inclined to talk—it was as though speech would destroy the magic. She looked up to catch an almost electric intensity in his blue-gray eyes. Their gazes locked for a moment, then he smiled and seemed to draw her slightly closer.

"You seem to have been born to waltz," he said.

"I do enjoy it." She sounded prim to her own ears, so she added, "But it does help to have a superb partner."

His smile broadened, white teeth flashing against a tanned complexion. "Indeed, it does."

"Of course, you must have danced the waltz hundreds of times in Vienna."

"A few times, certainly. The Viennese are very proud of their own contribution to Europe's ballrooms."

She changed the subject slightly. "I have heard that Vienna is a very lovely city."

"I suppose it is. It was a very *lively* city with half the crowned heads of Europe there for the Congress. But

I much prefer the smaller, quieter Salzburg, surrounded as it is by majestic mountains."

"His lordship is a mountaineer," she teased. "And do you yodel?"

"Only a little." He laughed. "Love of the mountains is in the Jeffries blood, I fear."

"Oh?"

"Our great-grandmother was a Highlander, daughter of a laird who was most unhappy when his favorite child stole away to marry a sassenach."

"One detects no trace of the Scots brogue in your speech. But then, in three generations, I surmise the southern blood has tamed the wild element." Again, her tone was playful.

"Ne'er think ye sich, lass," he said in a deliberately exaggerated brogue. "Ken ye no' the Scot is ne'er faer frae the surface?"

She laughed merrily, pleased that he felt so at ease with her as to engage in such frivolity. All too soon the dance was over and Marcus was relinquishing her to her next partner. Was he as reluctant as she at their parting?

The rest of the ball passed in a blur. In the carriage on the way home, Harriet's mind dwelled on their waltz and the easy rapport of their conversation. She was not ready to let go of the evening. Nor, it seemed, was Marcus.

"May I interest you ladies in a small glass of wine before we retire?" he asked as they shed their cloaks in the entranceway. "Aunt Gertrude? Harriet?"

Aunt Gertrude stifled a yawn. "Oh, not for me, my dear. I fear you young people have far more stamina than I for these evening affairs."

"Harriet?" he repeated.

She hesitated only a moment. She would be alone with him—but Lady Hermiston seemed to think nothing amiss with that—and it was not as though Harriet

Knightly were some green girl whose virtue needed guarding. "I—I think I should like that very much."

They bade Aunt Gertrude good night and then Marcus steered her into the library, where she took one of the wing chairs at a marble-topped table. He found a decanter of wine, poured two glasses, and handed her one. She felt again that shock of awareness as their fingers touched. He took the opposite chair.

Aware of the intimacy of their situation, it occurred to her that perhaps this was not such a good idea after all. She sought refuge in polite conversation. "It was a very nice ball. The Hatterlees seemed pleased with their turnout."

"Yes." He nodded equally polite agreement.

"The music was exceptional. I think I might have danced the night away."

He set his glass down and rose, extending his hand. "Come, Harriet, dance with me now."

Laughing nervously, she allowed him to pull her to her feet. "But, Marcus, we have no music."

"We shall make our own music." He took her in his arms and began to hum. "Come," he encouraged. "Join me."

She added her low voice to his in nonsense syllables of the piece to which they had danced earlier. She had no idea how long they danced about the room in tight but graceful little steps. She was lost in the sheer presence of this man. Had she really dreamed of this moment her whole life? Their feet slowed and finally stopped.

"Harriet?" he whispered. He put a finger under her chin to lift her face to his. His mouth settled on hers in a kiss that was exquisitely sweet. Stunned at the sensations he evoked, she was still for the briefest moment, then her lips returned the pressure of his.

He lifted his head to gaze into her eyes for an instant. "I—Harriet!"

His lips on hers were now fiercely demanding. His hands stroked her back, pulling her ever closer. She could not help herself—did not *want* to do so. She responded in kind, giving even as he gave. They seemed to come to their senses simultaneously and pulled apart, though he still held her firmly.

"My God!" he murmured. "I—I apologize. I had no right."

She pushed against his chest and he loosened his hold on her. "Please. Do not refine upon it," she said. "I expect we were both carried away by the spirit of the ball."

"Nevertheless, I hope you know it is not my custom to take advantage of a guest in my home."

"It had not occurred to me that you were, Marcus."

"Still, I am sorry I lost control."

"You are sorry you kissed me?" Her tone, both curious and challenging, also carried a teasing note.

"Actually—no." He grinned at her. "But I shall endeavor to see you are not subjected to a repeat mauling."

"We shall both simply forget it happened." She knew—even as the words slipped past her tongue—that she would be wholly incapable of forgetting that searing kiss. "Good night, Marcus."

Marcus sat in the library long after she had gone. Whatever had possessed him? How totally unlike him to forget himself so. He realized now he had wanted to kiss her for days—perhaps since that first moment in her drawing room.

Still, it was a stupid thing to have done. There was absolutely no point in complicating the situation between them. It was quite enough that they must make rational, considered judgments regarding the ward they shared.

Thinking to give both himself and Harriet space to remove any awkwardness between them, he absented himself most of the next day. The evening meal proceeded as usual, and he adjourned to his club afterward. The following day they met casually and, except for an occasional inquiring glance, their lives resumed a semblance of normality.

One afternoon a few days after the ball and its startling aftermath, Marcus entered the library to find all three of "his" females there, each with her nose firmly imbedded in some sort of reading material. Aunt Gertrude appeared to be reading a manual; Harriet sat with an open book; and Annabelle appeared to be engrossed in a magazine article.

On his entering the silent room, they each looked up to greet him. Harriet and Aunt Gertrude indicated ready willingness to be distracted from their particular reading matter, but Annabelle could scarcely tear her eyes away from hers. Her mouth dropped in surprise, and a look of distress crossed her features.

She emitted a shocked gasp. "Oh, my goodness. This is terrible. Yes." She seemed to be holding discourse with the writer. "Yes. Something should be done!"

Marcus strolled over to Annabelle's chair to glance over her shoulder. "What *is* it, Annabelle, that has captured your attention so?"

She looked up, her eyes filled with concern. "I picked up *The London Review* at the bookshop today. Oh, Marcus, really—you would not believe it. But it must be true—the writer seems so sincere."

"*What?*" he asked again in amused impatience. He thought she must be reading one of those serialized gothic novels.

"This is an exposé of terrible abuse of small children—some with scarcely more than four years."

She had the attention of all three adults, who seemed surprised at her choice of reading matter.

Harriet spoke first. "But I thought you were reading the latest installment of *The Count's Revenge.*"

"I finished that earlier," Annabelle said. She held up the magazine. "This article reveals some shocking information about society's indifference to the plight of poor children. Some are kidnapped—kidnapped!—to serve as chimney sweeps. And—even more appalling—some are actually sold into slavery by their very own parents!"

Aunt Gertrude said, "I doubt a young lady should be reading such material, my dear. It is sure to give you bad dreams."

"Well, perhaps people such as we *should* have a few bad dreams about situations of the sort this writer describes!" Annabelle's voice carried the shocked indignation of youth discovering injustices in life.

"That may be true," Marcus said mildly, "but I doubt the writer intends his material for England's schoolrooms."

"But, Marcus—" Annabelle's voice rose. She sounded to him as though she were on a campaign-for-a-cause. "The very people who will eventually right the wrongs of our society are probably *in* schoolrooms now."

Marcus looked at Harriet, who seemed somewhat uncomfortable—alarmed?—at the tenor of this conversation. He kept his tone indulgent as he asked Annabelle, "Oh? And are there other 'wrongs' you will seek to right?"

She held up her magazine. "Yes. Many of them."

"Such as?"

"Treatment of the poor. Are you aware that this country has no effective way of dealing with those suffering the degradation of poverty? It is up to individual parishes—and *they* often chase their poor away. And then there is the way women are treated."

Marcus could hear his own voice growing somewhat chilly. "The women of my acquaintance are not precisely suffering. They are very well taken care of."

"But that is precisely the point," Annabelle said. "They—we—are treated like favored pets—if we are lucky—and like work animals if we are not."

Marcus was taken aback. This sounded vaguely familiar to him. He had read or heard such exaggerated positions quite recently—but where?

Harriet broke in. "Annabelle, where did you get this—this material?" She pointed to the *Review* in Annabelle's hand.

"This one I picked up at the bookshop today because I recognized this author's name. Letty and I had two other of his essays. But Mrs. Hepplewhite confiscated those, too."

"As well she should," Marcus grumbled. "Just who is this writer?"

Annabelle's voice was eager. "He calls himself the Gadfly, but—"

"What?!" Marcus reached for the magazine. "Let me see that."

Chastened by his tone, Annabelle meekly handed it over and said in a small voice, "I—I do not think that is a real name."

"Of course not," Marcus said, impatient. "The cocky fellow has delusions of grandeur."

Harriet seemed to choke on a small cough. "D-delusions of grandeur?"

"Yes. Delusions of grandeur. Fancies himself some sort of Socrates—always badgering the government to do something about problems that are none of the government's business."

Annabelle gave a little squeal of delight. "Oh! I did not see that allusion to Socrates. But of course. It is perfect. Socrates did call himself 'the gadfly.' How very clever of our modern Gadfly."

Marcus snorted in disgust. "You *do* remember the end to which Socrates came, do you not?"

"You think this writer will be forced to swallow hemlock?" Harriet asked, her tone neutral.

"No, but if he does not stop spewing out his own brand of poison to corrupt young minds such as we see here, he may find himself in serious trouble."

"Is it not lucky for Gadfly that English people have certain rights in being able to express their own minds?" Harriet asked—a shade too sweetly, he thought.

"Good heavens! Am I to assume you knew about this?" He waved the magazine in her direction. "Is *this* part of the course of study you supervise?"

Two spots of color appeared on Harriet's cheeks. "No, my lord, it is *not* part of Annabelle's studies. I was not aware that she had purchased this publication. However, I see nothing wrong in either the Gadfly's views—or in Annabelle's knowing of them."

"Oh? You see nothing wrong in this man's unrelenting criticism of your government? A government that has brought the country through an unparalleled crisis—a whole generation of war with France—not to mention that ugly little sideshow with the former colonies. A government that has brought unprecedented prosperity despite these hardships?" He knew he was ranting, but he could not help himself.

"This government did have remarkable success in defeating Napoleon," she conceded, "but at a cost infinitely greater than it should have been."

He was outraged. "You measure a moral victory over anarchy and tyranny in terms of *money?*"

"I was thinking more of lives lost needlessly as the government you defend so nobly dithered in their reluctance to accord the army proper support. And the truly tragic losses—because they were so unnecessary—in what you label 'that ugly little sideshow with the former colonies.'" She took a deep breath and went on. "Unprecedented prosperity? Try that argument with people being forced off the land by enclosures—or returning soldiers unable to support their families—or workers whose jobs have been eliminated by new machines."

"Obviously," he said in a dry tone, "Annabelle is not the only one well schooled in the work of this . . . this . . . jackanapes. He needs to learn—and may I remind you, madam—that the prosperity of a nation never begins with the lower orders. Jobs are created by having men of conscience and vision as leaders. As they prosper, the wealth is passed on to those lower down."

"At a snail's pace," Harriet muttered.

"May I also remind you that Rome was not built in a day?"

"It would be nice, though, if some of this prosperity finally made its way *down* in our lifetime."

"Are you advocating a revolution in England? One would have supposed the recent example across the Channel would have curbed such radical thought."

Harriet drew a deep breath and enunciated each word precisely. "No. I am not advocating revolution."

"Well, this fellow is!" Marcus waved the magazine.

"Gadfly does nothing of the sort," she said heatedly. "Why is it that the very people who should bring about reforms in our society see the specter of revolution in every suggestion of change?"

"And why is it," he shot back, "that people like this Gadfly see only the ills and ignore genuine efforts to provide remedies? Reform in this country *will* come— but without the government's meddling in private business. There will be no Napoleons *here!*"

He was suddenly conscious of a look of alarm on Annabelle's face, and Aunt Gertrude cleared her throat and gave him a speaking look.

"Marcus. Harriet." Her tone was mildly admonishing. "I—I think . . . the two of you are allowing emotion to cloud your views."

Marcus felt slightly chagrined. He looked at Harriet and thought she, too, had been taken aback by the vehemence of their exchange.

"Aunt Gertrude is right. May we return to the issue at hand?" He tapped the magazine with his finger. "I would prefer that such treatises not become part of the regular course of study for any ward of mine."

"Did you not hear me say that it has not been?" she asked with an exaggerated show of patience.

"Truly, Marcus—my lord—" Annabelle sounded anxious and uncharacteristically meek. "I discovered this writer on my own. Are . . . uh . . . are you forbidding me to read such?"

He was thoughtful for a moment. Then he spoke slowly. "No. . . . Despite this writer's raising havoc among members of the House of Lords, I do not condone the practice of censoring anyone's ideas. However, I would ask that you consider other views on all issues."

He thought all three of his companions breathed easier at this. He handed the *Review* back to Annabelle.

"That seems reasonable," Aunt Gertrude said.

Harriet nodded, but he did not think she was totally mollified. Aunt Gertrude pointedly introduced another topic of conversation, and the evening ended on a pleasant note.

Later Marcus lay awake, replaying the entire scene in his mind. Obviously, the woman with whom he shared the guardianship was far more of a "reformer" in her thinking than he had thought. Ah, well, it should not prove to be too much of a problem. Annabelle—and, indeed, Harriet herself—seemed to have some sense of when and where it was appropriate to expound such liberal views.

By Jupiter! Harriet was beautiful with her eyes ablaze—her very being animated by an idea. Even now his body remembered the passion of her response to his kiss. Harriet Knightly was a woman of strong emotions and fervently held views. He would do well to remember that.

Luckily, in the grand scheme of things, females had little genuine influence. It was men like this Gadfly who posed a real threat to the nation—stirring up emotions and agitating for immediate and radical reform—and doing so behind a barricade of anonymity, at that.

"Gadfly, indeed!"

Six

His lordship's chamber was not the only room whose occupant was sleeplessly pounding pillows. Harriet was decidedly annoyed.

"Delusions of grandeur, indeed!"

She deemed "Gadfly" a very fitting pseudonym—Lord knew she could not use her own name. No one would take such ideas seriously if they were known to come from the pen of a woman. Women wrote novels such as Mrs. Radcliffe's or moral treatises such as Hannah More's—females did not venture into the male domains of public policy and politics. Even Marcus assumed the writer was a man.

Initially, she had not wanted her writing to prove embarrassing for her sister and her own friends. Now it was more important than ever to keep Gadfly's identity secret, for discovery would reflect upon Annabelle, too.

She smiled triumphantly to herself. If the oh-so-noble Earl of Wyndham's reaction were any indication, Gadfly must be rather effective. What had Marcus said? "Raising havoc among the members of the House of Lords." That was it. Good! It was about time some of those august personages were jarred out of their complacency.

She had to admit, though, that one of that number had jarred *her.* She had fully expected him to answer Annabelle's question by forbidding her to read any more of Gadfly's work. Instead, he had been fair and seemed open-minded about it.

"Seemed," she reminded herself. There was little doubt that Marcus Jeffries, Earl of Wyndham, shared the opinions of others in power, all of whom appeared to view their world in lofty abstractions. They paid but little regard to the realities of individual people affected by their policies.

This view of the Earl of Wyndham as a public figure contrasted with her feelings for the private man. His kiss had unnerved her. Her own response had unnerved her even more. She recalled very clearly the exquisite torture of her infatuation with him when she was a mere child. That those feelings had resurfaced— albeit in a more mature manner—was nothing short of embarrassing. She would have to ensure that the scene in the library was not repeated—no matter how she might long for his touch.

In early November, when the principal residents of Wyndham House had spent two evenings running in one another's exclusive company, Marcus made an announcement that at first alarmed Harriet.

They had gathered in the drawing room. Aunt Gertrude busied herself with some embroidery. Harriet was teaching Annabelle to play backgammon. Marcus had been idly playing some light tunes on the pianoforte, a practice that had surprised Harriet earlier, for relatively few men of the *ton* indulged in actually playing an instrument. He ended a tune with a flare and turned on his seat.

"I think," he said in a demand for the others' attention, "that we should all repair to Timberly until after the Christmas season."

He waited like a little boy for their approval. Aunt Gertrude was the first to respond.

"That would be marvelous."

"Why?" Harriet held the dice cup, suspending play.

Caught completely off guard, she had not once thought of such a possibility and had no time to consider the ramifications now. Her mind worked furiously as she set the cup down.

"We Jeffrieses always spend Christmas at Timberly," he replied. "With most members of Parliament out of town, there is little pressing business here."

"Spoken like a true member of the established order." Harriet smiled, her tone more teasing than cutting.

"It is true," Aunt Gertrude said, "that the city is now devoid of much in the way of diverting company."

"What say you, Annabelle?" Marcus asked. "Would *you* welcome a sojourn in the country?"

"I . . . I have no idea. Wha-what would I do there?"

He waved a hand airily. "Why, more or less what you do here, I suppose. Some lessons would have to be curtailed, but most would continue."

It occurred to Harriet that this suggestion of going to the country was less spontaneous than it had at first seemed. Clearly, this presumptuous man expected Annabelle's principal instructor simply to pack up and follow wherever he chose to lead!

She sat up straighter. "I am afraid this would be impossible for me, my lord." She could not keep the chill formality from her tone. "I had planned to spend the Christmas season itself with my sister at the Knightly estate. Travel to and from Timberly—in the opposite direction from London—would be most inconvenient. And I do not believe *all* of Annabelle's lessons should be suspended for such a long time."

There was also the matter of Gadfly, she thought. How would she get her essays to Mr. Watson? But she could hardly offer that issue as a reason for staying in town.

She added, "And . . . and I have commitments here in town. . . ."

"Can you not be freed of them for a few weeks?"

"Perhaps. . . ." Yes. She *might* prepare Gadfly's next articles ahead of time. One at least was nearly finished. "But my sister—"

"Invite her and Berwyn to join you at Timberly. It would mean a much shorter distance for them to travel, would it not? Your sister might enjoy visiting scenes from her childhood."

"True—on both counts," she conceded. Drat the man. How was it that he always seemed to make short work of her objections to a scheme?

"And," he went on enthusiastically, "we shall invite my brother, Trevor and his wife, Caitlyn. Aunt Gertrude, did you not tell me Trevor and Berwyn served together?"

"Yes. They did," his aunt said. Her eyes twinkled with amusement. "Are you aware that you are planning a rather large house party?"

He shrugged. "Perhaps as many as twenty people—that is hardly a large party."

"Not counting young children, who must, of course, accompany their parents at this season," Aunt Gertrude replied.

He looked at his aunt beseechingly. "I had rather counted on your helping me . . . ?"

"Of course, my dear. And you should include Melanie and Andrew as well. Your sister would be sorely put out were she excluded."

"I know. I *had* planned for them. How many children will that entail? I forget."

Aunt Gertrude ticked them off on her fingers. "Let me see. Trevor and Melanie have three each. And how many little ones did you tell me your sister has, Harriet?"

"Two. A boy and a girl. And Berwyn's sister lives with Charlotte and Tom when she is not away at school. She is sixteen and will surely be with them for the holiday season."

Annabelle clapped her hands in glee. "Oh, good. I shall have a confidante."

"And there is Andrew's ward," Aunt Gertrude said. "He usually spends school holidays with Melanie and Andrew."

Harriet began to see the proposal in a more positive light. Perhaps exposure to others who were off to school would lead Annabelle to entertain the notion of returning to school.

Marcus had turned back to gaze directly at Harriet. "So? Will you come?"

"Yes. If Lady Hermiston will allow me to help her."

"I had already counted on both of you to help." Aunt Gertrude's smile included both Annabelle and Harriet.

"If there are others you would like to invite, Harriet, please feel free to do so," Marcus said. "I shall be glad to extend the invitations."

"Thank you, Marcus."

Ten days later they were on their way to Timberly in three carriages, accompanied by a wagon for luggage. Besides personal servants, several of the staff from Wyndham House would augment that of Timberly. There would be the day-to-day entertainments of houseguests at Timberly to see to—as well as a larger party to which local residents would be invited. Extra servants would also be needed to provide for traditional Christmas festivities.

Harriet had met Mr. Watson in a bookshop and given him two essays for his monthly magazine, *The London Review.*

"Two?" He raised his eyebrows in surprise.

"December and January. I shall be back in town in time to give you the February article."

"Very good, madam. We have had quite a response to the one on chimney sweeps."

"Not all of it negative, I hope."

"Not all of it. Even the hardest of hearts find it difficult to approve the exploitation of small children."

Harriet tapped the sheaf of papers. "This one on the rights of women will probably ruffle some feathers in the gentlemen's clubs—but so be it."

Mr. Watson carefully tucked the papers into a portfolio he carried and then pretended to be pointing out a book to Harriet as another customer approached. "Perhaps this the book you were seeking, madam."

Charlotte had written that she was thrilled to receive an invitation to Timberly, and Harriet looked forward to seeing her sister after several months apart.

It had been a remarkably mild late autumn, so the roads had not yet produced the hazards of great chuckholes and rivers of mud the travelers might have encountered. They stayed at respectable inns along the way and amused themselves during the journey by reading aloud or playing twenty questions.

It had been years since Harriet had left what had been her father's estate. Now, as she began to see familiar landmarks, she felt the thrill of recognition and recalled warm memories of her childhood. She and Marcus were sitting opposite each other. Near the outskirts of the village of Ammerton, Marcus pointed out the window.

"Look, Harriet. Is that not the tree your overzealous kitten climbed and then was afraid to come down?"

She looked and—sure enough—there was the very spot where a nine-years-old Harriet had fallen in love with a resplendent young Marcus. Then she mentally shook herself. Fallen in love? What kind of poppycock was that? Aloud she said with a laugh, "So it is. And you risked life and limb to rescue him."

"What I risked—and ruined—was a new waistcoat of which I was inordinately proud at the time."

"Oh, how very sad." Her tone was exaggerated. "I shall have my man of business replace it for you. Better late than never."

"Good heavens, no! It was a ghastly color." He chuckled, then added with a gesture, "All this was once part of your father's estate, was it not?"

She nodded. "Yes. It was."

"Would you like to visit it? I am sure we could arrange with the current viscount for you and your sister to be shown around."

Mention of the present holder of her father's title sent a shudder of revulsion through her. She stifled it and said simply, "That will not be necessary."

"Have you no interest in seeing your childhood home?" he asked with obvious curiosity.

"Some. But it is often best to keep things as they were in happy memory." And not sully them with subsequent events, she thought

"It shall be just as you wish." He gave her a concerned glance before turning his attention to the others. Aunt Gertrude was giving Annabelle a running history of Timberly and pointing out items of interest to the girl.

Finally, they arrived in sight of the magnificent edifice that had been the main seat of the earls of Wyndham for nearly three centuries.

"Oh! How wonderful!" Annabelle's eyes were bight with pleasure. "It truly *is* a castle!"

"Well, of course, dear." Aunt Gertrude tone sounded slightly puzzled to Harriet's ear. "Did I not tell you as much?"

"You did, indeed, my lady, but I supposed you were

perhaps exaggerating somewhat." Annabelle's was the ingenuous honesty of youth.

"Exaggerated? I *never* exaggerate," Aunt Gertrude said with exaggerated hauteur and a wink at the others.

"Oh, my lady, I did not mean to imply—" Annabelle started to say, then seemed to realize Aunt Gertrude was teasing her. Annabelle's laugh joined the others.

"There was once a wall and a moat around the main buildings," Marcus explained. "The wall has long since disappeared—served as a quarry for many a cottage. And the moat was drained and filled in during the last century."

"What a setting for a romantical tale." Annabelle sat forward on her seat for a better look.

"Mrs. Radcliffe, give way. Our Annabelle is about to challenge your position," Marcus teased.

"Well, not quite yet." Annabelle gave a self-conscious laugh. "But maybe someday . . ."

"Novels?" Harriet was surprised and not altogether approving.

"I enjoy writing." Annabelle seemed slightly defensive.

"Yes, dear, and you write very well," Harriet reassured her. "Such talent could be quite effective on serious work."

Marcus raised one of his expressive brows. "You do not think a novelist takes his work seriously?"

"He—or *she*—may well do so, but the purpose of a fictional story is certainly less profound than that of a serious work."

"By serious work you mean an essay?" he asked.

"Well . . . yes."

"I find the delightful characters created by the lady writer of the novel *Pride and Prejudice* to present far more interesting commentary on human nature than the ponderous sermons of the Reverend Fordyce. Do you not agree?"

Harriet was nonplussed. "Well, I . . . I agree that they are more *delightful*. One always takes more *delight* in being entertained than in being educated. . . ."

"But that lady does both," he insisted. "The foolish Lydia, the prattling Mrs. Bennet, the fatuous Mr. Collins, the arrogant Lady Catherine—how could an essay full of thou-shalt-nots be nearly so effective?"

Annabelle's expression of stark amazement reflected Harriet's own reaction to this discourse. Even his aunt seemed taken aback. He grinned and added, "Ah-ha! I took you all by surprise, eh?"

Aunt Gertrude was the first to recover. "That you did, my dear. I had no idea you were so familiar with that novel."

"I admit that I do not share many of the Prince Regent's enthusiasms, but he has the right of it in endorsing this writer."

Harriet sniffed. "I would not consider the Prince's approval any ringing clarion of what is fit and proper."

"Nor would I, madam. Nor would I," he said. "Write whatever you like, Annabelle. Just try to ensure its quality, whatever it is."

Harriet was feeling chagrined. She had not meant to sound so pompous. The fact was, she agreed with much of what he had said. Still, she could not quite approve of Annabelle's talent being wasted on fiction. However, as *she*, not his lordship, was Annabelle's principal teacher, she would simply guide the girl toward more serious work.

Ten minutes later they were enmeshed in the controlled chaos of their arrival. It was not until much later that Harriet reflected on the conversation in the carriage and realized she had been shown an entirely different side of the increasingly enigmatic Earl of Wyndham.

* * *

Marcus had spent little time at Timberly since ascending to the title. Early on, he had been preoccupied with the details of quitting his diplomatic post and managing the Wyndham affairs in London. Because of his experience with the diplomatic corps, he had, as a member of the House of Lords, often been called upon to help set government policy in the nation's foreign concerns. This, too, had kept him in the city.

Thus he had left the affairs of Timberly in the capable hands of his steward, John Trenton. Trenton, who had served Jeffries men for nearly two decades, was not overly imaginative, but he was honest and followed orders conscientiously. Marcus's principal order had so far been to carry on whatever programs his father and brother had started, for one should not tamper with success—and the books showed Timberly as quite successful.

Now, however, it was time he took a closer interest in the detailed workings of his properties. In the few days he had before his younger brother and other guests arrived, he intended to go about the estate with Trenton and study the books more assiduously than he had done before. At times he felt overwhelmed with how much he had yet to learn. After all, it had been the ill-fated *Gerald* who had been slated for the earldom.

Timberly, like other great estates in Britain, had always been farmed with tenant labor working small plots of open land in common. In the last two decades or so, this practice had been changing as landowners enclosed their properties in large fields to raise crops and cattle, especially sheep, far more efficiently. Marcus noted that the process on his own land had begun gradually but then accelerated rapidly.

"You see, my lord," Trenton responded to Marcus's question, "your father thought to move folks off the land slowly so as not to cause too much hardship."

"How did he mean to do this?"

"He sort of waited till men became too old to work the land—or died—before he took over or moved folks. Some of the younger farmers emigrated to the colonies, too. And your pa often helped those who wanted to do so."

"And my brother?"

"Lord Gerald, he wanted things accomplished a lot quicker. 'Tis mostly done now," Trenton said with a degree of pride.

"What happened to the people?"

Trenton shrugged. "Gone. Emigrated to the colonies. Took jobs in the Midlands in the mills there. Went to the city."

Marcus wondered briefly what a farmer or sheepherder would do in the city, but Trenton seemed to have little real interest in what happened to people displaced by the enclosures. As other matters vied for his attention, Marcus, too, allowed the matter to slide to the back of his mind.

The morning after arriving at Timberly, he had invited Aunt Gertrude to join in his meeting with the housekeeper and the butler to inform them of the anticipated guests. They were also told that Aunt Gertrude would be overseeing matters in that regard as well as acting as Lord Wyndham's hostess. Later he scheduled a meeting with the head of his stables and inspected those facilities, pleased with what he found. Even later, he summoned Seth Connors, the gamekeeper to his office. Connors, a wiry fellow with thinning straight black hair and a surly demeanor, had been hired shortly before Marcus's father became ill. Marcus had never particularly liked the man but did not feel that was sufficient reason to dismiss him.

"We got problems, my lord," Connors announced in an authoritative, almost accusing tone.

"Of what sort?"

"Lack of game."

"Are you not engaged in breeding new stock to be released into the forest and fields to replenish the supply of game?"

"Yes, sir, but poachers—they get lots of 'em."

"Poachers?"

"They get bolder an' bolder, my lord."

"I believe our practice has traditionally been to overlook poaching to *some* degree. After all, the poor must feed their families."

"Yes, sir. But it's gotten much worse of late. I put out mantraps, but they avoids 'em despite how I change the locations."

"You put out mantraps?" Marcus kept his voice cool though hot fury coursed through his body.

"Yes, sir. Your brother ordered 'em—an' a good idea it was, too. Caught a couple of poachers that way," he said with notable pride.

Marcus spoke through clenched teeth. "You will go immediately and retrieve every last one of those contrivances and see that they are given to the blacksmith to be refashioned into useful tools."

The gamekeeper seemed totally taken aback. "But, my lord—"

"No buts—just do it." Marcus remembered all too well having to put down a favorite mount which had tangled with a mantrap. Besides having been broken, the horse's leg had been hideously mangled. "Those infernal things can cause serious—even permanent injury to a man."

"An' that's exactly what makes poachers back off, if I may say so."

"No grouse or hare is worth that sort of misery." Marcus's emphatic tone left no room for argument.

"Yes, my lord," Connors said grudgingly. "But . . . but I sure hopes you won't be holdin' me to blame when poachers overrun your land."

"We shall find an assistant to help you patrol."

"Thank you, my lord," Connors said, but gratitude was markedly absent in his tone.

When the man had left, Marcus found his anger at Connors abating—after all, the previous Earl of Wyndham had ordered the things—but he began to chastise himself for not having taken a keener interest in Timberly earlier.

Seven

Harriet had mixed feelings about returning to scenes of her childhood. In general—until the death of her father—hers had been a happy youth. But with his death, poverty and responsibility had come crashing in upon her. Now she tried to concentrate on the happiest moments. And those always came back to her as feelings for the then Lord Wyndham's second son. These feelings were entangled with her current feelings for the present Lord Wyndham—that second son grown up.

She recognized a strong physical attraction for him and was certain he felt such, too. She reminded herself that she had been content in her marriage and that she was now enjoying the sheer freedom that being a widow accorded her. She was answerable to no one.

Not that Raymond Knightly had been so very restrictive in dealing with his wife. Still, he had curbed her behavior some and forced her to modify her thoughts—or at least her expression of them—now and then. She knew he would never have approved of the Gadfly's writings, for instance. At first she had felt downright disloyal when she wrote something she knew would have drawn a disapproving frown from him. But after all, she was her own person, and they were *her* thoughts, and why should she inhibit herself now? She became bolder in such expression as time put distance between her and her erstwhile mentor.

Along with her newfound intellectual freedom, she was aware that widows also enjoyed more social freedom than unmarried ladies, no matter their age. Even had she not known this, certain rakes of the *ton* had lost little time in trying to disabuse her of her supposed ignorance. Harriet Knightly was not about to settle for a "slip on the shoulder." Nor would she enter into another marriage of convenience, no matter how well the first had turned out.

No. If she married again, it would be for love—and at this stage of her life, *that* was an unlikely possibility. Now, why should the image of Marcus Jeffries float into her musings with that thought? How utterly foolish. It was just that being here at Timberly had brought back memories of bygone yearnings.

Harriet delayed going about much until Charlotte's arrival. Meanwhile, she busied herself with Annabelle's lessons and helping Lady Hermiston plan accommodation, meals, and entertainment for the influx of visitors.

In the event, Charlotte arrived one day, and the earl's brother and then his sister, with their families, the next. In the flurry of greetings and introductions, there was little time for the sisterly "coze" Harriet had anticipated.

On the second day of Charlotte's visit, the gentlemen had gone off for an early morning shoot, taking young Ned, Andrew's ward, with them. The ladies were enjoying a leisurely breakfast, when Lady Hermiston, ever sensitive to the needs of others, suggested, "I am sure, Harriet dear, that you and Mrs. Berwyn would like to go about and renew acquaintance with some of your particular friends. Marcus has put a carriage and coachman at our disposal, as you know."

"But we should not be so rude as to exclude others," Harriet said with a smile for Caitlyn Jeffries and Melanie Sheffield.

Melanie laughed. "On the contrary, we are the rude ones. Caitlyn and I have planned a long ride this morning—and I believe Annabelle and Celia have some sort of adventure planned."

Harriet had been pleased to see that all three of the young people appeared to get on well together.

"And I intend to spend some time doting on Caitlyn's toddlers," Aunt Gertrude announced, referring to Caitlyn's twins, who were but fifteen months old.

Catching a nod from Charlotte, Harriet smiled in agreement. "In that case, we should be happy to accept the offer of the carriage."

As soon as they were settled in the vehicle, Charlotte pounced.

"So—tell me what is going on with you and Lord Wyndham."

Harriet drew in a sharp breath. Trust Charlotte to cut to the quick without preamble. "Why—why, whatever do you mean? We share guardianship of Annabelle—that is all."

"Please, Harriet. Do not try to gammon *me!* I see the two of you tiptoeing around each other, the looks when you think no one notices."

Harriet felt herself blushing and hoped the overcast day made the interior of the carriage dim enough to hide her heightened color. "Charlotte Louise," she reprimanded, "you always did have a vivid imagination."

"Very well." Charlotte made a dismissive gesture. "If you do not want to discuss it, so be it."

"There is nothing to discuss."

"I said 'very well,' " Charlotte repeated, and then went right on. "But he *is* a very handsome man. You could do much worse, you know."

Harriet sighed. The only way to deal with Charlotte was head-on.

"Yes, he is. And yes, I could—*if* I were interested

in marrying again. But I am not. What is more, the
Earl of Wyndham—*when* he chooses a bride—will undoubtedly settle on some young miss fresh out of the
schoolroom." Harriet paused, swallowed, and added
in a quieter tone, "One who will be able to give him
an heir."

She could not explain to herself—and had no time
at the moment to dwell upon—just why that thought
was so painful. Was it the image of Marcus making
love with another—younger—woman? Or was it her
own failure to produce a child with Raymond
Knightly?

"Oh, Harry, I am sorry. I—I did not mean to open
an old would."

"Never mind. I know you intended no meanness."

"Nor do I intend to cause further pain, but I must
say this—you are not as old as our mama was when I
was born. And you cannot be sure you were at fault
in your having no children in your marriage. Mr.
Knightly and his first wife had no child either."

Harriet had no chance to reply as the carriage drew
up at the vicarage and the footman jumped down
from his post at the back of the coach to open the
door. Mr. Henderson had accepted his position as
vicar in Ammerton when Harriet was a young child.
He and his wife greeted Harriet and Charlotte warmly
and offered refreshments.

When the four of them were seated and tea had
been served, Mr. Henderson spoke.

"What a pleasure it is to have you both back in our
little world. And to have the earl at Timberly."

"The villagers have not been so excited since before
the old earl left us," his wife added.

"A sad time, that." The vicar shook his head. "Folks
had hardly adjusted to that loss, when Lord Gerald was
gone, too. He held the title for a such a short time."

Mrs. Henderson sniffed delicately. "Long enough
to wreak genuine hardship in some quarters."

"Now, Martha," he admonished. "We must not speak ill of the dead."

"Nevertheless, we all breathed a bit easier when Lord Marcus came into the title," the vicar's wife assured her visitors.

Harriet and Charlotte asked about other acquaintances, and the discussion was more general for a few moments. Harriet carefully avoided asking about her father's successor and her old home. Charlotte was not so particular.

"I believe the viscount is currently in residence," Mr. Henderson replied to the query, "but we do not often see him at services."

"Talk among the servants is that he leads a rather dissipated life since his wife died," Mrs. Henderson said. "Frail little thing she was. Died of the fever that swept through the parish, taking some good people. The same one that took Lord Gerald."

"The viscount has not remarried, then?" Charlotte asked.

"Not yet. Probably hanging out for a rich wife. They do say he has all but exhausted what he inherited from his mother—and from his wife's marriage settlements."

"And the estate?" Harriet asked softly.

Mr. Henderson shook his head. "Still not doing well. His tenants are among the poorest people of the parish."

They sat in silence for a moment, then Harriet asked if Mr. Henderson still raised prize roses. She knew the vicar was justly famed throughout the county for his garden.

His chuckle contained a degree of pride. "Yes. In season I continue to try."

"He has added orchids to his gardening interests," his wife said.

"Orchids! In this climate?" Harriet asked.

"I have a very small solarium," he explained. "Would you like to see it?"

" 'Tis his pride and joy," his wife said.

It *was* small. With all the plants—a number of other tropical varieties shared space with the orchids—there was barely enough room for another person. Charlotte and Harriet took turns "oohing" and "aahing" over the exotic plants.

They then took their leave to visit the graveyard where their parents lay side by side. There were other graves to visit as well—those of retainers, neighbors, and friends, including that of Terrence Jeffries, who had died in a racing accident some eight or nine years earlier.

"He was so young . . . and so handsome and full of fun," Charlotte murmured.

"Yes. Trevor took his twin's death very hard. Jason's, too. Blamed himself for both of them the longest while."

"They were all three rather wild in those days," Charlotte observed.

Afterward, since the threatened rain still had not materialized, they walked around the village, stopping in at the few shops. It was a leisurely process, as they were hailed frequently and warmly. They paused at the outer edge of the village to call briefly upon the blacksmith's wife, Jenny, who had played with the Glasser girls in former times. The blacksmith's forge was in a shed attached to his house.

As Charlotte and Harriet were leaving, a young man drove a small cart into the blacksmith's yard with a good deal of clanking to accompany his arrival.

"Hey, Smitty," he called. "Where ya want these things?"

The blacksmith came to the opened wide door of his shed. He was a big man, his sandy hair tousled, his freckled face shining with sweat and smudged with ash. He wore a leather apron and held a huge hammer in his hand.

"What have we here?" he asked in a mild tone.

"Traps. Mantraps." The youth grinned. "Lord Wyndham, he said ol' Connors had ta get rid of 'em."

The blacksmith's eyes lit up, and his grin mirrored the youth's. "Did he now?"

"Sure did. Where you want 'em?"

"Around the back there." The smith gestured and shot a look at his wife as the boy followed his directive. "Didn't I tell you our old friend wouldn't like them things?"

"That you did, my love."

Hers was the agreeable tone wives used to placate husbands. Harriet smiled at the obvious affection and understanding between the couple.

She and Charlotte made their farewells and walked toward their carriage, which had been parked in front of the inn. Their driver and the footman were apparently enjoying a pint as a local boy held the horses. Just as they approached, the door of the inn opened and a well-dressed gentleman emerged. He glanced in their direction, stopped abruptly, and gazed boldly.

He lifted his hat to show thinning blond hair. His pale blue eyes lit up. "Ah, my fair cousins." He sounded unctuous. "Well met, ladies."

"Lord Sefton," Charlotte said as Harriet nodded her greeting. Neither sister offered her hand. They would have moved on, but he stood in front of them, effectively blocking their way.

"I had heard you were visiting a neighboring estate." He slapped his beaver hat idly against his leg. "I wonder you did not choose to stay at Sefton Hall. You would be most welcome, you know."

He smiled invitingly at Harriet, his calculating glance taking in her entire appearance. He licked his lips in a manner she suddenly remembered, and she stifled an inward shudder.

"We were invited to Timberly," she said in a neutral tone but with slight emphasis on the word *invited*.

"Oh, to be sure," he said. "Had I but known my fair

cousins were desirous of visiting the area, I should have extended the invitation myself."

"How kind of you." Charlotte's tone was polite emptiness.

He reached for Harriet's gloved hand and spoke in a solemn voice. "Ah, cousin. You and I have suffered the same terrible loss in the last few months. What consolation we might have provided each other."

Harriet tugged her hand, which he reluctantly released. "Mr. Knightly has been gone nearly two years," she said.

"Of course, my dear. And I am sorry for your loss."

"Thank you." She breathed an inward sigh of relief as the Wyndham driver and footman came from the inn. "Now, if you will excuse us . . . ?"

He stepped aside, then said, "Allow me." He extended his hand to help first Charlotte, then Harriet, into the carriage as the footman held the door. The viscount squeezed Harriet's hand. "I shall see you at the Wyndham Christmas affair, I am sure." He made it sound like an assignation, she thought.

At last the door was closed and they were on their way.

"Insufferable boor!" Harriet muttered.

"He is that," Charlotte agreed. "Unless I miss my guess, he will be pursuing you."

"Pursuing Knightly's fortune, you mean." Harriet had no illusions about what a man of Sefton's ilk pursued.

"And *you,*" Charlotte insisted. "He did so once before. Knightly's fortune makes you a suitable prospect as a *wife* now."

"Ugh." Harriet shuddered in disgust.

Harriet knew that twice a year Timberly hosted celebrations to which local residents as well as guests from farther away were invited. In her youth she had looked forward to the large three-day festival at harvest time. Road conditions and weather usually limited the Christmas party to a much smaller affair but one she had always enjoyed.

Now she began to dread this year's fete. Her father's successor would surely be invited. Marcus would not deliberately cut a neighbor without reason, and Harriet could not bring herself to request that he eliminate the Viscount Sefton from his guest list.

Timberly's Christmas party was a family affair to which all but the very youngest children were invited, swelling the guest list even more. A huge Yule log was brought in for the outsized fireplace in the Great Hall. "Kissing boughs" of mistletoe were hung from each of the chandeliers. Garlands of greenery and holly festooned the room, giving it a pleasant piney scent. Mummers would enact traditional Christmas plays and carolers would perform.

The party was in full swing when Viscount Sefton arrived. Observing his absence before, Harriet had begun to breathe easier. But there he was, making quite a scene with fulsome compliments to his host and members of the earl's family.

"It is such a pleasure to be in your elegant abode, my lord. Such grandeur and such beautiful ladies to grace it." This last was expressed as he bent over Melanie's hand.

Seeing Melanie momentarily roll her eyes heavenward, Harriet felt a twinge of embarrassment at the man's being even remotely related to her.

Harriet happened to be standing near Charlotte and Berwyn. Charlotte gave her sister a look of sympathy, for it appeared Sefton was heading straight for them.

And he was.

"Ah, my dear, dear cousins," His voice was effusive. Harriet murmured ironically to Charlotte, "What was it Hamlet said? 'A little more than kin and less than kind'?"

Charlotte gave her a quizzical look.

"Never mind." She turned to her encroaching relative and bent her knees in the slightest of curtsies by way of greeting. "Lord Sefton."

"Oh, come, come, dear lady," he boomed, seemingly for the benefit of bystanders. "After all, we are family. You must call me George. Or, at the very least, Cousin George."

"As you wish, sir."

"George," he insisted.

"Cousin . . . George," she said, hoping her distaste was not conveyed to others.

"Cousin Charlotte, you must introduce me to your husband. I have heard much of this brave man who fought so gallantly with our forces in the Peninsula."

Harriet could see that Charlotte had little choice but to comply. She also noted that her brother-in-law was only distantly polite to his new acquaintance.

The viscount seemed unaware. "So nice to have you in the district again. We must plan a family get-together, just the four of us, one day soon—perhaps two days hence?"

"I . . . I am not sure . . ." Charlotte hesitated.

"We must, of course, accommodate any plans of ours to those of our host," Harriet explained, quickly racking her brain for a suitable excuse.

"Of course. I understand perfectly." And for just a moment his glittering eyes told her he did. Then he veiled his look and added in an affable tone, "I shall send a man around with a note. Surely, his lordship will understand family obligations."

"Obligations?" Harriet could not repress the edge in her voice.

"Interests, then," he said smoothly. "Family interests may take *some* precedence."

"Sir—" Harriet started to add in a firm tone.

Aunt Gertrude's voice cut in. "Excuse me, Mrs. Knightly, but I wonder if I might have a word with you about the mummers?"

"Of course, my lady." She excused herself and strolled away with Lady Hermiston. "What is it, my lady?"

"Nothing. Nothing at all, my dear. I merely thought you needed rescuing."

Harriet laughed softly. "I did. But now we have left poor Charlotte and Berwyn to fend for themselves."

"No, we have not. I have enlisted support, you see."

"Support?"

"I have commissioned Caitlyn and Trevor to go over and talk babies and war. That should send that encroaching toad off soon enough. Oh! I do apologize, dear. I quite forgot for the moment that he is a connection of yours."

Harriet smiled and patted the older woman's arm. "*You* are a marvel, Lady Hermiston. I quite like the way you marshal your forces. And there is no need to apologize for calling a spade a spade."

They approached a group whose members included Melanie, Andrew, and Marcus as well as two other couples—and a beautiful brunette who stood very close to Marcus. He gave Harriet an inquiring glance, then smiled, and his gaze held hers for an instant. She felt a familiar flood of warmth and returned his smile.

Marcus drew Harriet and Aunt Gertrude into his circle, introducing Aunt Gertrude to the couple she did not know—a former navy officer and his wife. He also introduced Harriet to those who were strangers to her—the navy couple, and Baron Thornton, his wife, and his daughter, Lady Teasler. There was no mention of Lord Teasler, so Harriet assumed the beauty was a widow like herself.

Those being introduced murmured appropriate responses, Lord Thornton noting that he been acquainted with Mr. Knightly. The Thorntons were dressed finely. He was a rather portly man who wore his evening dress with great dignity. His wife was nearly as tall as he, and Harriet thought her hair color had benefited from a generous dose of henna. Her elegant lavender gown hung on her angular frame almost as though the dressmaker had envisioned a more curvaceous body for the garment.

Lady Teasler's gown, a bright emerald green, was a direct contrast to her mother's, and showed off a voluptuous figure to great advantage. The color of the gown had clearly been chosen to reflect her ladyship's brilliant green eyes. With hair the color of a raven's wings and an oval face with fine arched brows, a straight, well-defined nose, and a rosebud mouth, the woman was one of the most beautiful Harriet had ever seen. Suddenly, she felt herself to be positively dowdy in comparison.

Dressed in conventional evening wear, the other couple seemed slightly less comfortable than the Thorntons and Lady Teasler. Harriet warmed to them immediately. Then Marcus added to his introductions by saying, "Captain and Mrs. Nichols have just joined the ranks of landed civilians."

Harriet's inquiring look at the captain and his wife invited an explanation which Mrs. Nichols supplied.

"We have taken leave from the navy—after twenty-five years of service." She laughed self-consciously. "We are *trying* to fit in among the gentlemen farmers around us."

Her husband clasped her shoulder. "We miss that rolling deck under our feet, don't we, my dear?"

"Oh, yes, of course." Her exaggerated tone was clearly teasing her husband. "And the storms at sea and the poor rations and cramped quarters and—"

"Enough." Captain Nichols threw up his hands in mock surrender.

Lady Teasler asked in a slightly disapproving tone,

"You could have stayed onshore, could you not, Mrs. Nichols?"

"I did—when our children were young—because it was necessary then. When they went away to school, I rejoined the captain on board ship."

"It *sounds* a miserable life." Lady Teasler gave a delicate shudder.

"Life aboard a navy ship does have *some* compensations." Mrs. Nichols's eyes twinkled at her husband. "You would perhaps be surprised at how gentle rough sailors can be. And, of course, Charles and I were *together.*"

And that was all the compensation you needed, Harriet thought. This couple had the same easy, subtle communication that she had seen between Jenny and her blacksmith. She also saw it in Caitlyn and Trevor Jeffries, in the Sheffields, and in her own sister's marriage. Lord, she was surrounded by happy, compatible couples. Had she and Raymond ever shared such closeness?

No, she admitted, they had not, for these couples treated each other as partners, as equals. Raymond had always been her teacher and she his prize pupil. He took great pride in showing off his achievement. He had guided her in everything, she thought now. Even the selection of her clothing. He had had excellent taste and she had been content to allow his choices. After all, did she not owe him that much?

"—would you not agree, Mrs. Knightly?" Melanie broke into her musings.

"I beg your pardon. I was not attending."

"We were discussing an article in the latest issue of *The London Review,*" Melanie said.

Even before anyone uttered another word, Harriet had a premonition about *which* article was under discussion. "I—I have not seen the latest issue." Well, *that* was true, she thought.

"A disgusting article on the rights of women," Lady Thornton said.

Melanie laughed. "I think her ladyship means *lack* of such rights."

Lord Thornton gave a derisive snort. "This Gadfly fellow would have one believe our women are worse off than black slaves in the colonies."

Harriet noticed that at mention of the Gadfly, Marcus broke off whatever he had been saying to Captain Nichols and the two of them attended this discussion now.

"Did the article say *that?*" Harriet asked, knowing full well it had not.

"Well, not in so many words, but that *is* what he meant," Thornton said.

"He wants women to be too independent. The man clearly has no idea of what women want." Lady Thornton's tone echoed her husband's, and Harriet thought neither of them was used to having anyone presume to disagree with them. She noticed the raven-haired beauty said little but appeared to be waiting to see what position others—especially Marcus—would take before voicing an idea of her own.

"Hmmm." Marcus grinned broadly. "I believe Chaucer explored the idea of what women want."

Harriet flashed him an answering grin. "In the Wife of Bath's tale!"

"Precisely."

Lady Thornton drew herself up piously. "The Wife of Bath's licentious tale was not part of the course of study when *I* was a girl."

Harriet decided to allow this put-down to pass. However, Aunt Gertrude rose to the bait.

"Nor in mine, my lady," she said, "but girls in my school managed to rectify the omission. We read it— *and* the Miller's tale—and laughed uproariously over both."

Lady Thornton pursed her lips, then opened them

to say, "Well, I certainly hope young girls are not reading such today—or such horrid stuff as this—this Gadfly is putting forth."

"Just what was it you found so offensive, my lady?"
Harriet hoped only curiosity showed in her tone.

"Why—everything."

"I am not sure I understand," Harriet said inno-
cently.

Melanie explained. "The Gadfly advocates that married women retain rights to their property, that an
abused woman be allowed to seek a divorce, and that
an estranged husband not be allowed to forbid his
wife access to their children."

"Sounds perfectly reasonable to me," Harriet said.

"I must say," Mrs. Nichols offered, "I have not read
the item in question, but those ideas seem to have
merit."

"Only if one chooses to fly in the face of custom,"
Lady Teasler said, placing a hand on Wyndham's arm.
"Would you not agree, my lord?"

Harriet thought Marcus seemed uncomfortable at
Lady Teasler's hint of intimacy between them.

"Gadfly holds views that are not traditional, but one
must admit he seems to hold women in high esteem,"
Marcus said, apparently choosing his words carefully.

"Why, his ideas go against the very grain of society,"
Lady Thornton huffed. "A wife is supposed to obey
her husband, to 'cleave unto him'—not behave in a
hoydenish, rebellious manner."

"That saucy fellow will be arguing next month that
women should be admitted to Parliament and vote!"
Lord Thornton's hearty guffaw indicated how preposterous *that* idea was.

No, Harriet thought. Next month's article is on the
rights of workers in mills and factories. But she wisely
held her tongue on that and said instead, "Unfortunately, there *are* women—even of the upper classes—
who are locked into miserable situations. Surely, you

yourselves know someone like that?" She could tell by the expressions around her that this idea hit home. "Perhaps it is these poor souls with whom the Gadfly sympathizes."

Morris, Timberly's butler, had stood near Marcus for some moments. Harriet heard him tell Lord Wyndham the mummers had arrived. Marcus then announced such to the company at large, and there was much scraping of chairs as the audience sought advantageous spots from which to view the performance.

Harriet was relieved to see the end of a discussion of Gadfly's views, though she thought she had come through that rather well. However, she was *not* best pleased to see the beauty commandeer their host's partnership for the rest of the evening.

Eight

With Christmas over, the inhabitants of Timberly entered a period of calm before the New Year celebration. Members of the local gentry made a point of calling on the Earl of Wyndham. Some of these calls were purely social, and some were more "official" as the callers sought to coordinate local policies and practices. Among the neighbors with whom Marcus conferred were Squire Davies, who also acted as the local magistrate in the earl's absence, and a baronet named Rogers, whose land adjoined that of Timberly.

"Heard you rid Timberly forests of mantraps," Davies said approvingly.

"That I did."

"Nasty things they are. Oughta be outlawed everywhere," Davies said.

Rogers shifted, apparently discomfited. "I cannot agree. They work to discourage poachers. Some of us have not the means to hire dozens of servants to patrol our woods."

Marcus knew this was directed at him. "I hired *one* assistant gamekeeper. I should be happy to instruct him and Connors to patrol into your woods where our properties meet."

"That will not be necessary, sir. I intend to keep my traps in place. And," he added in a firm tone, "I intend to have offenders prosecuted to the fullest extent of the law."

"Transportation," Davies said.

Rogers nodded. "Transportation."

"Seems an excessive price to pay for trying to feed one's family," Marcus observed.

"Well, now," Rogers said, "*if* they were only feeding their families, that would be one thing. But half these fellows have made a thriving business of stealing our game and selling it to coachmen, who then resell it in the city."

Davies nodded. "That is true in some instances."

There seemed little else to be offered on this topic, so they moved on to discuss crop rotations and breeding stock. This led to the question of enclosures. Again Davies and Marcus disagreed with Rogers, who was determined to continue transforming his small tenant farms into larger, more efficient tracts of land.

Marcus could not approve of the pace with which this was being done. Nor could he condone the lack of concern Rogers exhibited for those being displaced. However, he did recognize that larger fields yielded greater returns for landowners.

Voicing his concerns to his male guests one evening, he found that he was far from alone in his views. The men sat over port and cigars after the ladies had withdrawn from the dining room.

"Seems to me," his brother Trevor said, "that you and Drew, here, are not unlike Berwyn and me."

"In what manner?"

"As diplomats, you two dealt with making policies, and as soldiers, Berwyn and I helped enact them—but all of us were pretty much removed from our fair country herself for a number of years."

"You do have a point?" Marcus prompted.

"It is not easy to change the whole direction of one's thinking to focus solely on domestic affairs," Andrew Sheffield noted.

"Probably harder for you, big brother, than for the rest of us." Trevor gave him a lopsided grin.

"Why do you say that?"

"We knew all along that we were coming home eventually to settle on our respective estates. I think you expected to be attached to the Foreign Office for some time to come. Am I right?"

"Yes."

Sheffield looked thoughtful for a moment, then spoke. "I think what Trevor is trying to say is that the transition from plain Marcus Jeffries, cog in a diplomatic foreign wheel, to Earl of Wyndham, major landowner and member of Parliament, is rather a huge step."

"And we live in interesting times." Berwyn refilled his glass as Andrew passed him the bottle.

"That we do," Marcus said, and added, his voice laced with irony, "and I believe it is the Irish who have a curse for their enemies, 'May you live in interesting times.' "

They all chuckled at this, and Berwyn elaborated.

"We have surely been cursed, then, for our times are extraordinary in the extreme."

"Because . . . ?" Trevor prompted.

"Methods of transportation are changing. Roads are improving. The canals are expanding."

"And if that Stephenson fellow's contraption proves out, we may one day move materials and people on rails," Trevor added in an eager voice.

Not to be left out of the discussion, Sheffield said, "Goods that were produced in cottage by hand ten years ago are being produced in huge manufactories by steam now."

Trevor grinned again. "Is progress not absolutely wonderful?"

Marcus gave an exaggerated groan. "Easy for *you* to say. You are not sitting in Parliament, dealing with the hundreds of issues thus created!"

"Who knows? We might all be there one day." Marcus recognized Trevor's tone as only half joking. "It *has* crossed my mind to set myself up for election to the House of Commons."

"Now, *that* would be interesting to see," Marcus said. "Come, gentlemen, shall we rejoin the ladies?"

Harriet observed that his lordship was not the only objective for many of the visitors. Melanie and Trevor had their fair share of callers. Harriet and Charlotte also had an occasional visitor. Therefore, she was only mildly surprised one afternoon just before the New Year when Morris came to tell her she had a caller who had asked for a private interview with her.

"I've shown him to the library, madam."

She paused just inside the door. The man had his back to her, but she recognized her cousin and drew in a fortifying breath.

"Yes? What is it you wanted, sir?"

"Ah, my dear Harriet. I thought we had agreed you would address me as George." He spoke with a show of sadness and came toward her.

"Will you have a seat, sir?" She gestured to a settee and quickly placed herself in a chair at some distance from him.

"I have come, my dear, on a very important matter. A matter vital to the future happiness of both of us, I may venture to say."

"I cannot possibly imagine any capacity in which my happiness would have aught to do with you, *Cousin* George." Harriet knew she sounded caustic, but she intended to quell any suggestion of further intimacy between them.

The viscount's skin was made of thicker stuff, however. He rose and knelt beside her chair. He seized both her hands, effectively trapping her, and said, "Dearest Harriet. Loveliest of women. You have quite won my poor heart. Please say you will become my wife. I have longed for years to have you in my arms again."

"What?" While the proposal itself did not come as much of a surprise, the speed with which it had come did. "You cannot be serious."

"But I assure you, I am. Given the attraction between us, I would have offered for you when you were younger, but it simply was not the practical thing to do then."

She clenched her jaw. "And now it is?"

"But of course. Come, come, my dear. We are both of this world. We know what is what."

Harriet finally jerked her hands free and stood abruptly, knocking the precariously balanced George onto his bottom.

"Oomph!" he gasped, and turned red in the face.

She stepped aside as he scrambled awkwardly to his feet.

"I find your suggestion, sirrah, almost as insulting as the one you made some years ago."

"Insulting? Insulting?" His voice rose as he became even redder in the face. "I offer you a title, invite you to return to Sefton Hall as its mistress, and you—a mere cit, if I may say so—would refuse such?"

He advanced toward her and she quickly put a chair between them. She felt her anger rising.

"Yes. Insulting. Your pretense of affection—a thin disguise of your interest in my late husband's fortune—is nothing short of disgusting."

"You go too far, madam." He moved again, more quickly than she had anticipated, and grabbed her, pulling her to him. "I shall enjoy bringing you to heel."

As he closed his wet, spongy lips over hers, she caught a whiff of stale drink. She pushed violently against his chest and broke free.

"You vile, repulsive toad." She spit the words at him.

"Oh, I see." He laughed scornfully. "You are of a

mind that you are too good for a mere viscount. You probably have an earl warming your bed these days."

"I beg your pardon? What an utterly despicable suggestion."

"But the truth, I'll wager. Well, well, well." He laughed—again without mirth. "He will never marry you, you know." He raked her person with a suggestive leer. "But—I must say—I envy him access to that luscious body."

"Sirrah, *you* go too far. How dare you? How *dare* you?"

Shaking with rage, she turned to leave, but he grabbed her again.

"Oh, I dare much, my love." Again he pressed his mushy mouth on hers, sliding his hands over her body. Struggling helplessly, she did not hear the library door open.

Marcus's voice broke into her consciousness. "May I ask what is going on here?"

George Glasser lifted his head. "You interrupt, my lord. My cousin and I were enjoying a little tête-à-tête."

Harriet pushed him, causing him to stumble slightly. "You disgusting piece of—"

"Now, now, my dear," Glasser said with oily smoothness, "his lordship is a man of the world. He understands."

"I understand when a guest of mine is being subjected to unwanted attentions. Mrs. Knightly, are you all right?"

"I—I think so." She smoothed her clothing with shaking hands.

Glasser sneered. "Do not be so sure the attentions were unwanted."

"I think, Sefton, you had better leave. No—not another word," Marcus said when it appeared the viscount would protest. "If you make any more such allegations, I shall be forced to call you out."

Glasser opened and closed his mouth—like a fish, Harriet thought incongruously. Her cousin picked up his hat and cloak from a nearby chair and strode toward the door with exaggerated dignity.

"Keep my offer in mind, dear, dear Harriet."

She stood in the middle of the room, still shaking with emotion as Marcus closed the door. He came back and silently guided her to the settee. He went to a cabinet and she heard the clink of glass.

"Here. Drink this." He thrust a goblet in her hand and sat beside her.

She drank, coughed, and felt the heat spreading through her. She handed the glass back to him. "Th-thank you—I think."

"Good. Your color is coming back. Are you truly all right?"

"I will be."

"What was that all about?" At her hesitation, he added, "You need not tell me if you had rather not."

"No. It is all right." She smoothed a loose strand of hair behind her ear. "He . . . uh . . . he offered for me and I refused him."

"I see."

"I—it made him angry." She drew in a shuddering breath, remembering the venom in Glasser's eyes and her revulsion at his kiss.

Marcus enfolded her in his arms. "It is all right now, Harriet. Let it go, my sweet." He pressed his lips to her temple and she clung to him, sobbing in earnest now. She was aware of the rough texture of his coat against her cheek and the spicy smell of his shaving soap.

Finally, she calmed and drew away from him. "I—I am sorry, Marcus. I usually do not go all to pieces like this."

"Oh? And is being accosted like that a usual occurrence for you?"

She knew he was trying to lighten her mood. She

smiled weakly. "No, of course not." She straightened and said in a more normal tone, "Thank you. I am fine now. I shall just go and make the necessary repairs."

Marcus sat staring at the door after she left. Thinking back on the scene as he had come upon, he felt again a wave of uncontrollable rage. He had wanted to kill Sefton—tear him limb from limb. His rage mixed with guilt and regret. He had failed to protect Harriet from what amounted to an attack. As her host, it was his duty to have done so.

Ah, as her host, was it? some bothersome imp asked.

Yes, of course, as her host. What else could it be?

Perhaps, concern for the woman herself—beyond her status as a guest?

Perhaps . . . no. It could not be.

Why not? She is a very attractive woman. Not to mention a comfortable companion. You could do worse. . . .

Worse? What? No!

You will have to marry one day—to secure an heir, you know.

Nonsense. I have an heir. Trevor. And he has not one but two sons.

A man needs a wife.

Well—*when* I feel such a need—my interests will be directed to some perfectly malleable young miss. Not a termagant such as Harriet Knightly. Why, that woman would drive a man to distraction.

He shook himself. He ignored the niggling idea that a "malleable young miss" might well *bore* him to distraction. He also tried vainly to ignore how perfectly right it had felt to have Harriet in his arms.

Lord! It was beyond time to get back to London.

* * *

Harriet tried to put the viscount's boorish behavior out of her mind. To this end, she dwelt on the aftermath—those few moments in Marcus's arms. She told herself repeatedly that he was just being kind, that she should not refine upon his taking exception to a guest's being treated rudely in his own dwelling. Besides, had it not been clear the other evening that Marcus had an interest in—maybe a *tendre* for—Lady Teasler?

This notion was solidified one afternoon when she happened to be in the drawing room with Annabelle and Celia. The men were off on some masculine jaunt, and the other ladies were occupied elsewhere. Harriet had been reading as the two girls dreamed over fashion plates in *La Belle Assemblée*. Harriet momentarily envied the two young girls their carefree interests. She had missed such in her own youth.

Celia sighed. "Ooh, do you not just love the way that dress drapes her figure?"

"Yes," Annabelle said, "but I prefer the square neckline on this one."

"It is quite low. My brother would have a fit if he saw me wearing the like."

"That is the fashion now," Annabelle said. "Lady Teasler's green gown was even lower."

"Well, yes, but she does not have to answer to a brother—or a guardian."

"Do you think she is . . . uh . . . *fast?*" Annabelle's question was filled with awe.

"Well, of *course* she is," Celia replied with the superior wisdom gained from being some eight months Annabelle's senior. "Prissy told me she was Lord Wyndham's mistress, but he gave her her congé several months ago."

"Who is Prissy? And how does she know?" Annabelle challenged.

"Prissy is my maid. And her cousin is an upstairs

maid in Lord Lynwood's establishment—and *she* knows all about it."

Harriet was herself keenly interested and felt the veriest hypocrite as she said, "Ladies. It is not seemly to repeat gossip about others as you are doing. Nor should one gossip with one's servants."

"Yes, ma'am." Celia's tone was contrite.

"But, Harriet—did you not hear? Marcus—and Lady Teasler?"

"Are grown people whose business must remain their own." Harriet's tone was firmly dismissive, but she was not surprised when the irrepressible Annabelle went on anyway.

"I met her at the theater when we went to see Mr. Kean as Shylock. She wanted Marcus to call on her."

"Annabelle!" Harriet said sharply.

"You saw Mr. Kean onstage?" Celia squealed. "Oh, how famous. Tell me all about it!"

The girls were off on the theater now, but Harriet was left to mull over the snippet of gossip Celia had thrown out. She was surprised but not shocked by what she had heard. Gentlemen did have certain needs. . . . Lady Teasler's intimate little gestures made more sense now. Was the woman trying to win him back? And—more to the point—was Marcus willing to be won?

Stop! she admonished herself. You just remarked on such conjecturing when Celia and Annabelle engaged in it.

She deliberately turned her attention back to her book.

Harriet had looked forward to the New Year celebrations such as she had enjoyed in her youth. Ammerton tradition included a huge bonfire in the village square to "burn out the old year." At midnight the church bells were tolled twelve times. On the twelfth bong of the bell, villagers gathered on the street erupted into cheers, wishing each other prosperity and happiness for the coming year.

Then as many as could be crammed into the public assembly hall repaired to that location for the "first footing." This office was performed by a tall, dark man from a neighboring village, for tradition decreed that it be an outsider who would make the first steps into the new year. He came bearing symbolic gifts of coal, salt, and cake—warmth, wealth, and food.

Afterward, there was more frolic and revelry until, finally, weary partiers made their way home to welcoming beds. Marcus had arranged a number of carriages—with lanterns and outriders to guide the way—to transport his guests to the community celebration.

The only blot on the celebration for Harriet—and it had been short-lived—came as her cousin made his presence known to her. She had been smilingly watching some little boys teasing each other with firebrands. Suddenly, there he was, murmuring in her ear.

"Ah, my fairest cousin. Well met, my dear." He put a possessive hand on her elbow. "Have you reconsidered your response to my offer?"

"Have I—?" She jerked away, but he did not loosen his hold. In fact, he tightened his grip and began to try to steer her away from the crowd. "Have you lost your senses?" she hissed at him. "Let me go or I shall scream."

"Come, come, my dear. You would not want to create a scene, now, would you? This coyness of yours is a bit tiresome. You know very well that at your age you are not likely to get a better offer." He patted his coat. "I have a special license right here."

"You *are* mad," she said.

She saw a flash of pure rage cross his features, but before he could reply, another voice broke in.

"There you are, Mrs. Knightly. We have been searching for you," Caitlyn, on the arm of her husband, called to her from only a few feet away. "Trevor says you know the whole history of this celebration. You *will* tell me all about it, will you not?" Caitlyn hooked her arm with Harriet's and said brightly to Glasser, "You will not mind if we steal her away, will you?"

For a moment Harriet thought she might become the object of a tugging contest between the two of them. Finally, with an assessing glance at Trevor and a curse she barely heard, he released her. In a louder voice he said, "Later, my dear."

"Thank you," she said to Caitlyn.

"Marcus sent us over. He thought you seemed uncomfortable."

"Did he now?" She felt a glow of pleasure at the thought that Marcus had been looking out for her.

Caitlyn and Trevor walked her over to where Marcus stood with Melanie and Aunt Gertrude.

"Where did the others go?" Caitlyn asked.

"They stepped just across the way to obtain something to drink for us," Aunt Gertrude replied even as the Berwyns and Sheffields returned bearing obviously full tankards.

In the mild confusion of distributing the drinks, Marcus moved closer to Harriet and asked in a low voice, "Are you all right?"

"Yes. Thank you for rescuing me yet again."

"Was he . . . uh . . . ?"

"Yes."

"Damn!" Marcus muttered, then immediately added, "I beg your pardon, madam."

Harriet smiled, again pleased at his apparent concern for her. "I am fine. There was no harm done." She forced herself to sound reassuring, but inwardly she trembled at what might have occurred had Marcus not seen what was happening.

"You must stay out of his way." Marcus echoed her own thoughts.

"I shall."

She then turned her attention to the gaiety of the New Year celebration.

Quiet descended on Timberly with the departure of the three young families for their own homes.

"I had quite forgotten how very fatiguing young children can be," Aunt Gertrude said with the last departure.

Marcus put an arm around his aunt's shoulder. "You held up quite well, my lady. I think we shall cancel that order for a wheeled Bath chair for you."

She gave him a withering look, at which Marcus merely grinned.

Annabelle sighed. "I shall miss Ned and Celia. We had such fun together—and long talks, you know."

Marcus caught Harriet's eye in a silent communication and then wondered at their seeming to share the same thought.

Annabelle retired early, leaving Harriet, Marcus, and Aunt Gertrude in the family drawing room. He broke the not uncomfortable silence.

"What do you two think about Annabelle?"

"What do you mean, what do we think?" Aunt Gertrude put down a piece of needlework.

"She seemed to relish the company of people her own age," he observed. "Might she be prepared to return to school?"

"No doubt she enjoyed the visit . . ." Harriet's voice trailed off.

"But . . . ?"

"I think she still needs the security of a family atmosphere."

"Family?" he asked.

Marcus saw Harriet's color heighten slightly. She looked away, then back at him. There was a defensive note in her tone. "That is the way Annabelle thinks of our . . . situation."

"I see . . ." he said, not really seeing at all.

"I agree," Aunt Gertrude said. "Annabelle was neglected at a very impressionable age."

"Neglected? She had quite adequate care, I believe."

"She was fed and clothed, if that is what you mean. But she felt lost and rejected," Harriet insisted. "And now—in her mind—she has created a family in which she feels secure."

"Do you agree with this assessment?" he asked his aunt.

"Essentially, yes."

"So where does this leave the rest of us?" he asked. "Especially you two?"

The two women looked at each other questioningly.

"What I mean to say is—this was to have been a rather temporary arrangement, and you *have* both disrupted your own lives. . . . If she were to return to school, your lives might be your own again."

"Are you looking forward to returning to the freedom of your bachelor existence?" Aunt Gertrude asked with an understanding smile.

"No." He was surprised at the truth of this. "I suppose—in all honesty—I am feeling guilty at the sacrifices you two are making."

"Harriet dear, do you feel yourself long-suffering in this?" Aunt Gertrude asked.

"Not at all."

"Would it not be better for Annabelle if she *did* return to school?" Marcus was genuinely confused. What did *he* know of a young girl's feelings and thoughts?

"Why not ask her to see how *she* feels about such a prospect?" Harriet looked from one to the other.

"And if she rejects the idea?" He waited as the two women considered.

"Well—"

"I think—"

They both started to speak at once. Harriet gestured for Aunt Gertrude to continue.

"Annabelle is a charming girl. She has blossomed into a secure young woman in the last few months. I would hate to see us destroy that."

Harriet nodded. "I agree. And, in point of fact, caring for her as we have has not required significant alterations in *my* life. I still see to my affairs and have my special friends and activities."

"Nor in mine," Aunt Gertrude said. "So—if Marcus is willing to endure a house full of females for a few more months, I see no real need to make changes."

"Then, we are agreed?" Marcus asked, feeling relieved somehow.

The next day as the ladies—all three of them—prepared for another jaunt in the village, Harriet popped into the library briefly, where Marcus labored over a set of ledgers.

"Annabelle is ecstatic that we are not shipping her off to school," she reported.

"Good."

He smiled broadly, not sure exactly *why* that was such good news, but it was.

Nine

In mid-January Marcus and his ladies returned to Wyndham House in London, for Parliament would be opening at the end of the month.

"Please—may we go and watch the royal procession for the opening of Parliament?" Annabelle begged of Harriet.

"You wish to see all that pageantry for yourself—is that it?" Harriet asked, considering the request.

"Oh, yes," Annabelle rhapsodized. "The elegant state coach and the Prince in all his finery. Letty told me all about it."

"Our Prince does know how to put on a remarkable show," Harriet agreed. "If the weather permits, I see no reason we should not go."

Annabelle clapped her hands gleefully and immediately began planning the outfit she would wear for such an outing.

However, when Harriet mentioned the venture to Marcus, he was less than enthusiastic about their going. Harriet waited until Annabelle and Aunt Gertrude had retired before bringing up the subject again. She and Marcus had had a minor difference of opinion over a point of geography and had repaired to the library to check with an atlas.

"See," he said with what she saw as male pride, "I told you the Ural Mountains were not so far east as you were placing them."

"All right, I concede to your superior wisdom—and the accuracy of your atlas." She turned away from the table on which the atlas lay and took one of the wing chairs in front of the fireplace. "Tell me, Marcus. Why do you object to our seeing the procession for the opening of Parliament?"

He took the opposite chair and crossed his legs in a relaxed manner. "Did I say I objected?"

"Not in so many words, but I detected a noticeable lack of enthusiasm."

"Let us just say I have some reservations."

"Why?"

He was thoughtful for a time. "As you know, the Prince is not very popular at the moment."

"That qualifies as an understatement of rather monumental proportions."

He chuckled. "Well, perhaps so. But the fact is, there are always great crowds to watch the royal procession to and from Westminster."

"Yes. Cheering crowds are part of the total picture."

"I fear there may be more jeering than cheering this year."

"Not without cause," she said flatly. "The Prince's extravagance at public expense is somewhat offensive to people who are out of work and hungry."

"I think you speak of extremes, but the point is there are likely to be a good many malcontents in the crowd this year. They could become unruly."

"A mob? Surely not."

"One would hope not."

"Do you think it could be dangerous?"

"I just do not know, Harriet."

"If we stayed near the carriage, we should be safe enough."

"Hmmm. Yes. That might eliminate any risk."

But it did not.

* * *

The excursion started well enough. Aunt Gertrude chose not to venture out, but both Harriet and Annabelle bundled up against the January cold and a groom placed hot bricks in the straw to warm their feet. When the carriage was ready, two footmen joined them. Harriet looked at them questioningly.

"Lord Wyndham said me an' Jamie should come with you," the largest footman in the earl's employ explained.

"He did?"

"Just to be safe, he said."

"Well, in that case, we are glad to have you—Henry, is it not?"

"Yes, ma'am." Henry was obviously pleased to be called by name.

The Prince's processional route ran from his residence, Carlton House, to the palace of Westminster, seat of Parliament. Harriet had timed their arrival along the route so as to watch the procession as it returned from Parliament. The streets were lined with a multitude of people, but they found a slightly less crowded area not far from Carlton House. Harriet deliberately chose a spot that seemed to be peopled with somewhat better dressed members of the citizenry. Still, she and Annabelle would stand out in their fine cloaks.

The coachman stopped to let them down, saying he would wait just down a side street to which he pointed. Henry opened the door to hand them out.

"I ain't so sure about this," he said.

Harriet tried to quell her own apprehension. "It will be all right."

"Why? What is wrong?" Annabelle asked.

"This crowd's a bit off, miss," Henry explained.

"Off? What does that mean—off?"

"Hostile, miss."

"Toward the Prince? A member of the royal family?"

"Yes, miss."

Harriet looked around to see that Henry's assessment was true of a good portion of the onlookers. Many had apparently been there earlier to watch the Prince's departure. She heard isolated comments critical of the Prince's appearance, his lavish lifestyle, and his estrangement from his wife.

"You and Jamie stay close to us," Harriet said to Henry as the carriage, impeded by the crowd, left them to make its way ever so slowly into the side street.

"Yes, ma'am." Henry and Jamie stood on either side of Annabelle and Harriet.

People in the immediate area sought to make room for the newcomers. Harriet noticed several nipping from bottles and flasks they carried. Shouts and catcalls passed between various factions of the crowd. Finally, a shout came out at a higher pitch.

"They're a comin'!"

"Here 'e comes."

"Ol' fat George hisself!"

The crowd surged forward, conveying Harriet and Annabelle with it. They could hear the clip-clop of the horses' hooves on the cobblestoned pavement before the entourage came into view, preceded by a company of horse guards. Another company brought up the rear. In between was the magnificent state carriage in which sat the Prince of Wales, waving to his subjects in a great show of royal grace and dignity.

"Fat toad." Some woman followed this epithet with a string of even stronger abuse.

"We need bread!" a group chanted repeatedly.

"My children are starving!" a man shouted, waving his fist.

Farther down, Harriet heard another group chanting, "Food! Shelter! Jobs! Food! Shelter! Jobs!"

Jamie leaned over Annabelle to get Harriet's attention. "Ma'am? This could get real nastylike."

"Yes, I think you are right. We must return to our carriage."

This, however, proved impossible with the crowd pressed in all around them. As the Prince's carriage passed, Harriet saw that the windows had been closed and the vehicle seemed to have been pelted with mud and dung from the street. Then she heard pebbles and stones hitting the carriage.

Some of the horse guards moved up and some back to form a circle around the carriage. Harriet thought they displayed great calm in the face of the hostility of the crowd. They merely used their animals to shield the Prince's coach. Slowly the vehicle came to where Harriet and Annabelle stood and began to pass beyond them.

Harriet expected the crowd to disperse once the state carriage had passed, but people seemed to hang about, voicing varying degrees of dissatisfaction with the regent. Then she heard a loud report of what might have been gunfire. Immediately the crowd lost any sense of organization or decorum.

"That was a shot."

"Someone shot the Prince."

"Is he dead?"

People were pushing and shouting and shoving, some apparently to see what was happening and others to escape. Horse guards now turned their animals deliberately into the crowd to put distance between the royal personage they guarded and the hostile mob around him.

The panicked crowd surged in every direction. Harriet felt herself stumble. She had an instant of terror as she envisioned herself trampled to death. Then she felt Henry's hand at her elbow holding her upright.

"I've got you, ma'am."

"Thank you."

"How are we to get out of this?" Annabelle's fear manifested itself in her high-pitched question.

Henry answered, "I think if the four of us link arms so we don't get separated, we might stand a chance."

"Excellent idea, Henry." Harriet promptly linked one of her arms with Annabelle's and the other with Henry's, and Annabelle linked her other arm with Jamie's.

"*Now* what, oh, noble leader?" Jamie asked in a voice loud enough to be heard above the cacophony around them. Harriet thought the young footman's bravado masked his own fear.

"Just try to reach the carriage," Henry answered, using his free arm to stop a woman who would have crashed right into Harriet. Slowly, awkwardly—often with one step forward and two shoved back—they reached the side street. Above the teeming crowd around them, Harriet could see that John Coachman was having a difficult time holding his team in check and fending off some ruffians who apparently tried to drag him from his perch. She saw him wield his whip repeatedly.

On this side street the mass of humanity had thinned somewhat.

"Jamie, you stay with us," Harriet said. "Henry, do what you can to help John."

Henry, tall and muscular, waded into the group around the Wyndham carriage and began to toss the assailants around like so many cloth dolls. Others quickly lost interest in this particular carriage.

Finally, Jamie and the ladies in his care were at the door of the coach. Henry opened it and the two females were bundled in with no regard whatsoever to ceremony. Annabelle collapsed on a seat, but Harriet rummaged in a storage compartment under the other seat.

"Here." She thrust a pistol into Jamie's hand. "Use it only if you must." She said a silent prayer of thanks for its being there, as Marcus had said it was during their journey to Timberly.

The sight of the pistol, along with the gigantic proportions of Henry, quickly removed any remaining daring of these ruffians. Slowly, the carriage made its way free of the congestion.

Marcus had rushed home in a highly agitated state. He had heard of what had possibly been an attempt on the Prince's life as the regent returned to Carlton House. Marcus feared the effect of such an event on an already unfriendly crowd. Why had he allowed Harriet and Annabelle to go off with inadequate protection?

"Have Mrs. Knightly and Miss Richardson returned yet?" he asked Heston on entering.

"No, my lord."

Aunt Gertrude came to the library door. "Oh. I heard the door and thought Harriet and Annabelle might have returned."

"You heard, then?"

"Yes. Oh, dear me. What a frightful event, to be sure. Lady Hennington was here earlier. She told me the Prince had been shot—perhaps killed. She said there was blood everywhere! I am so worried about them."

There was no need to wonder whom she meant by "them," for he shared that worry. Having thrust his greatcoat and hat into Heston's hands, he followed her into the library.

"What shall we do?" Aunt Gertrude clasped and unclasped her hands.

"I came as soon as I heard, but I took a circuitous route to get here. It has been over an hour." He ran his hand distractedly through his hair and had a fleeting image of his valet, Fenwick, tsk-tsking over the damage thus wrought. "Had Lady Hennington been present? Was hers a firsthand report?"

"I think not. She heard the story when she called at the Bennett place and a visitor there had conveyed the news."

"Her degree of accuracy may be suspect, then. All

we heard at Westminster was of a *possible* attempt on the regent's life. No one was certain that a shot was even fired."

"He was not injured, then?"

"I think not."

"But what about Harriet and Annabelle? They are out there all alone."

He glanced at the ormolu clock on the mantel. "We must wait a while longer—hard as that is—and if they have not returned in an hour, I shall go out looking for them. And they are not *totally* alone. I sent Henry and Jamie with them."

"Oh. I did not know. Well, surely they are all right then." Marcus thought his aunt was trying hard to believe this.

In the event, it was not quite an hour before Harriet and Annabelle arrived—disheveled, but indeed all right. Marcus and Aunt Gertrude rushed into the foyer on hearing the commotion of their entrance. He noted the disarray of the women and the two footmen right behind them.

"Oh, my goodness! You will never believe what happened!" Annabelle announced.

"You *are* all right?" Marcus directed his question to Harriet, who nodded, and he felt himself relaxing. "I shall speak with you later," he said to Henry.

"Yes, my lord."

There was a mild flurry as Harriet and Annabelle removed their cloaks and bonnets and gave these up along with their gloves to the waiting Heston. Then they were ushered into the welcoming warmth of the library.

Annabelle, in a high degree of excitement, and Harriet, more calmly, related the events of their morning.

Harriet ended by saying, "I wish to thank you, Marcus, for sending Henry and Jamie along. Who knows what might have happened had they not been with us?"

"I am glad they were there."

"And," she added, "John Coachman handled himself pretty wonderfully as well."

"I shall see they are properly rewarded," he said.

His interview with Henry gave Marcus a slightly different perspective on the events of the morning than the one with Harriet and Annabelle. Henry was clearly impressed with the way Mrs. Knightly had kept her head about her in a crisis. It occurred to Marcus that Harriet had quite unintentionally made a conquest.

Afterward, he sat in thought for some time. Obviously, Parliament should take some sort of action. Even if it turned out not to have been an attempt on the regent's life, something had to be done about such civil unrest. This was England, not France, where an unruly mob could commit regicide with impunity. On the other hand, this was England—and the government should not be using draconian measures to crack down on its own citizenry.

Unfortunately, in the days ahead, Marcus found his was the minority view in government circles. He knew that many in power were genuinely alarmed by the unrest among the populace. But he also knew that some seized upon a good excuse to advance their own interests at the expense of those less fortunate than they.

Parliament suspended the Habeas Corpus Act, which had required sufficient evidence to show cause for arrest and incarceration. Now anyone under mere suspicion could be summarily thrown into jail and kept there indefinitely. It was no use protesting this breach of citizens' rights. Another act prohibited meetings of more than fifty people within a mile of Westminster. There was also a bill declaring any action against the King or the regent to be an act of treason.

Marcus, of course, knew about these measures before they were made known to the public. He and his cohorts had tried—vainly—to temper them. When they were published in the newspapers, he found Harriet fairly sputtering at breakfast one morning.

We'd Like to Invite You to Subscribe to Zebra's Regency Romance Book Club and Give You a Gift of 4 Free Books as Your Introduction! (Worth $19.96!)

If you're a Regency lover, imagine the joy of getting **4 FREE Zebra Regency Romances** and then the chance to have these lovely stories delivered to your home each month at the lowest price available! Well, that's our offer to you and here's how you benefit by becoming a Regency Romance subscriber:

- **4 FREE** Introductory Regency Romances are delivered to your doorstep

- **4 BRAND NEW** Regencies are then delivered each month (usually before they're available in bookstores)

- Subscribers save almost $4.00 every month

- Home delivery is always **FREE**

- You also receive a **FREE** monthly newsletter, which features author profiles, discounts, subscriber benefits, book previews and more

- No risks or obligations...in other words, you can cancel whenever you wish with no questions asked

Join the thousands of readers who enjoy the savings and convenience offered to Regency Romance subscribers. After your initial introductory shipment, you receive 4 brand-new Zebra Regency Romances each month to examine for 10 days. Then, if you decide to keep the books, you'll pay the preferred subscriber's price of just $4.00 per title. That's only $16.00 for all 4 books and there's never an extra charge for shipping and handling.

It's a no-lose proposition, so return the FREE BOOK CERTIFICATE today!

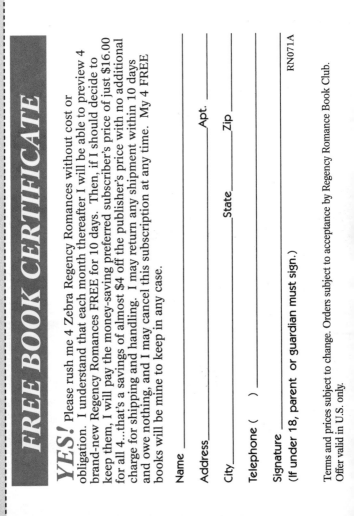

Their "family" breakfasts had evolved into very casual affairs. A discussion might involve only two, or three, or all four. Just as frequently, each of them would have some sort of reading material at hand— the mail, a magazine, or a newspaper. On this morning Marcus was idly checking his mail; Aunt Gertrude and Annabelle were discussing a visit to an art gallery the day before; and Harriet was absorbed in a newspaper.

"Well! I never—! Oh! This is the outside of enough! Outrageous! Treason, indeed!" she muttered.

She now had the attention of her three companions. Aunt Gertrude asked, "What is it, Harriet?"

"Did you *know* about this?" Harriet challenged Marcus, her hazel eyes flashing.

"I might be better equipped to answer that question if I knew what *this* referred to," he said mildly, though he had a sneaking suspicion that he did know.

She looked from him to his aunt. "It is now an act of treason—*treason*, mind you!—to throw mud at the Prince's carriage!"

"What?" he expostulated. "Where did you get that idea?"

"Right here." She tapped the newspaper. "Parliament, it seems, deems any act against the Prince to be *treason*. Those people protesting and throwing mud that day were *traitors* yet! How utterly preposterous!"

"Now, now, dear," Aunt Gertrude murmured.

"You are taking a rather extreme view," Marcus said.

"It says 'any act against the King or the regent'—I assume that means 'any act.' Do you not agree?"

"I doubt anyone would be prosecuted for throwing mud."

"No." Her voice was laced with sarcasm. "They would be arrested and tossed in jail on *suspicion* and never heard of again."

"Good heavens, Harriet." He was becoming impatient

with her extremism. "Give the magistrates *some* credit for common sense."

She was silent for a moment, then spoke more calmly. "I think this—and the other restrictions of late—are extremely dangerous. They violate every principle for which Englishmen have fought for generations."

"You cannot expect Parliament to sit back and condone anarchy," he said flatly, and rose. "I should like to continue this intriguing discussion, but unfortunately, I have a meeting to attend this morning."

"Coward," she said with a smile.

He returned her smile and felt the slight tension in the room ease. He touched her shoulder as he left the room. His tone was gentle. "I do hope, Harriet, that you will not broadcast these views too vehemently outside our circle. It might not be wise in these times."

Ten

Harriet was deeply shaken by the apparent attempt on the Prince's life, by seeing firsthand the desperation in the faces of the people in the crowd. Their animal-like savagery had unnerved her. Her dominant emotion, however, was anger—anger that people could be driven to such extremes in a modern country whose leaders professed to care about the welfare of its citizens.

Widowed Harriet Knightly, whose political standing was nil and whose social standing was respectable but by no means exalted, could do and say little about these matters. But the Gadfly could. And did.

Meeting with Mr. Watson at yet another bookshop, she gave him her latest essay. She was surprised when, instead of merely tucking the papers into a portfolio as he usually did, he began to peruse the document. His brow knit in a worried frown.

"Is something amiss?" she asked in a low voice.

"This is . . . uh . . . very volatile."

"Too strong, you mean? But it is all true. Every word is factual."

"I know. But since that business at Spa Fields a few months ago, persons in authority are taking a dimmer view of anything they consider threatening. And this attack on the Prince will likely make matters worse."

"The Spa Fields incidents were largely exaggerated rhetoric, I think." Harriet had been at Timberly so was not in London during what some newspapers had labeled the "Spa Fields Riots." She had, however, heard and read detailed reports of the incidents since.

"Those fellows came dangerously close to preaching revolution to a receptive crowd," Mr. Watson said.

"Mr. Hunt and Mr. Castle were simply carried away with their own enthusiasm, I am sure."

"That may be. 'Orator' Hunt is a firebrand on a speaker's platform. But Castle's attack on the King and the Church—even only a verbal attack—did not sit well."

"Are you worried that *you* will come under suspicion?"

"I already have," he said simply.

"Wha-at?" Surprise pitched her voice higher than she intended.

He took her elbow to steer her deeper among the shelves of books. He spoke in a low tone. "And—what is more to the point—so have you."

"I?" It was an alarmed squeak.

"Indirectly. Two men—they were from the government—came to me seeking the identity of this Gadfly person."

"I trust you did not reveal it."

He gave her a brief glare of impatience. "Of course not! Told them even I did not know the proper identity of Gadfly. No sense letting people like that know more than you need them to know."

She chuckled. "Thank you, Mr. Watson. I appreciate your support."

"Well . . ." He colored slightly and cleared his throat. "Hmmm. I probably should not say this—I mean, after all, I am in the business of selling magazines—and Lord knows Gadfly sells magazines! But if things keep going as they have, Gadfly might be in danger. Have a care, madam."

"I shall take your words as a caution, and I am grateful for them. But, really, I think government authorities have merely panicked and will soon return to their staid, indifferent selves."

In the days that followed, however, Harriet had to admit that the current government was not easing any of the restrictions passed in the panicky reaction to the Spa Fields events and the attack on the Prince. Instead, Parliament—which she knew to be dominated by men who owned large tracts of land and who controlled the major exports—passed even stricter curbs on civil freedoms.

"Seditious libel," wrote Gadfly, "is so loosely defined in these new acts that any magistrate may jail anyone he merely *suspects* of being opposed to a local lord's edicts. Did this nation not just fight a war against a tyrant who used such measures?"

"And that is the least inflammatory of his statements!" Marcus said, slapping the back of his hand against the pages he read.

The four chief residents of Wyndham House had settled in the family drawing room after the evening meal. It was March, and, as the Season was not yet in full swing, these four often enjoyed such an evening, though Lord Wyndham would occasionally be off to his club. Harriet felt particularly content when he joined them, though she realized this in only a vague sort of way. On this day, Marcus had come across *The London Review* with Gadfly's latest treatise.

"It is true, is it not?" Harriet asked. "The magistrates *have* been given such powers."

"Well, yes, but it is clearly a temporary measure."

"A repressive one," she said.

"We have to have order. A nation cannot thrive in chaos." This comment seemed an automatic response as he continued to peruse the article. "Oh, good grief!" he muttered. "What balderdash!"

"Really, Marcus, what *is* it that has you in such a pelter?" Aunt Gertrude asked.

"This . . . this Gadfly—again! The fellow is a rabble-rouser of the first order."

Annabelle looked up from a copy of *La Belle Assemblée* through which she had been leafing with an occasional remark or observation to Harriet. Now she said in a mild tone, "I do not understand why you read such, when it so clearly disturbs you."

"Sometimes I wonder myself," he said with a rueful chuckle. "But one wants to understand the opposition. And . . . well . . . the fellow *is* amusing."

"Amusing?" Harriet felt her hackles rising at this trivializing of important issues. "Amusing? You find egregious taxes and extreme discrepancies in wealth *amusing?*"

"No, that is not what I meant. He repeatedly overstates his case, but his writing style is quite pleasing." He paused and looked thoughtful for a moment, then said, "Have you ladies already read this? Cosgrove gave it to me only this afternoon, and he said it was an advance copy."

"I have not seen it," Annabelle said. "So, do go on, my lord."

"Nor I," Aunt Gertrude said, "but then, political tracts are not my first choice in reading matter."

"Harriet?" he asked.

"No. I have not yet seen the latest issue of the *Review.*" She was glad the others' comments had given her time to phrase her response carefully. "Why do you ask?"

"Because that is what he discusses here." Again he slapped the pages. "Taxation policies and, as he puts it, 'an egregiously unfair distribution of this nation's wealth.'"

"Oh." She frantically searched for a way to respond. "Those topics seem to have been on the minds of many people of late."

"Hmmm. I suppose so." He continued to read. "Oh. Now, this *is* the outside of enough."

"What?" Annabelle asked.

"Yes. Do share," Aunt Gertrude urged.

Harriet braced herself for what his lordship would find "the outside of enough."

Marcus read, " 'In these sad days the rich are becoming ever richer whilst the poor wallow in ever more debilitating poverty—poverty that snuffs out ambition and leaves whole families mired in filth and disease. Indeed' "—here Marcus's voice rose—" 'many of the very people who fought so valiantly against the Corsican tyrant are probably *worse* off than they might have been had he been the victor instead of the vanquished.' I tell you, the man goes too far." Marcus tossed the magazine on a chair and rose. "If you ladies will excuse me . . ."

When he had left, Annabelle snatched up the magazine and proceeded to read choice passages aloud.

"Well," Aunt Gertrude said, "Marcus is right about that being a clever writer."

"However," Harriet said, "I cannot help thinking Lord Wyndham's critique went more to style than substance."

Aunt Gertrude stifled a ladylike yawn. "Perhaps. The fellow does seem overly enthusiastic in his views, though."

Later it was this gentle criticism rather than his lordship's harsher "Balderdash!" that fixed itself in the mind of Gadfly's creator.

Occasionally Marcus found ideas from their conversations about Gadfly popping into his musings. There was something about the last discussion that nagged at him, but he could not pinpoint exactly what. In any event, why should *he* be so concerned with the scribblings of the intellectual counterpart of some street rabble-rouser?

What he found more disturbing in himself was the way Harriet Knightly occupied more and more of his waking—and sleeping—thoughts. Every day he discovered something new to intrigue him. He became aware of the way she would slant her head slightly as she contemplated an idea. He came to look for that loose curl, which—no matter how smooth and controlled her coiffure—would, in the course of the evening, slip out in front of her left ear. How his fingers itched to touch its softness! He began to notice the presence or absence of the faint flowery scent she wore. But most of all, there was that intense awareness if their hands chanced to touch or they brushed against each other.

Marcus had always liked and enjoyed women. He had even fancied himself in love once or twice. However, his status as a younger son had been something of an impediment in romantic ventures early on. Twice he had lost out to men of greater rank and fortune. In neither instance had he felt great personal loss—other than the blow to his pride. Other women had been happy enough to assuage a young man's wounded ego.

The instability associated with his work for the Foreign Office had also prevented his seriously pursuing any relationship in the last few years. Now—since coming into the title—he found himself actually the quarry—a prize to be won on the marriage mart.

He was not wholly comfortable with this position. Despite his training as a diplomat, he had little patience with the senseless prattle that passed for conversation at most *ton* parties. That, of course, was why he enjoyed conversing with his houseguest. She was never insipidly shy—even when the topic was light and foolish, as it was often enough.

On the contrary, she was the most opinionated female he had ever met. One day he challenged her on this. He had come upon Harriet and Annabelle in the library, where they were reading aloud from a recently published portion of Lord Byron's *Childe Harold*. He knew from an earlier discussion that Harriet read it with great delight and Annabelle had fallen in love with the so-called Byronic hero.

"Melancholia and self-absorption—is that what attracts the modern woman?" Marcus was only half teasing in his criticism of the poet.

"Oh, but he is *so* romantic," Annabelle crooned. "So sensitive."

"Sooo insipid," he teased.

"You just have not the romantic soul of a poet," Annabelle said dreamily as she floated out of the room, clutching the book to her bosom.

He glanced at Harriet to see her lips pressed firmly together to keep from laughing aloud, though her eyes danced with mirth.

"I suppose you agree with her?" He was hard pressed to contain his own laughter.

"That you lack the soul of a poet?" She did laugh now. "Frankly, I have not thought about it. But let me see . . ." She put her fist to her chin in a parody of deep thought.

"You know very well, madam, that I was referring to that . . . that popinjay scribbler!"

She sobered but kept her smile. "Lord Byron's public image is rather less than decorous—"

He gave a derisive snort as he took a chair opposite hers.

"But," she continued, ignoring his derision, "I think he is a very fine poet."

"Do you do that intentionally? Or do you merely find the role of devil's advocate irresistible?"

"Do I do what?" Her voice had lost its trace of laughter.

"Take the contrary view all the time."

"I was not aware that I did so," she said icily.

"Well, you do." His tone was mild but matter-of-fact.

"I beg your pardon." She enunciated each word precisely. "I was under the—apparently mistaken—impression that one could speak one's mind with you. Do you indeed prefer toadyism?"

He could see that she was suddenly angry, but for the life of him, he did not understand why. "Wha—? Of course not. Why would you think so?"

"You seemed to object to my expressing a view different from your own."

"Object? To what did I object? I merely ask if you enjoy the role of devil's advocate."

"There! You see? I said I liked Lord Byron's poetry and you link me with the devil. Very unchivalrous of you, if I may say so." She lifted her chin.

"Chivalry? How did we get to chivalry? I thought we were talking about the melancholy poet which has taken all female London by storm." He thought it would be safer to put the discussion back on a less personal track.

"His poetry is not melancholy. Actually, it is quite merry. Nor is it just women who admire his work. Some discerning gentlemen are able to look beyond the public antics of the creator to read the work itself."

Her tone left him no doubt about his own exclusion from the company of "discerning gentlemen."

"While I may not qualify as one of your 'discerning gentlemen,' I *have* read Byron's work." He hated that he sounded defensive.

"And . . . ?"

"And what?"

"What did you think? Be fair now."

"I find that he is not unlike another writer that you admire much more than I do."

She looked at him with a little frown of consternation.

"Gadfly," he said.

"Oh." She seemed startled, and then recovered.

"Oh, but they are nothing alike—nothing. You cannot compare imaginative poetry to expository prose."

"Why not? Both writers exhibit a good command of the language. Both are eminently readable. And both lean to extremes, overstating their positions, exaggerating in their descriptions."

"That is most unfair! Lord Byron is attentive to the emotional impact of his work. And Gadfly is meticulously careful about stating only such facts as are known to be true."

"How do you know that?"

"How do I know what?" Her expression took on a guarded quality that he could not read.

"How do you know that this Gadfly takes such care to be accurate? Oh! I say! You know him, don't you? Is Gadfly a friend of yours?"

"I . . . uh . . . yes. You might say Gadfly and I are acquainted."

He thought she seemed rather uncomfortable. "I should have realized—"

"Why?"

"You have always been so . . . so defensive about him."

"Defensive?" Her defensive tone brought a smile from him. "It just happens that I agree with Gadfly's positions."

"*All* of them?"

"Yes. All of them."

"Then he must be a very close friend, indeed." He could not say why that idea annoyed him so, but it did.

Fortunately, Harriet thought later, Aunt Gertrude had come in at that point and saved her from having to tell any out-and-out lies. Still, she was not comfortable about deliberately misleading Marcus. She had always prided herself on being scrupulously honest. This deception went very much against the grain.

Moreover, she had, in the last few weeks, gained a good deal of respect for the Earl of Wyndham—respect quite apart from the attraction she felt for the man Marcus Jeffries. True, he was rather high in the instep on most matters, and perhaps he took himself a bit too seriously. But there was in the earl much of the young man she had once known.

She dreaded his discovering her deception, yet she was realistic enough to recognize that eventual discovery was probably inevitable. But by then surely she would no longer be directly in his life.

Meanwhile, Gadfly aside, there was Annabelle's education to see to. The girl continued to be an apt pupil. Her aversion to school as an institution did not carry over to the fact of her studies, though she still professed an intense dislike of mathematics. Her real academic talent lay in an area close to Harriet's own heart—writing.

However, it was here that Harriet often felt somewhat thwarted. As teacher, Harriet would assign a composition on an historical event or an analysis of a Shakespearean sonnet. As pupil, Annabelle was likely to weave an imaginative tale around the incident in history or compose a parody of the Shakespearean work.

"This is *not* what I asked you to do," Harriet said sternly as she read Annabelle's latest effort. "You were to write of the life of Eleanor of Aquitaine after she lost favor with her husband, King Henry II."

"But I did that," Annabelle protested.

"Only indirectly."

"No. Do you not see?" Annabelle sounded genuinely hurt. "I *have* focused on the Queen's loneliness and her futile attempts to continue to have a role in matters of the kingdom."

"You wrote about her pet *dog!*"

"Yes. He gives us a different perspective from which to view the Queen. The dry facts in the history books do not tell us anything of the woman—of the person she was. I have tried to see her through the eyes of someone who loved her unconditionally."

"But a *dog*? Do you not think you detract from Eleanor's achievements—achievements made despite the great restraints on women in her day?"

"Did I leave out any important facts? I tried to include the major events."

"No . . ." Harriet glanced back over the paper. "They seem to be all here. . . ."

"Well, then . . . ?"

"It is just that I would have you be more direct, more scholarly, if you will."

Annabelle's shoulders slumped in disappointment. "I suppose I *could* write that way—but do you not see? It wouldn't be *me.*"

"Just try it—please? For me?"

"All right," Annabelle said with a little pout. "But honestly, Harry, sometimes you sound exactly like Marcus!"

Eleven

By mid-April, most of the *ton* had returned to the city and the social season was picking up. Invitations poured in to Wyndham House for balls and routs, musicales and suppers. Attendance swelled at meetings of civic-minded groups like the Antiquities Society and the Society for Saving the Overlooked Unfortunates of Our Nation. Harriet was finding grist for Gadfly's mill.

Annabelle, who was still a year or two away from making her debut, was not included in the invitations, but Harriet allowed her to join in when callers were received at Wyndham House. Also, Annabelle often accompanied Aunt Gertrude or Harriet—or both—in making calls or in attending certain meetings of groups to which the adult women belonged.

Harriet knew that Marcus had a keen interest in such activities as they concerned Annabelle, so, as a matter of courtesy, she often consulted him about when and where Annabelle should be allowed to go. To this end she sought a private interview with him one morning.

He ushered her into the library, invited her to be seated, and took a chair opposite. "What is it you wish to discuss?"

"Annabelle, of course."

"Is something amiss?"

"No. Actually, she is, as you know, a bright and capable student."

"Is she any nearer to agreeing to return to school?"

"She *might* be . . ." Harriet said slowly. "Not at the moment, but perhaps at the end of the summer. That would, of course, be the logical time for her to make such a change."

"I suppose so," he said absently.

"However, that is not what I wished to discuss. Annabelle needs more exposure to the world."

"Schoolroom misses have little need to be worldly wise."

"I disagree."

He grinned. "Now, why am I not surprised at that?"

She emitted a small exasperated sigh. "Many a young woman might have avoided mistakes in society if only she had had a bit more polish."

"Or if her father or husband had held a tighter rein."

"Or," she countered, "if her education had been more inclusive."

"Perhaps. So what are you proposing?"

"There is to be a reading of Lord Byron's poetry at a meeting of the Royal Literary Society."

He frowned. "I thought Byron was out of the country."

"He is. Italy, I believe. The reading is being done by a group of actors from Drury Lane."

"I see. Hmmm. Well—there should be no harm in that. Is there anything else?"

"Yes. Annabelle wants to teach in an infants' school for deprived children."

"She wants to do *what*? Now where on earth did *she* get *that* idea?" His tone was accusing.

"Where? In your own drawing room, my lord."

"*That* will bear some explaining."

"As you know, your aunt is very active in an organization dedicated to helping people who have suffered misfortunes."

He rolled his eyes. "An organization bearing an unwieldy name and attracting a good many ne'er-do-wells who take advantage of softhearted people like my aunt."

She gave him a sympathetic smile. "Yes. I agree. But they also do some remarkably good work for people who truly suffer. Including an infants' school that has been set up in the Chapel of St. Catherine. Annabelle heard about it when the Reverend Mr. Hale called on Lady Hermiston."

"And Annabelle wants to work in this school?"

"She is very fond of young children. She would be working with those having four or five years."

"Am I to understand you approve of this venture?"

"I see no reason to disapprove—it is held in the basement of the chapel and conducted by ladies of the parish. And I quite admire Annabelle's wish to do something truly useful. That is not what one expects of a girl her age."

"True. However, I should not like to see her turned into one of those do-gooder bluestocking types."

Harriet wondered fleetingly if that was how he saw herself, but she stifled her annoyance and smiled. "Oh, I hardly think you need fear our Annabelle has lost her sense of fun."

"I am concerned about the riffraff with whom she would come in contact. Such children are not likely to be progeny of pillars of the community, and that is not the most pleasant part of the city."

"True. But she would be doing this only two or three hours a week."

"Still—"

"And either Lady Hermiston or I would always be present as well."

"In that case, I shall—reluctantly—agree. I cannot be wholly at ease with *any* of you spending time in that very rough part of the city."

"I think it truly rough only at night," she said. "And we shall simply never be there after sunset."

"I should hope not."

"Now—there *is* one more thing, my lord."

"I thought we agreed some time ago on Marcus and Harriet."

"That we did. Marcus."

"Go on, please."

"You are aware—are you not?—that Annabelle has been corresponding with Lady Letitia Atkinson."

"Yes. Her precious Letty. I must frank three letters a week for her."

"I am glad you do so. Annabelle has far too little contact with persons her own age. Neither Lady Hermiston nor I is a proper confidante for a young girl."

"Still, one wonders how anyone can have *that* much to say! It is quite beyond me."

She chuckled. "That is because you were never a young girl in the teen years."

"You noticed that, did you?"

"Oh, yes." She felt a blush of embarrassment as she remembered just how much she, as a young girl in her teens, *had* noticed him. And, truth to tell, still did.

"So what has the duke's daughter to do with anything?"

"Letty has convinced Annabelle that one's life cannot be termed complete until one has visited Vauxhall Gardens."

"Vauxhall? Do you think that is wise? The place is fairly overrun with questionable characters."

"I know. Mr. Knightly and I visited the gardens twice. But the attractions there can be very enticing— the gardens themselves, the music, the acrobats and other acts . . . We saw a reenactment of the Battle of Vitoria there. It was quite spectacular."

"Hmmm." He considered the idea for so long, she thought he would surely forbid such an outing. Finally, he said, "All right—*if* you are adequately escorted. The gardens are not the safest place in London—and unescorted females would simply invite trouble."

She grinned at him impishly. "I was rather hoping *you* could be prevailed upon to accompany us. Lady Hermiston has indicated interest in going as well."

She thought he seemed pleased at being asked, and he readily agreed. "I think I can tear myself away for one evening," he said dryly.

"It will not be immediately," she said. "The gardens will not open until mid-May, but I wanted to secure your concurrence before mentioning such a venture to Annabelle."

Marcus was pleased that Harriet had consulted him on these matters, though he did wonder how she might have reacted had he refused his permission for any of them.

In the days that followed, he noted that Annabelle seemed to enjoy her work with children. She had initially been shocked to learn that the mothers of her charges were, in some instances, barely older than herself. Another shock for Annabelle had been the almost total absence of fathers.

All this had come to light one afternoon when Marcus happened to be present as Harriet, Aunt Gertrude, and Annabelle received callers. Among their visitors today were Harriet's sister, Charlotte, Charlotte's husband, and his sister. The Berwyns had come to town for the Season and brought Celia with them "for a bit of town bronze before she makes her come-out next year." Annabelle had been telling Celia of the rewards of working with underprivileged children.

"Here I have been feeling deprived because my parents were taken from me—but at least my mama and papa loved me and were able to ensure my well-being. So many of these children have no one—and nothing." Annabelle was, he noted, genuinely moved by their plight.

"No doubt your work with them provides a pleasant interlude in their lives," he said, aware that he sounded slightly condescending to his ward.

"If only we could do more, though." Annabelle's eyes shone with youthful intensity. "If only we could, as Harriet says, give them hope and ambition—something to look forward to."

"I should think those would be qualities developed from within, not something that could be bestowed from an external source."

Harriet spoke up at this. "Children who grow up amid degradation and decay have precious little chance to develop such noble traits. Occasionally, a flower flourishes among weeds, but usually it is choked out."

"Is it not up to their parents to cultivate a better garden plot, then?" He smiled, pleased at being able to pick up on her image.

"He has you there, Harriet," Berwyn said, but Marcus noticed that none of the females in the room appeared to agree with the baronet.

"I think not," she said to her brother-in-law, then turned back to Marcus. "Their parents have already been overwhelmed by the weeds around them. These little seedlings need to be nurtured."

"Hear! Hear!" Annabelle and Aunt Gertrude said in unison. Charlotte gave her sister a smile.

Marcus threw up his hands in mock surrender. "Very well. You win. I give up. You have my permission to continue your 'good works' in any way you please."

"Actually," Harriet said in a serious tone, "we need rather more than your permission."

"Uh-oh. Watch out, Wyndham," Berwyn teased.

"More than my permission?" Marcus was smiling but wary.

"Yes." Her tone was firm, her words precise. "That our government should condone such abuse of children is nothing short of disgraceful."

"Abuse of children? And here I thought you were helping them." He winked at Berwyn.

"Marcus!" Aunt Gertrude admonished. "How can you make light of this situation even in jest?"

Harriet glared at him in exasperation. "My *lord*—I do believe you are contriving to be deliberately obtuse."

"Perhaps—a little." He was serious himself now. "Mostly, I was attempting—futilely—to divert the conversation. I should have known. . . . However, in my opinion, the government should not be involved in the rearing of children."

"Laissez-faire with children as well as business? Is that it?" Her tone was sarcastic.

"Yes. Hands off business. Hands off incidental problems in society."

"That is all very well to *say*, but it simply is not done."

"What do you mean? It is stated policy for the current government to remain disinterested in regulating business affairs."

He saw Berwyn nod his agreement. Expressions on the female faces ranged from the curiosity of Celia and Annabelle to mild interest on the faces of Aunt Gertrude and Charlotte and impatient annoyance on Harriet's.

"Oh," she said sweetly. "Is that why we have the Corn Laws protecting our producers of grains? And is *that* the reason we continue to pay high taxes on most goods despite the war having been over nearly two years?"

"Producers of English goods have a right to protection from outsiders."

"But children do not?"

He gestured impatiently. "I did not say that. Broad economic measures have little to do with the way individual parents rear their children."

"So say you—and other Members of Parliament. But out-of-work fathers might have a different view."

Marcus glanced around at the others. He himself always enjoyed sparring with Harriet, but he could see that others were not entirely comfortable. He caught his aunt's gaze.

"Harriet dear," Aunt Gertrude said in an obvious effort to change the subject, "Mrs. Berwyn tells me Miss Berwyn plays exceptionally well. Perhaps we can prevail upon her to demonstrate her skill."

Charlotte added her encouragement, and Celia readily agreed to play the pianoforte for them. Marcus settled himself to endure the plunking of a schoolroom miss. To his surprise, Celia was an accomplished pianist, and the afternoon ended very pleasantly indeed.

For Harriet the truncated discussion of the plight of children had been frustrating. She had been longing for days for an opportunity to bring up such matters to Marcus, who was, after all, as a member of the ruling Tory party, deeply involved in government affairs. She had to admit, though, that Lady Hermiston had been right in diverting that particular drawing-room discussion to a lighter vein.

She wondered if Marcus and his parliamentary colleagues would be amenable to what Gadfly would say on such issues. She was well aware that they rarely *liked* Gadfly's message—but they *did* read it, did they not? Perhaps some of it would get through. That very night she outlined her ideas, and over the next two or three days, she produced what she knew to be her most powerful piece yet.

Her subject was, of course, the plight of children—innocents who bore no responsibility for the circumstances of their birth and who were often preyed upon by the most despicable elements of society. Her focus was on the so-called "flash houses," which were in effect schools for crime and corruption.

She had first learned of these havens of crime in an academic way from attending political meetings devoted to other matters. Only recently had she gained firsthand knowledge from some of the "graduates" of such. These were, in some instances, mothers of children with whom Annabelle worked. Some were former prostitutes who had started their venture into the world's oldest profession through the flash houses. Much of Gadfly's information came from these damaged human beings.

"Flash houses," Gadfly's readers were informed, were set up to provide bed and board to dozens—sometimes hundreds—of youngsters in their earliest teens and younger, most of whom had been orphaned or abandoned by their parents. The harsh economic realities of this postwar period had swelled the numbers considerably. The owners of such places were mostly women—"women who have forfeited every semblance of maternal feeling," Gadfly wrote, "as a sacrifice to the great god Mammon, for pursuit of coin dominates their lives."

In terms clearly meant to appall readers of *The London Review,* Gadfly went on to relate that young boys were trained to become experts at thievery—pilfering, burglary, and picking pockets. For girls, life was even worse. The flash house "mothers" introduced them early on to prostitution. When they became too old to please those truly disgusting sorts who preferred child or childlike partners, they had little choice but to join an established brothel. The girls became inured to such a lot in life, because from their first initiation onward, they were seldom allowed to draw a sober breath. Gadfly ended the essay in a resounding call to arms.

> *Thus does this proud nation treat its innocents. We condemn mere children to be enslaved in lives of unspeakable debauchery. If a nation may be rightly judged*

*by the manner in which it treats its most vulnerable
citizens, this nation will, indeed, have much to answer
for on judgment day!*

*Until such time as divine retribution may be effected,
citizens should be able to look to His Majesty's government to redress such terrible wrongs. When will our
Prince and his henchmen in Parliament deign to open
their pleasure-befogged eyes and their hardened hearts?*

A few days after the latest issue of the *Review* appeared, Harriet learned that Gadfly's revelations had
become a prime topic in the men's clubs and a shocking *on-dit* to be shared in titillating whispers during
morning calls.

In Wyndham House, as Harriet had expected, the
article produced lively discussion. One evening the
four principal residents had gathered in the drawing
room, awaiting the announcement of dinner. The latest edition of *The London Review* had appeared only
that day. An appalled Annabelle, who had devoured
every word, was ready to embark on a crusade.

" 'Tis shocking. Truly shocking," she said in a
shaken voice. "Can *nothing* be done?" She addressed
her question to Marcus.

"In time," he said. "The wheels of government are
like the mills of the gods—exceeding slow."

Aunt Gertrude, seated on a settee with Annabelle,
patted the girl's hand. "You must not become so emotional, my dear. I dare say such problems have been
with the human race forever."

"Are you saying we must simply accept them, then?"
Annabelle's tone was disbelieving.

Aunt Gertrude answered gently. "No, of course not.
We do what we can."

"In any event," Marcus said, "that fellow has—as
usual—overstated his case. Not to mention putting yet
another untoward demand on the government."

"How so?" Harriet challenged.

"Well," he responded in what she thought to be a deliberate show of patience, "I doubt not that there *are* orphans and abandoned children who become prey to unscrupulous persons, but I seriously doubt the problem is as monumental as your Gadfly suggests. And it is certainly not an issue for Parliament."

"Not an issue?" Harriet nearly sputtered.

"For Parliament."

"Why not?"

"Because," he said with that same show of patience, "this is a moral issue that need not be legislated. There are private charitable organizations to handle such matters. Public law and government money should not be involved."

"Some of your 'private charities' are run by those same 'unscrupulous persons' you mention—profiting from activities that *are* immoral—and they are illegal as well."

"That *may* be so—but hardly to the extent depicted there." He pointed to the magazine lying on a table.

"It would appear," Harriet said tartly, "that certain men in His Majesty's government should venture forth from the hallowed halls of Westminster Palace—or the smoky rooms of their clubs—into the streets of the city to see what really goes on."

Seeing a flash of annoyance in his expression, she immediately wished she had been less blunt.

"And it would also appear," he said, imitating her tone, "that certain men should tone down their rhetoric which seeks to arouse the emotions of gullible females! That man is a menace." Again he pointed at finger at the magazine.

Annabelle picked up the offending publication and leafed through it. "You know—the name Gadfly *is* a pseudonym. . . . Who is to say the writer might not be a woman?"

"Wha-at?" Harriet's surprise and fear at this observation drove out her anger at Marcus's condemnation of "gullible females."

"Well, it *could* be." Annabelle sounded defensive.

"Not likely," Marcus said.

"Why not?" Annabelle challenged.

Before Marcus could respond, Harriet said, "Because his lordship considers the inferior mind of a female incapable of such reasoning."

"That is not what I said—and certainly not what *I* meant." His voice was tinged with anger. "You will have to agree, however, that those who write on such topics are usually men."

"Really, Harriet," Aunt Gertrude said in her usual role as peacemaker, "that *is* a bit unfair. Marcus has never indicated he holds women in such low esteem."

Immediately, Harriet knew her emotions had overwhelmed her caution. "I apologize, Marcus. That *was* unfair." She gave him a tentative smile. "But so was your labeling women as 'gullible.' "

He looked a bit chagrined. "I accept your apology and offer you my own. Shall we cry *pax* and go in to dinner?"

All of them had become aware of Heston at the door to announce the meal.

"*Pax.*" She offered him her hand and felt that familiar flutter when his hand enclosed hers.

Dinner passed in amiable conversation, and then the three adults were off, Marcus to his club, Harriet and Aunt Gertrude to a musical presentation given by Lady Drummond-Burrell.

Just before she drifted off to sleep that night, it occurred to Harriet that she had had a narrow escape. It also occurred to her that the dispute with Marcus had been more distressing than such a difference of opinion with another might have been.

* * *

Marcus found himself out of sorts most of the evening. He ordinarily enjoyed a casual game of whist now and then. Tonight he did not. Nor did he enjoy the usual male conversations centering on sport, politics, or women. Something kept niggling at the back of his mind.

When someone introduced the topic of Gadfly's latest treatise, Marcus decided he had had enough. He would go home and find a good book. But a book—even a good one—failed to hold his interest this night.

He had gone to bed and was in that delicious stage between being awake and being asleep when it hit him. Once again he heard Annabelle's innocent question: "Who is to say the Gadfly might not be a woman?"

Could *he* be a *she*?

No.

Well, it *could* be, Annabelle had said.

And now he had to admit it *was* possible. . . .

But who?

And suddenly he was wide awake, staring at what he could see of the underside of the canopy over his bed. The dim light from a banked fire in the hearth told him nothing, but his gut instinct had supplied the answer.

Of course.

Why had he not seen it before?

The cadence of sentences, the word choices, the tone—they were all there in Gadfly's offerings!

Harriet Knightly was the Gadfly!

Twelve

The trip to Vauxhall Gardens was planned for an early evening in mid-May. The days were getting longer now, and the Wyndham party would have time for their supper there and enjoy a leisurely stroll in the gardens between the demonstrations of showmanship, which included magic and music as well as acrobats on this night.

Annabelle's excitement was contagious, and Marcus was pleased that the event apparently exceeded her expectations. Her eyes shone and she repeatedly expressed her delight and thanked him and Harriet for allowing the outing. They had wandered through the gardens before darkness fell, but after the show Annabelle wanted to see the gardens lit with the myriad of Chinese lanterns placed strategically within the foliage. Marcus suspected she wanted to prolong the evening—and, in truth, so did he.

The rest of the party eagerly joined her. Annabelle and Aunt Gertrude ambled along several feet ahead of Marcus, Harriet on his arm.

"I am glad we did this for Annabelle," Harriet said.

"Only for Annabelle?" he teased.

She smiled up at him, and he found himself lost momentarily in the depths of her gaze. Then a movement ahead of them caught his attention.

"What the—" he muttered just as Annabelle screamed in startled fear.

A child had dashed from behind a bush to grab Annabelle's reticule. In a flash, Marcus loosed himself from Harriet's hand on his arm and gave chase as the child ran. The boy did not get far before Marcus gripped his shoulder. The child struggled, but Marcus held him firmly. He brought his captive back onto the path, where a number of people had gathered in response to Annabelle's scream.

"Ah, good. Ya caught the little thatch-gallows," an onlooker said.

"Best turn 'im over to the watch straightaway," someone else said.

"Why, he is only a child!" Harriet exclaimed.

"Still a thief," yet another voice observed.

Marcus examined his catch. He *was* a mere child—having perhaps eight years. He felt the thin shoulder bones through a ragged, dirty coat that was too large for the small body. The boy's trousers, also too large, had been cut unevenly at his ankles and were attached to the hipless little form with a piece of rope.

"Let me go!" he shouted in a high, thin voice, and tried to scratch and bite at the hands holding him. The kicks he aimed at Marcus's legs were largely ineffectual, as his feet were bare.

"Here, now." Marcus gave him a shake. "Calm down!"

Marcus took the reticule which the child still held and returned it to Annabelle.

"Let me go!" the boy shouted again, and aimed another kick at Marcus.

" 'Tis a real shame such filth is allowed to accost decent folks." A well-dressed matron on the arm of a portly gentleman sniffed and swished her skirts away from the center of their attention.

Others among the onlookers muttered agreement. Still others watched to see what would happen. Those of the lower orders seemed resentful but remained silent. An adolescent boy with dark red hair on the edge of the group caught Marcus's attention, but the youth quickly averted his gaze and Marcus focused on the explosive little bundle in his hands.

He gave the child another shake. "Stop it!" His tone was such that the child did as he was told.

A man identifying himself as a member of the security forces hired by the Gardens pushed his way into the center where Marcus still gripped the child's shoulders and where the two of them were surrounded closely by Annabelle, Aunt Gertrude, and Harriet.

"I'll take care of this little rat," the security man said. "See how he likes goin' off to the detention center—*after* I give 'im somethin' to discourage doin' this again."

"Right. A bit of a whip will teach 'em!" some faceless voice growled.

"No!" Harriet protested. "Marcus—please—you cannot let this happen."

"Harriet. He is a thief. What would you have me do with him?"

"He is a mere child. Look at the poor thing!" She put her hand on Marcus's arm, and the little boy twisted up a face with tear-smudged cheeks to look at the two of them.

"Please. Jus' let me go," he begged.

"Absolutely not!" The burly security guard stepped closer. "Just hand him over to me, sir. I'll take it from here."

"Wait," Marcus ordered. He knew he should turn the child over to what passed for authority here, but with Harriet's beseeching eyes gazing at him intently, he knew he would not be able to do that. Then Annabelle added her plea.

"We cannot let him be beaten . . . can we? Perhaps . . ." She was obviously thinking furiously and clutching at straws. "Perhaps Reverend Hale can find a place for him."

"We cannot just put him on Hale's doorstep tonight

like some . . . some foundling," Marcus said. "Besides, he may have family looking for him."

"I do not think that likely." Harriet touched the boy's chest gently. "Where is your father?"

"D-dead."

"And your mother?"

"Sh-she's dead, too."

"Could we not take him home until tomorrow, then?" Annabelle begged.

Harriet added her plea. "Surely we can deal with this one small urchin in the morning."

"Aunt Gertrude?" he asked.

"It would appear that you are taking in a stray, my dear," his aunt said mildly.

"Oh, good grief." He muttered his capitulation and his exasperated glance took in the three females. "As you wish."

"You're amakin' a mistake, mister," someone said.

"I feel quite sure you are right." Marcus picked up the child about the waist and carried him kicking and yelling all the way to the carriage. Only once did the boy try to throw himself from the moving vehicle.

In the closed carriage it occurred to Harriet that the rank odor assailing their nostrils was not merely from the street.

"I do believe the first order of business should be a bath," she said.

"Not to mention inspection for vermin," Marcus responded. "What a sapskull I am to have allowed you three to talk me into this!"

Harriet merely smiled to herself, suspecting his bluster covered a heart every bit as soft as her own, if he only knew.

"What is your name, young man?" Aunt Gertrude asked.

"F-Freddie." There was a sob of fear.

"Freddie is a nice name." Aunt Gertrude's voice was soothing. "I once knew a brave soldier named Freddie."

"I ain't no soldier," the boy replied with a show of spirit that Harriet admired.

"No, you are not," Aunt Gertrude agreed calmly, "but I think you must be a brave lad all the same."

The boy seemed to relax slightly at her tone and did not say a word the rest of the way to Wyndham House. Harriet noted he kept twisting his hands spasmodically between his knees.

As they arrived at the town house, Marcus turned the child over to a footman with instructions to "hold on to him." He then set other servants to the tasks of opening the long-unused nursery and arranging for the bath that Mrs. Benson would supervise.

Harriet noted that the housekeeper looked at Freddie with a skeptical expression but assured her employer she would "have him cleaned up in no time."

"Put him to bed in the nursery," Marcus ordered. "Those windows have bars to prevent falls, but I want a footman posted at the door all night. No sense taking chances. He could likely pick the lock."

With that, the servants went about their newly assigned tasks as Marcus and the ladies retired to their rooms. Harriet had removed her bonnet and cloak, and Betsy was helping her out of her dress, when they heard a tremendous howl from the nursery. It was followed by sounds of grunts and thumps and more yelling. Harriet hastily redid the fastening on her dress and made her way to the nursery on the next floor.

She pushed open the door to disclose a chaotic scene. Freddie stood on one side of a large tub of water, still fully clothed, though he and Mrs. Benson and the footman all bore watery signs of the struggle that had been taking place. There were puddles of water around the tub.

"What *is* the matter?" Harriet asked.

"He refuses to take his bath, ma'am," the footman Jamie explained.

"I told him I had raised three boys of my own," Mrs. Benson said.

"Won't let her take his clothes off. An' won't let me, neither."

"I ain't takin' no bath," Freddie said. There was a high-pitched note of fear in his voice.

"Of course you are." Harriet tried to soothe him. "But if you prefer, we women will leave the room and Jamie will see to your bath." A glance at Jamie told her that the footman did not welcome that prospect at all.

"No!" The note of sheer terror in Freddie's one-word response surprised Harriet. "No. It ain't decent to be all naked and wet all over."

"Nonsense." Harriet was losing patience. "No one here means you any harm. But you *will* have a bath and you *will* wear that clean nightshirt Mrs. Benson has laid out for you." She gestured to Jamie and Mrs. Benson, and with the three of them against one little street urchin, Freddie was caught like the small, frightened animal he seemed.

He sobbed wildly as Jamie held him and Mrs. Benson and Harriet began to remove his dirty clothing.

"Oh, my goodness!" Mrs. Benson gasped as the naked little body emerged.

"Jiminy! *He*'s a *she!*" Jamie blushed a furious red.

"Freddie?" Harriet was nonplussed for a moment. Then she told Jamie, "Mrs. Benson and I will handle this."

"Right." The still-blushing Jamie hurried toward the door. "Me an' Henry will be taking turns guarding this door all night."

When the footman had gone, the now-naked Freddie was more docile and submitted to the bath, though she complained bitterly about soap in her eyes as Mrs. Benson washed her hair. The child that emerged was far too thin, but she had enormous brown eyes, a close-cropped shock of dark carroty-red hair, and a sprinkling of charming freckles across her cheeks and nose.

Jamie was dispatched to the kitchen for some bread and cheese and an herbal tea. Soon the child was dried and attired in a too-large but clean nightshirt. She ate the bread and cheese ravenously and drank the tea with relish despite her obvious apprehension. Meanwhile, Jamie removed the tub. When a maid took away the soiled clothing, Freddie squeaked a protest.

"Now," Harriet said at last. "You are clearly not a Freddie. What *is* your name?"

"F-Freda."

"Freda. Freda what? Do you have a surname?"

"Freda Milton."

"I see. How old are you?"

"N-nine. Almost."

"Well, Freda Milton who is almost nine years old—you are a very pretty girl and you will be safe here. So you crawl into that bed and go to sleep. Mrs. Benson and I will stay here until you do, and tomorrow we will see what can be done for you."

The little girl did as she was told, and in a very short time she was clearly fast asleep. "Worn out from all that fretting," Mrs. Benson said, and Harriet agreed.

As she returned to her own room—now exhausted herself—she paused only long enough to speak briefly with Jamie. He assured her that his lordship had been informed of the turn events had taken.

Soon Wyndham House had settled into its customary nighttime tranquillity.

At first Marcus had no idea what had awakened him. Then he heard a shout and a thump from the floor above. The nursery? Then he remembered. He struck a tinder to light a candle, quickly donned a pair of breeches, slipped his arms into a robe, and slid his feet into a pair of slippers. He held the candle up to view the clock on the mantel. Three-thirty in the morning. There was another thump and a yowl that carried more exasperation than pain.

As Marcus dashed up the stairs, his robe flying, he heard doors opening behind him. The scene that greeted him might have been amusing had he not been witnessing it in his own home. There was Henry, whose size alone would intimidate most adversaries, trying to fend off blows from two small red-haired beings, one in a too-large nightshirt and the other a larger intruder in rags similar to those Freda had worn earlier.

"You leave my brother alone!" Freda yelled, snatching at one of Henry's arms.

"Here! What is going on?" Marcus grabbed Freda and held her away from the other two, though her arms and legs moved wildly.

Henry was able to get a firmer hold on the intruder and managed to keep him still. "This fellow tried to sneak in, my lord. I heard the back stairs creak and I pretended to be asleep. Caught 'im just as he was about to do me in with that vase." Henry pointed to an urn lying on the floor.

Annabelle and Harriet arrived and spoke simultaneously.

"What is it?"

"What happened?"

Right behind them, Aunt Gertrude murmured, "Oh, dear."

"Who are you, boy?" Marcus addressed the one in Henry's grip even while Freda continued to struggle in his own hands.

"Let me go!" she shouted. "Don't you dare hurt Charley, you big bully!"

"Bloody damned Earl of Wyndham. Killed my dad

and now he's gone and kidnapped my little sister," the boy yelled, and struggled against the iron grip holding him. But the frail, obviously undernourished Charley was no match for the strapping footman.

Marcus tightened his hold on Freda. "Stop it now. Both of you." He glared at the boy. "And *you* watch your language!"

"Answer his lordship." Henry gave the boy a shake. "Tell 'im who you are."

"Name's Charley Milton." The boy glared back at Marcus defiantly. "An' I come to get my sister. You got no business to snatch her." He pointed at Annabelle. "That one done got her purse back."

Marcus looked at the lad and recognized him as having been in the crowd at Vauxhall Gardens. As more members of the household poured into the hallway, Marcus steered his charge toward the nursery door.

"Let us go in and *try* to sort this out. Heston, get these people back to their beds. And bring us some coffee."

"Yes, my lord."

"Annabelle, Aunt Gertrude, Harriet—you may as well as go back to bed, too," Marcus said.

"For what purpose?" Aunt Gertrude asked. "Do you seriously think we could sleep—consumed by curiosity?"

"I am staying." Harriet's tone brooked no opposition.

He looked up as she spoke. Her hair trailed down her back in a thick braid. Despite having so recently wakened, her eyes shone with bright awareness. She folded her arms across her breasts in a stubborn stance. This action caused her cleavage to be more pronounced at the V neckline of her dressing gown. He was sure she had no idea what that was doing to *his* body.

When the principal figures of this little drama had

all crowded into the nursery, Marcus sat Freda and Charley on a settee. The others took various seats in the room, while he himself stood near the faintly glowing fire. He noticed Freda snuggling closer to Charley, and the boy took his little sister's hand. Marcus just looked at them for a moment.

"It'll be all right, Freddie," Charley said, but Marcus heard doubt and fear in his voice.

"Now," Marcus finally said to Charley, "suppose you explain yourself."

"I just come for my sister."

"How did you know where to come?" Annabelle's curiosity would not be contained, Marcus knew.

"I followed you to that coach an' then I asked around. 'Twarn't hard to find this place." There was a defiant sneer in his voice. "I watched and seen all the lights up here. Figured you was keepin' her here."

It occurred to Marcus the boy was not only intelligent, he had a remarkable sense of direction. "How did you get in? The doors are locked at night."

The boy squared his shoulders. "Ain't many locks goin' ta keep Charley Milton out if he wants in."

"Do you usually invade houses that are occupied?" Harriet asked.

"No, ma'am. But this was special."

Marcus was surprised at the boy's polite response and, catching Harriet's eye, he saw that she was, too.

"Now," Charley said with an obvious show of bravado, "if you will give her back her clothes, me an' Freddie will leave you folks alone." He tried to rise, but Henry's hand on his shoulder held him firmly in place.

"You are not going anywhere." Marcus gave him a stern look. "Your sister tried to rob one of us, and now you have broken into my house. Those are serious charges, young man."

Charley pointed at Annabelle again. "Like I said, she got 'er stuff back. An' I didn't take nothin'. An' besides—maybe you owe us."

"Owe you?" Marcus could see his was not the only surprised reaction in the room. "Perhaps you had better begin at the beginning."

"Our dad—he was a tenant farmer at Timberly. Got run off when the land was enclosed. Our cottage was tore down so's we'd hafta leave. Da found us a hut by the marsh. But Ma caught a fever there an' died."

"An' we didn't have no food," Freda put in plaintively.

"Leastways, not enough," Charley continued. "Da, he thought to try an' get a rabbit for the pot, but he got caught in one o' them mantraps. Tore 'is leg up something fierce. The wound festered real bad an' Da, he was outa his head most o' the time." The boy swallowed hard and shrugged. "He died, too."

"And then . . . ?" Marcus prompted as he tried to digest what the boy had already said. The others in the room had gone very still as the boy started to talk.

"Me an' Freddie—her name's Freda, really—come to Lunnon and hooked up with Ma Parker's house. Not much of a ma, though, if you was to ask me."

"A flash house?" Harriet asked, a note of horror in her voice.

"Yes, ma'am. I guess that's what they's called. You know—a place to put up. But ya've got ta earn your keep."

"But . . ." Annabelle's puzzled tone indicated her curiosity was kicking in again. "But why was Freda dressed as a boy? I do not understand."

Charley gave her a look of scorn for her ignorance. "Safer that way."

"Safer?"

"Ol' Parker puts the females to work right away. It don't matter how old they are."

"I still do not understand," Annabelle said.

The adults all looked embarrassed, and Marcus was grateful when Aunt Gertrude said, "Never mind, dear. I will explain later."

Then Annabelle apparently *did* understand. She gasped, blushed, and subsided into silence.

But Harriet did not. She turned to Marcus in shocked fury. "How *could* you? How could any human being be so utterly unfeeling as to destroy a family like that? So lacking in conscience as to condemn innocent children to such a wretched form of existence? You are just like the others."

"I—" Marcus groped for a response.

"Hey!" Charley looked at her with an expression of surprise. " 'Twarn't 'im what done it to us Miltons. The other one afore 'im done it. I heard he died—an' I was downright glad to hear it." He added this last with a defiant look around him.

"Here, now." Henry squeezed the boy's shoulder.

"Never mind," Marcus said absently. "But thank you for that exoneration." He was still reeling from Harriet's outburst and the intense pain it had caused to realize what she truly thought of him.

She looked at him with regret. "Oh, Marcus. I am so sorry. I should have known."

He looked away, not wanting to hold her gaze lest she perceive how her words had affected him. "It is not important." He gestured dismissively and welcomed Heston's arrival just then with a tray bearing herbal tea and biscuits as well as the coffee Marcus had ordered.

He watched as from a distance as the two children tried to be polite but obviously feared they would not have another opportunity at such abundance. The atmosphere in the room was subdued, and an undercurrent of tension prevailed through some desultory conversation.

Finally, Marcus set his cup down. "We shall finish sorting this out later. For now, everyone back to bed. Charley, there is another bed here in the nursery for you. Henry, lock the door—but stay on guard until Jamie relieves you." He started for the door.

Harriet rose to follow him. "Marcus—"

"Later, if you please, madam. We are all tired and out of sorts."

She gave a small gesture of defeat. "As you wish."

Coward, he admonished himself. He knew very well he simply did not want to face the fact that she had thought him capable of such indifferent brutality. He might be tempted to throttle her!

Why did it matter so much anyway?

Thirteen

Harriet chastised herself as she returned to her own chamber. "You stupid fool! You certainly demonstrated more hair than wit in that scene." How *could* she have lashed out at Marcus like that? Had she not a short time earlier noted his "soft heart"? Would such a person be a party to what she had laid at his door? Hardly. Belatedly, she now recalled his destroying the mantraps and that Ammerton folks had not only applauded the action, they had expected little else of Marcus.

Once again reason had fallen prey to emotion. Would she *never* learn?

Most devastating was the thought that she had destroyed a growing sense of camaraderie between them. She remembered how right—how utterly natural—it had felt to stroll with him in the Gardens. Feeling the hard strength of the arm beneath her fingertips, she had been more intensely aware of him than of any other human being in her entire life.

She had not imagined that he tightened his arm to press her closer. Nor had she imagined the warmth in his teasing gaze. . . . Nor the coldness a few moments before. He would not even allow her to apologize—he was that angry. And Lord knew he had cause to be. . . .

She slept very little in the remaining few hours before rising. Then her glass glared back at her, showing dark smudges under her eyes. Marcus was not in the breakfast room when she arrived.

"He was just finishing as I came down," Annabelle said in answer to Harriet's casual question. "He was out riding really early this morning."

Working off some of his anger? Harriet wondered, but aloud she made some innocuous comment about the weather.

Annabelle and Aunt Gertrude, apparently understanding that the children above stairs would be a sensitive topic, conversed amiably about the sights they had all seen at Vauxhall the previous evening.

Harriet tried to keep up her part in the discussion, but she was aware that her responses tended toward such substantive comments as "Yes," "No," "Hmmm," and "Is that so?"

Finally, she asked, "Did Marcus say what he intended about Freda and Charley?"

"No, he did not," Aunt Gertrude answered. "He ordered their breakfast sent up to the nursery. And he had Mrs. Benson send a maid to the attic for some clothing for them. The Jeffries children all spent a great deal of time here as they were growing up, you know."

This information merely served to intensify Harriet's guilt. A man who thought of attire for such children was certainly not the monster she had depicted last night.

"Marcus would like us to meet with him and the children in the library later." Aunt Gertrude named the hour.

Harriet reported to the library earlier than the appointed time, hoping to find Marcus alone so she could tender her apology. He was not there. In fact, he was the last to arrive. The children had been ushered in to exclamations of delight over their appearance. Freda fairly preened in a lovely yellow muslin, and she could not seem to stop swinging her legs to look at the shoes on her feet. Harriet had heard her whisper "Real shoes!" to her brother.

Charley seemed less comfortable and far more apprehensive than the little girl. Harriet wondered if he had balked at the bath as Freda had. He was dressed in a pair of brown trousers, a white shirt, and a dark blue jacket on which the sleeves had had to be turned back. His hair was neatly combed and he, too, wore real shoes. The siblings looked very much alike, with the same reddish hair, the same brown eyes, and the same sprinkling of freckles.

Marcus came in, flashed an approving glance at the children, and took a seat behind the heavy mahogany desk. So, Harriet thought with an inward sigh, this is going to be a formal interview.

"I have given this situation a great deal of thought," he announced. "Young Mr. Milton is at least partly right about my having a degree of responsibility for his plight."

Harriet saw Charley squirm nervously at this.

"Therefore," Marcus continued, "I am quite prepared to offer them positions on my staff. Cook tells me she could use another tweeny in the kitchen, and she will welcome Freda. Also, we need another man to help in the stables." He paused, then addressed the boy. "Would that offer meet with your approval, Milton?"

The boy's eyes glowed, and he glanced at his little sister. "Oh, yes, my lord."

"Very well," Marcus said. "You may go on back to the nursery now. Heston will be up to sort you out after the midday meal."

Charley stood and Freda slipped her hand into his.

"Does this mean we don't have to go back to Ol' Parker?" Freda wondered of her brother.

"Yes." He squeezed her hand and executed a passable bow to Marcus. "Thank you, my lord. Me an' Freda will earn our keep, never fear."

The two children left, the face of each aglow with hope.

"I knew you would think of something for them," Annabelle exulted.

"They both seemed pleased." Aunt Gertrude cast a fond smile at her nephew. "Did you not think so, Harriet?"

Harriet tried—and failed—to quell her fury. "Oh, yes, no doubt *they* were pleased at his lordship's largess."

"But you are not?" His lordship's voice was a study in neutrality, though she noted his clenched jaw.

Aunt Gertrude looked quickly from one to the other. "I think Annabelle and I will check on the children. Come, Annabelle."

Annabelle seemed reluctant to go, but she readily obeyed the gentle command. Harriet felt a moment of panic as being left alone with the angry earl, but her own anger gave her strength. She had come here prepared to apologize for misjudging him, only to find he lived up to the arrogance associated with the nobility. Indeed, it seemed Marcus Jeffries *was* just like all the rest.

"You object, madam, to the provisions made for these street waifs?"

She took a deep breath. "I object to your high-handedly assigning them to a life of servitude as a scullery maid and a stable hand with no knowledge or understanding of their abilities."

"Freda is hardly old enough to have developed 'abilities,' and Charley has had precious little opportunity to gain any experience."

"Precisely! He has had no opportunity. And you are offering him none now."

"Is that so?" he challenged.

"Yes, that is so." She enunciated each word clearly for emphasis. "A mere accident of birth separates them from dozens of other children."

"I suppose you have a better plan?" He was clearly trying to keep his temper under control.

"They should be educated."

"By whom?" His voice rose.

"I shall do it myself if you are unwilling to accept such an obligation."

"And what about Annabelle?"

"I shall simply remove Annabelle and the Miltons to my estate in the country and hire proper tutors for all of them."

She had no idea where this notion had come from, but now she was determined to stand by it. She said a silent prayer of thanks that Raymond Knightly had left her in a position to be able to follow through on this plan.

Marcus rose and leaned across the desk on his splayed hands. "Oh, no, you will not!" he said fiercely. "I already have a legal right to thwart any such plans for Annabelle. And I doubt not that I could secure such authority over the other two in a twinkling. You are not taking them anywhere." It was his turn to enunciate each word distinctly. He resumed his seat.

Harriet was stunned at his outburst. She stared openmouthed for a moment, then felt her shoulders slump in defeat. His title and his wealth—not to mention his gender—would automatically ensure his success in any court of law.

They sat in heavy silence for several moments. She thought he seemed as taken aback by the vehemence of their argument as she was.

Finally, he said in a subdued tone, "Shall we start over, madam?"

"I—I suppose you will want me to go now."

"Go? Go where?"

"Leave. Annabelle is fairly settled now. And . . . and I have no doubts anymore about . . . about the quality of her care. As for the other two, their situation breaks my heart, but it *is* within your power to do as you will."

She could not keep the despair out of her voice—nor, she suspected, from her eyes. She tried not to look at him directly.

She watched as his hands fiddled with articles on the desk, lining up the blotter pad just so and placing pens and the inkwell very precisely in relation to each other. Despite the incongruity of doing so in the heat of this moment, she noted that his hands were well-shaped, suggesting both gentleness and strength. She looked up into his rather bleak gaze.

"So," he said, "you plan to simply run away and leave me to handle all three by myself?"

"I—I thought that was what you would want, my lord."

"Well, it is not what I want." His tone was testy. "And for God's sake, stop 'my-lording' me, Harriet."

"Don't you dare swear at me!"

They paused and looked at each other in glaring challenges. Then he grinned ruefully, she smiled, and they both burst into laughter.

The ice having been broken, they reached a compromise. The Milton children would spend half of each day in the schoolroom with Harriet and half working in the stables and the kitchen.

"That will make them neither fish nor fowl with the rest of the staff, I am sure," Marcus said, "but it will be all right until autumn at least."

"And will allow Charley to save face," Harriet observed. "I think he truly wants to earn his own way—and Freda's."

"Yes. The boy does have spirit."

In the following weeks, Marcus knew Harriet had thrown herself into the task of teaching her two new students even as she continued to oversee Annabelle's work. He surmised that Harriet felt she had a point to prove with the Milton children.

The tension between the two of them had been eased considerably, but they had not achieved the comfortable camaraderie they had once enjoyed. When she tried again to apologize for blaming him for what happened to the Milton parents, he had politely turned the discussion to other matters. He could tell this did not sit well with her.

He felt remorse for thus hurting her feelings. He also suffered some remorse in not being totally honest with her during the argument in the library. The truth was, he could not allow Annabelle or the other two to go off with the Gadfly—not when the essayist was coming under more and more fire within government circles. On the other hand, his own sense of integrity—or was it pride?—would not allow him to confront her about the Gadfly so long as she wanted to keep that secret.

And there was another factor. Despite being angry and hurt over her misjudgment of him, he wanted her near. Yes, she could be dogmatic and infuriating, but she was also generous, caring, and witty—and he simply enjoyed her company. Nor was he unmindful of the physical spark between them. He thought she was aware of it, too, but neither of them seemed to trust the other—or themselves—fully. So there had been no more kisses, though the Earl of Wyndham would have welcomed an opportunity for such—Gadfly notwithstanding.

Invitations continued to arrive regularly, and Marcus happily escorted Harriet and Aunt Gertrude on those occasions when his social obligations coincided with theirs. This was the case one evening as the three of them were to attend a ball given by Lord and Lady

Brompton to honor their daughter, who was making her come-out this year.

Harriet had appeared in a dazzling gown of what he had come to recognize as her favorite shade of green. It was silk shot with threads of gold that caught the light enticingly as she moved. Her hair was piled on her head in some variation of the classical style so popular at the moment. He raised his eyebrows and cocked his head in an approving nod. She smiled in return.

The Wyndham party made their way through the reception line, and Marcus was immediately accosted by a middle-aged man who wanted to discuss some business of Parliament that could just as well have waited. Later he was annoyed to find all the dances with Harriet had been bespoken.

"Had I but known," she said, "I could have saved you one."

"Ah, well, I shall have to have *two* at the next such affair." He grinned to mask his disappointment.

She gave a soft laugh. *"That* would start tongues wagging."

When she then appeared on the dance floor twice with Dexter Taverner, he wondered about that comment. Had she no concern about gossips linking her and Taverner while taking exception to their linking her and Wyndham?

He knew Taverner to be a perfectly eligible *parti*. A younger son, he had little wealth of his own—but Harriet had enough for the both of them. And more, Marcus thought glumly. Besides which, Harriet seemed delighted to be in Taverner's company, judging by the way she smiled up at him ever so invitingly. When she allowed Taverner to waltz her out through the French doors to the terrace beyond, Marcus gritted his teeth.

"And just what is it that has brought such a scowl at a ball?" It was the throaty tones of Cynthia Teasler.

"Nothing," he lied. "My mind was elsewhere."

"I just happen to have the next dance free," she said with a flirtatious smile.

No gentleman could ignore such a blatant invitation. It was, however, the supper dance, and Marcus knew this would suggest to the gossips a renewal of their previous relationship. He suspected she was as aware of this fact as he.

"What have you done with Lynwood, then?" he asked as they sat with plates of lobster patties and other delicacies.

"Oh, he is here somewhere," she said airily. "The card room, perhaps."

But Lynwood was not in the card room, Marcus noted only a moment later. He had stood in the doorway, briefly searching the room, and when his gaze lighted on Lady Teasler, he turned and left. It occurred to Marcus that the lady had ulterior motives in maneuvering him into dancing with her. Ah, well, if she wanted to use an old lover to tweak the interest of a new one, so be it. He supposed he might oblige her with no harm to himself.

She was, after all, a pleasant companion and, while she had produced a monumental temper tantrum at their parting, she now apparently saw it to be to her advantage to be on good terms with one earl as she sought to bring another up to scratch. She was a very beautiful woman. Since when did it hurt one's standing to be seen in the company of such a beauty?

Across the room he noted with some annoyance that Harriet Knightly seemed to be thoroughly enjoying herself as Taverner offered her a tidbit from his own plate. The intimacy of such a gesture was not lost on the watching Earl of Wyndham.

"Marcus?" Cynthia raised her perfect brows. "You have not heard one word I have uttered!"

"Uh . . . sorry, Cyn. What was it?"

"Never mind. And what is it—or who is it—that holds your attention so?" She twisted around, gawking this way and that. "Taverner and Mrs. Knightly? They were an item some months ago. I was not aware it was still going on."

"That so?" he murmured, trying to sound disinterested. He was certainly not going to gossip about Harriet with Cynthia—or with anyone else for that matter.

"Oh, yes," she went on, oblivious to his tone. "Taverner is a bit of a rake, of course, but he is also a good friend of Lord Elgin's, you know. The whole lot of them were keenly concerned with those tiresome marbles Elgin brought from Greece."

"Has your brother returned from the Continent?" he asked in a determined effort to change the subject. "I heard he had gone to Greece."

"No, he has not, and Papa is furious—thinks Robert should take more interest in the title and lands he will inherit."

They discussed the merits of travel as an extension of one's education and then went on to other topics—all of which were interesting enough, but Marcus was not unhappy when it came time to release his companion to her next dance partner, the patient Lord Lynwood.

For her part, Harriet had been genuinely sorry to find every dance promised when Marcus approached her. But then, he *would* leave the asking until the last minute. A part of her longed for his partnership in a dance, but a whimsical part of her was glad to show him that unlike Harriet Glasser, Harriet Knightly was no wallflower needing the pity of one accustomed to taking in strays.

Then her attention was diverted by Dexter Taverner, who began by paying her fulsome compliments. She merely laughed and accused him of offering her Spanish coin. She turned the subject by asking him, "How is your translation of Thucydides coming along?"

He expressed mock horror and looked around in exaggerated furtiveness. "Oh, dear lady, never let any of this lot know of such!"

"Dex, you are such a humbug! Why are you so ashamed of that very fine mind you possess? Not to mention the splendid education your father afforded you."

"Ain't ashamed. Just trying to maintain my standing with the ladies."

"Ah, well, then—far be it from me to expose your deep, dark secrets." She laughed again but quickly sobered as he offered her a question.

"And have *you* no deep, dark secrets of your own, dear Harriet?"

"I—what do you mean?"

He shrugged. "A secret love? A secret ambition? A secret vice—do you hide chocolate truffles in your jewelry box?"

"Oh, my, you have found me out!"

"Only fair, considering you know of my translating. And"—he turned serious now—"it is going quite well. I know my version will be *accurate*, but I want it to be readable, too."

"I feel certain it will be. Your own writing style is generally pleasing."

He gave her a deep bow of self-mockery. "Thank you, dear lady. Now—shall we dance?"

Somewhat later she allowed him to waltz her out onto the terrace. As did so many *ton* hostesses, Lady Brompton had invited half again as many people as her ballroom would comfortably hold. It being midsummer as well, the room was excessively warm. Despite a conscious effort to divert her own attention elsewhere, Harriet was always attuned to where Marcus was in any gathering. Thus, she was aware that his eyes followed when she and Taverner left the ballroom.

Let Marcus Jeffries make of it what he will, she thought rebelliously. The truth was she and Dexter might flirt superficially, but beneath such foolery there was a serious friendship. Both of them knew it would never be any more—nor did either of them want anything else of their relationship.

Harriet was grateful to Dexter for his honesty with her in a friendship that had begun when her husband was still alive. Taverner had needed a female sounding board as he experienced the throes of unrequited love for the Season's reigning beauty one year. The accomplished rake was unused to rejection. The Knightlys had teased him out of his depression, and they had all become fast friends. Later Dexter had lent her much-appreciated support when Knightly died.

As she recalled the Brompton ball in the next few days, Harriet knew that Marcus probably entertained a distorted notion of her friendship with Mr. Taverner, but she saw no reason to disabuse him of it. After all, he obviously still enjoyed the attentions of the lovely Lady Teasler. Let him think what he would.

Meanwhile, in Wyndham House life proceeded at an orderly pace, running smoothly enough on the surface. However, Harriet was aware—and she thought Marcus was, too—of undercurrents that might one day erupt into major waves.

The waves came sooner than either of them might have expected.

Fourteen

Gadfly's next treatise was a vehement defense of certain persons brought up on charges for speaking out against His Majesty's government. The final paragraph was a thinly disguised questioning of the necessity of the crown itself and those who hung "like leeches on the body politic."

Marcus sought a private interview with Harriet one afternoon following ringing speeches on the floor of the House of Lords and heated discussions in both the halls of Parliament and in the clubs. When she appeared, he was standing, staring unseeing out the library window.

"You wanted to see me, Marcus?"

He turned as she came fully into the room. The late afternoon sun picked out golden highlights in the tendrils of soft brown hair around her face. She reached to brush one behind her ear and his fingers itched to perform that service for her. He noticed an ink smudge on her cheek and her fingers showed similar stains. More of Gadfly? he wondered.

"Yes, I did want to speak with you."

"Something about the children, perhaps? They are doing remarkably well—little Freda absorbs learning like a sponge. Why, she already reads as well as children her age who have had far greater advantages."

Marcus thought she was babbling nervously, but he loved her show of enthusiasm and pride in the achievement of her charges. "No, it is not about your pupils."

"Oh. What, then?"

"That." He pointed to the latest issue of the *Review* lying on his desk. He saw a subtle change in her expression. "I assume you know what Gadfly's latest essay covers."

"Uh . . . yes, I do."

"Harriet, this matter is becoming very serious."

"What is? I do not understand."

"Your friend's views have angered and disturbed people in very high places."

"They are intended to do so."

"But this one goes too far in the use of inflammatory rhetoric. That comment about leeches was a particular irritant. And Mr. Canning is furious about Gadfly's defense of that buffoon who questioned his parentage."

"Are you saying these very powerful politicians have taken exception to a single writer's work? Gadfly is but one among many of the government's critics."

"Yes, but he is particularly popular."

"How wonderful." She smiled in obvious pleasure.

"No, it is *not* wonderful. It is, in fact, dangerous. Very dangerous. You must see that Gadfly understands that this work is considered by some to be nothing short of sedition."

She looked thoughtful for a moment, then shrugged. "All that talk about sedition is somewhat exaggerated, I think."

He closed the distance between them and grabbed her shoulders. "Harriet! You sweet, wonderful little peagoose! Are you not listening? It is very hard to mount a defense against a charge of sedition. And it is punishable by a severe prison term—or transportation to a penal colony. Gadfly is in grave danger."

She looked up, holding his gaze, and he could see her finally understand the full impact of what he was saying. Without thinking he pulled her closer and lowered his mouth to hers. At first she seemed startled, then her arms were around his neck and she was responding as he had dreamed she might—when he had allowed such dreams. The temptation, the frustrations, the misunderstanding and fear—all melted away in mutual yearning and need.

He came to his senses reluctantly. "Harriet, I—"

She put a finger to his lips. "Shh. I know."

He still held her, and she seemed in no hurry to disengage herself from his embrace.

"Tell him to be careful—very careful," he murmured.

"I . . . I shall . . ." She stepped away from him. "Um . . . Marcus?"

"Yes?" He held her gaze, but then she looked away. "N-nothing."

"Nothing?"

"Only . . . only that I am sure Gadfly's rhetoric will be toned down. And . . . thank you."

She turned and left the room.

Had she been about to tell him the truth concerning Gadfly?

Harriet carried out her usual activities in the next few days, but she often relived the scene in the library, savoring the memory of that kiss. Though it was not repeated, it had done much to erase the residue of tension between them. Both were more at ease, enjoying once again discussions of the profound or the trivial and treasuring the occasional comfortable silences.

Keeping him apprised of the progress of their charges, she assured him again of Freda's eagerness to learn. They had been walking in the garden one afternoon and paused to sit on a stone bench.

"Turning her into a bluestocking, are you?" he teased.

She laughed. "No, but she may well do that to herself."

"What about Charley?"

"Charley is an apt pupil, too. . . ."

"But . . . ?" he prompted her.

"But what?"

"I heard a definite 'but' in your tone."

"It is just that his interest is not as strong as hers. He tolerates lessons. She welcomes them." She sat straighter. "Still—he will make a wonderful clerk one day. Perhaps I will speak to my solicitor about an apprenticeship for him."

"*If* that is what he wants . . ."

"Well, of *course* he wants to better himself," she said.

"And our Annabelle?"

"I think she has finally given up the idea of writing silly novels. She wrote a very informative essay on the Battle of Hastings. You should read it."

"I shall—later. Right now I have an appointment." He rose and took his leave. She chose to remain in the garden to savor the sun for a while.

And try to make some sense of her emotions.

There was no hope for it—she was in love with Marcus Jeffries, Earl of Wyndham. Despite his reactionary political views and his faintly condescending attitude toward women, he was quite simply the most fascinating—and innately generous—person of her acquaintance. And despite cherishing her freedom, leaving him at the end of the summer was likely to prove the most difficult action of her entire life.

She wondered if he suspected the truth about Gadfly? If she were discovered, the subsequent scandal could be very damaging to Marcus. After all, his government work had always been vitally important to him. If she *were* found out, it would be best if she were not in proximity to Marcus when it happened.

It rankled that she should have to curb her views so, but she also recognized that these were precarious, if not downright dangerous, times. Fear—fear of revolution—was the driving force of those in power. Unfortunately, fear inspired increasingly repressive measures. She knew—and not just from Marcus—that there were important men who favored reforms, but they were—so far—a minority.

"Reform," Marcus said one evening, "is inevitable, but it is likely to be a slow process. And probably *should* be."

She gave a ladylike sniff. "Reactionary thinkers putting up obstacles at every turn merely condemn more people to misery."

"Nevertheless, some changes should be instituted slowly," he insisted. "We in this house have seen firsthand the results of proceeding too hastily—on enclosures, for instance."

Harriet mulled this over for a moment. "The pace of any proposed change is always set by the particular interests of people wielding the most power."

He nodded. "Yes, sometimes that is all too true. However, you will be glad to know, I am sure, that Parliament has appointed a Select Committee to investigate such things as flash houses."

"Truly?"

"Truly. Hastened, no doubt, by the outcries of Gadfly and others."

"Just so something positive comes of the Committee's work."

"There is more," he said. "Sir Robert Peel's call for a national police force seems to be finding some willing listeners."

"Oh, Marcus, how wonderful."

" 'Tis a *start.*"

These were but small steps, she knew. Nevertheless, she wanted to hail them from the rooftops. She wanted to rush right to her desk and pen demands for more, but she had committed herself to toning down the rhetoric, had she not? She had contracted with Mr. Watson for one more Gadfly essay, and she would deliver it as promised.

After that Gadfly would be forced into quiet—and permanent—retirement.

Marcus harbored no doubts about Gadfly's identity—and the knowledge was a major source of worry to him.

Despite small concessions made to reform, the bulk of power in government lay with the most adamant of conservatives—those least amenable to the very idea of change. Since armed hostilities had ended and the troublesome Bonaparte had been permanently banished to the small island of St. Helena, the conservatives had gained a powerful addition to their forces—a national hero, no less. Already there were those who whispered of the Duke of Wellington's becoming prime minister one day.

If anything, Marcus knew his own comment that reform would be slow was an incredible understatement. Repression continued to be the watchword of the day. In the Midlands, men who tried to organize textile workers or coal miners were jailed or, in some instances, transported. Such sentences came on the basis of the flimsiest of evidence.

The calls for suppression of a "radical" press were stronger than ever. Lord Bixby had been most vocal in charging "sedition" against people like the Hunts and Mr. Castle. Marcus knew that Bixby—a pompous know-all defender of the status quo—was especially eager to ferret out the identity of Gadfly and hold that troublesome writer up to severe judgment as a warning to others. Quite by accident, Marcus learned that Bixby was nearing his goal.

Marcus was sitting in his club, enjoying a glass of brandy with Lord Hanford, when they were joined by another club member named Jenkins.

"Have you heard the news?" Jenkins asked in the tone of one always eager to be first with new information.

"Depends on what news you have," Hanford said.

"Bixby says he can find out who this Gadfly fellow is."

"Does he now?" Hanford shifted in his seat. "The fellow has eluded detection so far."

Marcus sat very still, almost afraid to say anything himself.

"Alistair Thompson publishes *The London Review*," Jenkins said, "and even he doesn't know who the Gadfly is. Or at least that's what he says."

"I know Thompson. He is an honorable man," Hanford responded.

Marcus finally trusted himself to ask, "So—who *is* this source Bixby has tracked down?"

"Some fellow named Winston or Watson—can't recall the name precisely. He's the editor—and the only one who seems to know. Bixby says he can put pressure on Thompson to put pressure on Watson. We should have the Gadfly soon enough." Jenkins assumed the same self-important tone of one "in the know."

When Jenkins had gone on to spread his "news" elsewhere, Hanford asked, "Well, Wyndham, what do you think? Is Bixby on to something?"

"I doubt Thompson will be persuaded to put undue pressure on his editor."

"Why?"

"It would amount to killing the hen that lays the golden eggs." Hanford gave him a quizzical look, so Marcus added, "This Gadfly sells their publication. They will not readily give up the writer's identity."

"True enough, I suppose. Still—probably only a matter of time." Hanford set his empty glass aside and took his leave. Marcus sat lost in thought. Hanford was right. Given Bixby's determination and his willingness to use any means available, it probably was, indeed, only a matter of time before Gadfly was exposed. Furthermore, given the mood of Bixby and others like him, they would not hesitate to prosecute a woman as readily and as severely as a man.

Marcus could not face the images thus conjured—of Harriet standing before a court, or languishing in prison, or—God forbid!—being transported to a penal colony. The simple truth was he could not face the idea of losing her. Now, *there* was a new idea. But it was so. Life without her would have lost its meaning. True—she was stubborn—decidedly mule-headed at times. And it was also true that she lacked restraint in expressing her views.

Caring passion was the very core of her being—and he suspected it colored every aspect of her life. Her approach to a given problem might be too vehement, her solutions too simplistic, but the substance of her criticism was generally on target. It came as a surprise to find himself admitting that fundamentally, he agreed with most of what Gadfly had said in the last few months.

But it was Harriet—not Gadfly—he wanted to—no, *had* to—protect. His title, his position and wealth—all those years of service to this very government—ought to count for something in protecting someone he cared for.

Cared for? *Cared* for? Admit it, Jeffries. You are head over heels in love with her. Of all the women he might have chosen to love, a more troublesome one did not exist. But then—he had not "chosen," had he? It was not a matter of choice at all. It just *was*.

How could he protect her, though? He could not just drag her off to his cave and lock her up, could he? On second thought, why not? He had planned to take the entire household to Timberly for the Harvest

Festival in a few weeks. They would just go earlier than
he had originally planned. She should be safe enough
in a county so distant from London. Still . . . how
could he absolutely ensure her safety?

The thought remained with him all the way home
and through the night. The next morning at breakfast
he broached the subject of their removal to Timberly.

Aunt Gertrude's response was one of complacency.
"I had assumed we would return for the Harvest Festival."

"I had given it little thought," Harriet said. "When
have you in mind to leave the city?"

"In three days? Perhaps?" he offered tentatively.

"Three days! Why, we cannot possibly be prepared
in a mere three days," Harriet cried. "Annabelle and
I have fittings at the mantua maker's. And . . . and
there are other appointments to keep."

"Very well. Five days, then. But not a moment more,
if you please."

"I do not understand the necessity for such haste,"
Harriet said.

"The festival is rather special this year. It will be the
first full-fledged celebration in three years. First my
father was ill. Then, during the last two autumns, the
family was in mourning—first for my father, then for
my brother." He was rather proud of himself for coming up with such a plausible explanation.

"And you need more time to plan the festivities—is
that it?"

"In a word, yes."

"Well, could not you go ahead and the rest of us
follow at a more leisurely pace later?" she asked in
reasonable tone.

"I *could* . . . but I should prefer not to do so. I was
rather counting on you and Aunt Gertrude to lend
me your sage advice on such matters."

She gave him an arch look. "And you believe blatant flattery will achieve your end?"

"It usually succeeds," he said smugly.

"Lady Hermiston?" Harriet queried.

"I can be prepared in three days—or five—as the two of you wish."

"Five days, then." Harriet's tone was adamant.

Marcus readily agreed, for he had business of his own to transact in the next few days—not the least of which was a trip to the archbishop's office in Doctor's Commons to secure a special license. This would be his ultimate insurance policy in his scheme to protect Harriet.

Now that her deadline had been moved up, so to speak, Harriet threw herself into writing Gadfly's "farewell missive." Her pride dictated that the last article should be a powerful piece. This one would also go to the very heart of corruption and self-serving special interests within the government. Her topics were the so-called "pocket boroughs," or "rotten" boroughs, and a voting system that was patently unfair.

The House of Commons should by its very name be of ordinary people and should serve their interests. Instead, we have one parliamentary body that is largely controlled by the other, for many of the boroughs fall within the purview of only a few powerful land-holders—who are themselves members of the senior legislative body.

A given landowner may, in fact, "own" more than one borough. It is he who chooses who will occupy a seat in Commons. Naturally, his choices share his political interests and views. Some "boroughs" in fact hardly exist as such at all, for property lines and population centers have shifted in the centuries since they were first established. Yet a given peer may still appoint one of his henchmen to that position—which member of Commons has a vote equal to that of members from the most populous boroughs!

At this point Gadfly pointed out specific locations and gave population figures so far as they could be determined. This section of the essay ended with the ironic question, "Is it any wonder that real reform is decades overdue?"

However, reform is unlikely so long as the voting system itself is also under the control of these same few. Only males owning specified amounts of land may vote—and lesser landowners must do so in a public arena overseen by a man who may wield a great deal of authority over the lesser man and his property.

The system is further skewed by denying a vote to many who have a vested interest in public policy but whose wealth is not tied directly to large tracts of land. In a crisis, merchants, shipping magnates, and bankers offer services to the nation as necessary as those of owners of huge tracts of land, yet they are denied a like voice in government.

Is this the way to ensure a government of men of conscience?

Arriving at Hatchard's to meet with Mr. Watson, Harriet found the popular bookstore and lending library busier than usual. The two of them regularly chose to meet in the sections of a bookshop dealing with classical history or farming—under the correct assumption that these areas of a shop in London would be less crowded.

"You are sure this is to be your swan song?" Mr. Watson asked with a touch of sadness as he took the manuscript.

"Yes. It must be. As you yourself have said, it may

well be too risky to continue—not so much for me as for others I hold dear."

"I understand. I—we at the *Review* will be sad to lose you."

"I may offer you something else one day—but it will not be political—and it most assuredly will not come from the Gadfly."

He handed her a folded sealed paper that she knew would contain a check for her latest effort. "It has been a pleasure to work with you, Mrs. Knightly—and I shall be glad to consider any of your work in future."

"Thank you, sir." She offered him her hand, which he took briefly. She started to leave, then turned back to ask quietly, "Mr. Watson, do you know that man?" She pointed surreptitiously at a fellow who had been sitting at a table placed so as to have a view of this particular aisle between shelves of books.

Mr. Watson looked over her shoulder and said, "No. Never saw him before. Why?"

"He appeared to be merely loitering in the front when I came in, and now his book does not seem to hold his interest."

"Hmmm. That could be cause for concern."

"I feared as much."

"I told you earlier about those two men who questioned me about Gadfly."

"Yes."

He wore a worried frown. "I *have* taken precautions to ensure I was not followed when I met with you."

"Perhaps he is merely waiting for someone."

"Perhaps. In any event, it is I he might be interested in—not a lady such as you."

She smiled. "Of course." And then in a tone just loud enough to be heard by the gentleman at the table, she added, "I am sure you will find this particular volume on crop rotation of value, sir. My late husband swore by it."

"Thank you, ma'am."

Mr. Watson took the book she extended and went to pay for a work she knew he had no use for whatsoever. As Watson left the shop, the man at the table shoved his book aside, rose, and followed the editor of the *Review* out the door.

Fifteen

Harriet hurried home to Wyndham House, where she penned a note to Mr. Watson detailing the man's following the editor. She then called in Jamie as one of Wyndham's least conspicuous footmen to deliver it. She cautioned him, however, to perform the errand in garb other than the distinctive livery of Wyndham servants. If Jamie thought this was an unusual request, he was far too well trained to say so. He took the missive and later reported its successful delivery.

Besides finishing the last of the Gadfly essays and the visit to the mantua maker, Harriet had a full social schedule in the few days before their departure for Timberly. One of these affairs was a musical evening to be followed by a light supper and dancing at the home of Lord and Lady Hanford. Harriet knew the couple were particular friends of Marcus's and she enjoyed a passing acquaintance with Lady Hanford. She also knew that what Lady Hanford billed as a "small gathering" was likely to be a "terrible crush" just short of a full-fledged ball.

And so it was.

Harriet and Aunt Gertrude had gone together, with Marcus planning to arrive somewhat later due to a previous engagement. Mrs. Knightly and Lady Hermiston soon became separated as they were taken up by different groups of friends. Harriet had been delighted to see Dexter Taverner among the guests. He immediately sought her out.

"You will be happy to know that I have finished my translation of Thucydides," he said.

"Very happy to know." She was genuinely pleased for him. "Do you have another project planned?"

"Planned, yes. But I intend to take a long holiday first."

"Oh?"

"I shall rusticate in the country in Wiltshire with my favorite aunt and her retired navy husband."

"In Wiltshire? Really?" she asked in surprise. "Where in Wiltshire?"

"Captain Nichols bought a piece of property—"

"Near Ammerton," she interrupted.

"How did you know?"

"I met Captain and Mrs. Nichols at Wyndham's Christmas party. They seemed very nice people."

"They are. She is my mother's sister. Spoiled me frightfully when I visited as a child. Fancy your knowing them!"

"Wyndham is removing the lot of us to Wiltshire in a few days. I am sure the Nicholses—and any houseguest of theirs—will be invited to participate in the Harvest Festival—not, mind you, that one *needs* an invitation to most things. It truly is largely a village affair."

"Oh, yes," he said. "Now I remember—you grew up in that area. I shall certainly call upon you, if I may."

"Of course."

They found seats for the musical presentations that were about to commence. Harriet waved discreetly to Lady Hermiston several seats away. They sat through performances by an only passable soprano and an excellent quartet of strings.

Later, during an interval, Harriet had gone to the ladies' withdrawing room to find it empty. As she prepared to leave, the door opened and Lady Teasler entered.

"Oh! Mrs. Knightly, is it not?" the newcomer said in a slightly condescending tone.

Harriet knew very well the beauty knew to whom she spoke. She inclined her head coolly and murmured, "Lady Teasler."

"Come, join me for a moment," the beauty said, taking a seat before a large looking glass. Lady Teasler fussed with her hair for a moment and pinched her cheeks to bring more color to them. "Time is so unkind to us women." She sighed.

"However, one must observe that you have managed to escape his cruel hand." Harriet knew the woman expected such a response, but it was the truth all the same.

"Why, thank you." There was a little trill of laughter. "I . . . uh . . . I did not see Wyndham with you and Lady Hermiston when you arrived."

"No. I believe he plans to turn up later."

"Marvelous. I fully expected to see him here. I do so enjoy the company of a handsome man." She gave Harriet a look of feminine conspiracy. "Do not you? I noticed you with Taverner. *Charming* rake, is he not?"

"Mr. Taverner is a friend," Harriet said stiffly.

"Of course he is." Lady Teasler again sounded condescending. Then she assumed a more intimate tone. "But tell me—truly—do you not love the freedom of being a widow? No more worry about chaperones or jealous husbands."

Taken aback, Harriet groped for an appropriate response. "Well . . . I— In truth, I do not recall my husband's having been jealous."

"Oh, but he must have been. With your looks? And the age difference . . ." Apparently seeing Harriet's shock at such forthright speculation from one who was not an intimate friend, Lady Teasler gave a little self-effacing moue and said, "Now see what I have done. I have offended you. Forgive me? Please?"

She was so beautiful and seemed so genuinely sorry that Harriet readily forgave her. The two of them left the room together, and just as they reentered the main salon, Marcus appeared before them.

"Oh, *there* you are, Marcus," Lady Teasler said, her tone and inflection indicating they may have arranged to meet here. "We were just sharing secrets about you." She laughed suggestively.

"Is that so?" he asked with a look at Harriet that she found hard to decipher.

"Oh, well—not *those* kinds of secrets." Lady Teasler obviously enjoyed his reaction. She linked her arm with his and said, "Come, Marcus. You must explain to me what that last piece of music was all about. You did hear it, did you not?"

He nodded and looked at Harriet, but before he could say anything, Lady Teasler spoke again.

"Oh, look. Here is Taverner. You sly thing, Mrs. Knightly. You *will* excuse us, I am sure."

And with that, the beauty—losing some of the shine of her looks with *one* of the Hanford guests—all but dragged a seemingly nonplussed Marcus away.

"What was that all about?" Taverner asked, handing Harriet a glass of lemonade.

"I honestly have no idea," Harriet answered in amazement.

"Saw Lynwood earlier. Thought she might have come with him—but maybe not."

Harriet changed the subject, and they spent the rest of the interval in pleasant conversation. Later Taverner was part of her group for supper, along with Lady Hermiston and others from the Antiquities Society. Harriet thought Lady Hermiston seemed rather tired, and the older woman protested only mildly when Harriet suggested they leave early.

Lady Teasler was still hanging on Lord Wyndham's arm as they left.

Having arrived at the Hanford soiree late, Marcus took a seat in the back. He looked around for Harriet and Aunt Gertrude and found his aunt first. Some distance away he found Harriet sitting with Taverner—apparently on very good terms with the man, judging by the way they had their heads together between numbers. With a definite twinge of annoyance, Marcus wondered just what there was between the two of them.

Later he had hoped to catch Harriet alone for a moment, only to find her in the company of Lady Teasler! That had come as a surprise. He had not known they were even acquainted—let alone sharing "secrets"—and about him yet! What did that mean?

When Cynthia had maneuvered him away from Taverner and Harriet, he had tried to press her on the matter. She merely laughed it off and continued to babble on in a gossipy fashion.

Finally able to get a word in, Marcus asked, "What is it with you and Lynwood?"

"Why do you ask?"

"I thought surely you would have brought him up to scratch by now—but here you are according me your singular attentions and he is on the other side of the room, dancing attendance on the Stimson chit."

"Edwina Stimson? She is a mere schoolgirl."

"Was. She made her come-out this year. Her mama seems eager to fire her off in a hurry."

"Tried to corner you, I take it?" she teased.

"She did. But do not seek to change the subject. Is Lynwood past history with you now?"

"Would it make any difference to you if he were?" She smiled up at him flirtatiously.

"No." He knew that sounded too blunt, so he

added, "Not in the usual manner of things, but I should like to see you happy."

"Thank you, Marcus." She patted his arm. "Lynwood is—shall we say—unsure of what he wants."

"And you?"

"Oh, I know well enough. Before autumn has passed—he is coming to the country for a house party my parents are having—I shall have convinced him, too."

"I doubt not you will." He chuckled. "Poor Lynwood."

"*Poor* Lynwood, indeed. You mean to say *lucky* Lynwood, do you not?"

"Of course. Is that not what I just said?"

They laughed together and went on to other topics in the comfortable manner of friends who understand each other.

After a while Cynthia said, "She left."

Marcus felt his face grow warm. "Who?"

Cynthia rolled her eyes in a show of impatience. "Mrs. Knightly. She and Lady Hermiston just bade the Hanfords farewell."

"Oh." He shrugged.

"I have seen you watching for her. Were *my* affections not engaged elsewhere, I might fall into a definite fit of pique." She expressed a little pout.

"Caught me out," he admitted.

"Only because I know you rather well. Your secret is safe with me."

"It is a rare woman who can keep a secret," he teased. But his thoughts immediately became more somber as he recalled the seriousness—not to say danger—of Harriet's secret. "A rare woman," he repeated.

"You might be surprised." Cynthia's voice was serious, too.

As Marcus quickly changed the subject, she gave him an arch look. The rest of the evening passed amiably.

* * *

The addition of Freda and Charley to the entourage setting out for Timberly did not appreciably inconvenience anyone. Charley happily rode on the driver's seat with John Coachman on the earl's own carriage. Tiny Freda squeezed in between two of the maids intended to augment the staff in the country. Harriet knew that both children viewed this trip as "going home."

This thought nagged at her a bit, for of course there would be more opportunity for a clerk in the city. Charley must surely realize that, though Freda was far too young to think of such matters. No need to fret about it, she reassured herself. It would all work out in the end.

The weather was warm and sunny. Therefore, Marcus spent most of the journey riding alongside instead of in the carriage. The ladies entertained themselves with the usual word games—and reading, when road conditions allowed. Still, Harriet found she had a good deal of time to think. And her thoughts dwelled much on her own future.

She had felt a sense of relief on giving Mr. Watson the last of the Gadfly material. Relief mixed with a certain sense of nostalgia. Gadfly had been a companion of sorts for months now. She would to have find something else to supply that sense of purpose in her life.

On the last day of the journey, Harriet glanced at Annabelle and smiled indulgently at the girl. Annabelle had come so far in this year. She had progressed from a lonely, rebellious child to an attractive, confident young woman. Harriet was sure that when the ward made her come-out in two years' time, she would break hearts as well as rules.

"Annabelle." Harriet drew the girl's attention from the book she held.

"Yes?"

"You promised some weeks ago to give your return to school serious consideration. Have you done so?"

"Yes, ma'am, I have."

"And . . . ?"

"And I would certainly consider some school other than the Chesterton-Jones school. Letty writes that she is attending the Westchester Seminary for Young Ladies. Her father finally agreed to let her change."

Aunt Gertrude had been watching the passing scenery. "Is that not the same school Berwyn's sister attends?"

"Yes, ma'am, it is. The three of us could have such fun together! I just know Celia and Letty will love each other as much as I love both of them."

This information came as a surprise to Harriet, who had fully expected Annabelle to continue to resist the idea of school. "Have you spoken with Lord Wyndham of this matter?"

"Only in a roundabout way. I think he will approve the Westchester school."

"There should be little objection," Aunt Gertrude said. "That school has always had a fine reputation."

"When did you make this decision?" Harriet could not help feeling somewhat left out. "And why?"

"Well . . ." Annabelle sounded thoughtful. "I suppose it has been coming for some time. Celia and I have talked it over. And Letty and I have covered it in letters."

"I see." Harriet nodded encouragement. "Will you be happy there, then?"

"Oh, I think so. I really do. But more to the point—I will no longer be a burden to you two—and to Marcus."

"But, dear—" Aunt Gertrude protested.

"A burden? No such thing," Harriet said.

"You are both very kind. And I truly do love you dearly for giving me this year of my life. But I think I have required enough of you—and of Marcus. It is time I stopped making such selfish demands on your time and attention."

"I am very proud of you, Annabelle." Aunt Gertrude, who shared the forward-looking coach seat with Annabelle, gave the girl a brief hug. "That is such a grown-up view to take. But really, dear, if you want to think about it some more . . ."

"By all means," Harriet said around the lump in her throat. Annabelle's statement of love and gratitude had brought tears to Harriet's eyes.

"You must not turn into a watering pot," Annabelle said in mock sternness. "You will have me crying my eyes out and they will turn all red and swollen and *ever* so ugly!"

At this, Aunt Gertrude chuckled, Harriet smiled, and Annabelle giggled—all of them through tears—as the carriages arrived at the posting station where they would have their midday meal.

"May a mere male know what it is that has the three of you in what appears to be an emotional state?" Marcus asked as he handed them from the coach.

"We shall tell you during our nuncheon," Harriet said as she turned to the business of seeing that Charley and Freda were being cared for.

When the food had been served in a private parlor for the four of them, the ladies did tell Marcus the news. Harriet found it difficult to read his reaction, but she thought he shared her own mixed emotions. On the one hand, it marked a milestone of maturity for Annabelle. But it also presaged changes in all their lives.

"Well!" He lifted his wineglass. "Such a decision deserves a salute."

"Hear! Hear!" The ladies lifted their glasses as well—of lemonade in Annabelle's case and watered wine for the other two.

"This puts special meaning on this holiday," Marcus

said. "But never forget, Annabelle—you will be expected to spend your school holidays with us."

With us? Harriet thought. What did that mean? She gave a mental shrug. Probably nothing.

Then Marcus turned to her. "You and I will need to discuss our other two charges in light of this turn of events."

"Yes. I suppose we will."

She was pleased that he intended to consult her about Freda and Charley. After all, she knew very well that he could simply ignore her wishes—or those of the Milton children—if he so chose.

For the remainder of the journey, Annabelle read silently, Aunt Gertrude dozed, and Harriet was lost in thought. Annabelle was not the only one who faced a milestone in her life. Harriet finally came to the conclusion that once Freda and Charley were provided for, she would probably hire another companion and perhaps travel on the continent.

Winter in Naples might be quite nice. . . .

Sixteen

As he had announced, Marcus intended this year's Harvest Festival to be something extraordinary. The occasion had a long tradition in the Jeffries family, and the festivities customarily included a prolonged house party as well as the festival itself. This year's guest list was a reprise of the Christmas group—plus a number of London connections. There would be some thirty adults staying at Timberly—not to mention attendant children.

The guests would begin arriving only a few days after the return of the earl and his immediate entourage. As he had anticipated, no one sent regrets. He looked forward to welcoming his brother and his sister, along with their families. He had also invited the Berwyns again, in part because he knew Harriet would enjoy the visit more if her sister were included.

Besides family, the guests reflected an eclectic gathering of interests, and included people from the worlds of finance and commerce, the law, politics, and the arts. "One should not want for interesting conversation, anyway," Marcus muttered to himself. He was happy to leave it to Aunt Gertrude and Harriet to sort out proper seating arrangements and such, for, privately, Marcus thought that kind of thing to be of more interest to women than to men.

Knowing that his time would be taken up later with entertainments for his guests, Marcus tried to take care of as much estate business as possible in the days immediately following his return. A meeting with his steward proved rather enlightening.

"Our gamekeeper has done *what?*"

Trenton grinned. "Connors took a job with your neighbor—Rogers."

"I assume he gave a reason for quitting Timberly."

"Said as how we was—how did he put it?—'too soft on poachers'—and the ban on mantraps just made his job too difficult."

Marcus returned Trenton's grin. "Indeed? I cannot say that his leaving comes as a disappointment, but what are we to do for a gamekeeper?"

"That feller—Starkle—that we hired as assistant seems to be working out fine. I had my doubts, him being crippled and all, but he's doing it all now that Connors is gone."

"He probably needs help, though—even if he did not have a damaged leg. We must consider getting *him* an assistant."

They discussed several other matters, then the steward left, armed with new orders. Marcus had been working at his desk for some time, when Morris announced that he had visitors. The butler ushered in the vicar, Mr. Henderson; the vicar's wife; and Jenny Hart, wife of the blacksmith. They had a rather determined look about them.

"I gather this is not purely a social call," Marcus observed after initial pleasantries.

"No, my lord, it is not, the vicar said. "We have come on a matter of importance to all of Ammerton."

"And surrounding areas as well," his wife added.

"I see." Marcus remained noncommittal, waiting.

Henderson took a breath, glanced at the women, and proceeded to explain. "Well, the truth of the matter is, my lord, our parish school is proving inadequate to the needs of the district."

"I am not sure I understand," Marcus replied. He

hated to admit that he had not even known there *was* a parish school. Not that it came as such a surprise. Many parishes had schools of a sort—to teach the rudiments of learning to scholars whose interest and attendance was likely to be erratic.

"Mrs. Hart and I have been working in the church for the most part," Mrs. Henderson said. "However, it is difficult to conduct lessons around the pews. When the weather permits, we take the children out-of-doors."

"But we need a real school," Mrs. Hart said. "The number of children seeking our services has steadily increased."

Mr. Henderson chuckled. "Their own success is coming to haunt them."

"So you are asking me to build a school—is that it?"

"Not precisely," Mrs. Hart replied.

"Then what—precisely?"

"We need your moral support—and, yes, a good deal of financial support as well," Mr. Henderson said.

His wife elaborated. "If *you* were to be in favor of such, you see, other landowners would probably follow along."

"If we can procure the materials, my lord, the men of the village will gladly build our school," Mrs. Hart said.

"Whom will it serve?" Marcus asked.

"Whom—?" Jenny Hart's eyebrows flew skyward. "Why, everyone, of course. Any child who desires to learn is welcome now—even though we *are* grievously overcrowded. We turn away no one, my lord."

"Despite there being many who say children of laborers and tenant farmers have no need to learn," Mrs. Henderson said darkly. Then she colored up. "Oh, dear, I do hope you are not one of those who feel that way, my lord."

Marcus smiled at her. "No, I am not one of those. I think you are doing something very fine. I will be happy to do what I can to help. So—tell me what is needed."

As they laid out the details of their plan, Marcus found his own enthusiasm growing. He was glad to lend his aid to such a project for "his" village. Having seen firsthand—well, secondhand, anyway—how their learning was broadening the vision of Freda and Charley, he had no doubt of its effectiveness for the village as a whole. Mrs. Henderson and Mrs. Hart—the parish teachers of older and younger students respectively—had also allowed their enthusiasm to extend to teaching illiterate adults who requested their services.

Marcus knew a good many people in his social milieu were opposed to making education available to servants and laborers. "Makes them needlessly discontented" he had heard more than one member of the House of Lords say. While Marcus had never opposed education for the lower classes, until his experience with Freda and Charley, it had simply never been a matter demanding his attention. Good Lord! he thought. He had held the earldom nearly two years—and he was *still* discovering new duties and responsibilities that came with the title.

Marcus offered to hire extra laborers to see to the building of a new school.

"That is very generous, my lord," the vicar responded. "However, it might be better if the people of Ammerton built their school themselves."

His wife nodded her agreement. "Somewhat slower, but better."

"I should think sooner is better," Marcus objected.

"Up to a point," Mrs. Hart responded. "We think parents might be more inclined to keep their children in school if they have a hand in it themselves."

"Makes them feel it is really theirs, you see," Mrs. Henderson added.

"Yes, I do see. And a very proper consideration that

is, too. You three would have been welcome additions at the negotiating tables in Vienna."

He could see that his joking compliment pleased them. They departed seemingly quite satisfied with their mission and convinced that support from the Earl of Wyndham would have others eager to follow his lead.

A day or so later, Harriet and Annabelle went into the village. The excursion was mostly a diversion for them, but Harriet intended to call on her friend Jenny Hart, and Annabelle wanted to check out the offerings in a small milliner's shop, for the woman who owned it was said to produce "the most *charming* bonnets."

Jenny spent most of their visit singing the praises of the Earl of Wyndham, who had, it appeared, agreed to the building of a real school for the village. As Harriet and Annabelle prepared to leave, Jenny offered to walk part of the way with them as she "had an errand or two to run."

The three chatted and laughed as they strolled along Ammerton's single thoroughfare. Suddenly, a middle-aged woman and a young girl appeared before them. The two seemed to be of the working classes. The woman wore a worried look, and the girl had her head down, her face obscured by a wide-brimmed bonnet. Then Harriet recognized the woman as the wife of one of her father's tenant farmers.

"Mrs. Twomey! How nice to see you." Harriet's greeting caught the woman by surprise.

"Ah! Miss Harriet—er—I mean Mrs. Knightly, ma'am." Mrs. Twomey executed a hasty curtsy.

"This must be your daughter," Harriet said. Still the girl did not look up.

"Yes. My daughter, Beth."

The girl mumbled incoherently, and Harriet wondered if she was somehow want-witted.

"Oh, Miss Harriet," the mother wailed. "We have fallen on hard times at Sefton Hall."

"I am sorry to hear that," Harriet said. "If there is something I can do—"

"Nothing, I am afraid," Mrs. Twomey said. "Only *look* what's happened to my Beth." She put her hand under her daughter's chin to force the girl to face the others.

Harriet, Annabelle, and Jenny gasped in unison. Beth's face bore a small cut, a swollen lip, a black eye, and a bruised cheek.

"Oh, my heavens! What happened?" Harriet asked.

"He beat her. In 'is cups, 'e was, an' 'e beat her."

"Her father did this?" Jenny's voice was full of indignation.

"Her father?" Mrs. Twomey responded in shocked denial. "Never. My Ben would never— No. 'Twas that blackguard Sefton. Needed a maid in the manor house, he said. Well, Beth here had to go into service somewhere . . . better close to home, we thought."

"I am so sorry," Harriet murmured.

"Heavens! 'Twarn't *your* fault," Mrs. Twomey protested. "I blame myself for letting her go. Lucky for Beth he was so foxed. She kept her virtue, she did."

"That bruise looks painful, though," Harriet said, and the girl nodded.

"An' *now* that poor excuse for a man is putting it about that my Beth tried to seduce *him.*" Mrs. Twomey made a determined gesture with her closed fist. "Ooh! If I were a man . . ."

"Unfortunately, there is never just punishment for such behavior." Harriet recalled her own close encounters with the lascivious viscount.

Mrs. Twomey sighed. "I know . . ." Then she glanced at the sky. "Oh, dear. We must hurry home to prepare the midday meal for Ben and the boys."

Harriet, her ward, and her friend were silent for quite some time. Gradually, they began to talk of other things. Soon Jenny bade them farewell and Harriet and Annabelle went on to the dressmaker-millinery establishment. Their mood was considerably lightened as they spent several pleasant minutes trying on bonnets. Annabelle found one she would have in a moment, if only . . . This, of course, was no problem for the woman who had made the headgear. She would simply alter it for the young miss.

The milliner walked them to the door. "I shall send word when the bonnet is ready," she promised on the step of her shop. "I must send to Bristol for that ribbon."

"Ah, Cousin Harriet," sounded a voice Harriet had hoped not to encounter. Viscount Sefton blocked their way. "And this must be your charming ward of whom all Ammerton hears such heartwarming tales."

He positively leered at Annabelle, Harriet thought. He was dressed in his usual finery, but his eyes and complexion reflected marked dissipation.

"Lord Sefton." Harriet accorded him only the barest civility. "Miss Richardson and I must be on our way." Harriet saw no need to grant him the courtesy of introducing Annabelle.

He laughed. "Surely you are not still smarting from our little contretemps last winter? Do say we can let bygones be bygones. Come—we can discuss it like civilized human beings."

"There is quite simply nothing to discuss," Harriet said, aware that they were attracting the attention of passersby as well as the milliner and her other customers.

But the viscount planted himself squarely in front of Annabelle and gave her a sweeping bow. "My dear Miss Richardson, my cousin seems to have forgot her manners, but I hope you will not take your cue from her. I am truly quite an amiable fellow."

"Yes," Annabelle said. "I can see that you are."

He began to preen at this and gave Harriet a triumphant glance. Then Annabelle continued in the same sweet tone.

"We have just seen splendid evidence of your extreme amiability, sirrah—we met Beth Twomey."

Color flooded his face, and he began to sputter. "Oh, I say—surely you have better sense than to take the word of that bit of baggage."

Annabelle looked at him directly, holding his gaze with a hard glare. "Her injuries spoke rather forcefully."

"And you think I— Oh! This is infamous. Simply infamous!"

"Methinks the gentleman doth protest too much," Harriet said.

Now he turned his fury on her. "You, madam, seem only too happy to malign me in the eyes of others. Well, know this, Harriet, and know it well—you will live to rue this day."

He turned on his heel and stalked away, his fury evident in every mincing step.

"That was an unfortunate encounter," Harriet said as she and Annabelle settled into their waiting carriage.

"A singularly unpleasant fellow," Annabelle agreed with a shudder. "I was lucky to have avoided him during the last visit."

In a matter of days the London contingent from Wyndham House had settled into a routine at Timberly. When they had been there nearly a fortnight, young Charley Milton requested a private interview with Lord Wyndham.

Marcus tried to put the obviously nervous young man at ease. "Have a seat, Milton."

"Thank you, my lord."

"Now—what have you on your mind?"

"Well, sir—" The words came out in a high squeak. Marcus saw the boy's Adam's apple bob as he swallowed, reddened, and started over in a deeper, more manly tone. "You see, sir, I've been talking with Mr. Starkle and Mr. Trenton. They tells me—tell me—that Mr. Starkle, he needs help."

"He does. Starkle is a good gamekeeper, but with his leg injury at Waterloo, the sheer size of this estate gives him far too much to do."

"I could help him." Charley's voice was full of youthful eagerness.

"You?"

"Yes, my lord. I could do it. I know I could."

"What do you know of gamekeeping?"

"Only a little now. But I like being out-of-doors—in the woods and the fields. An' Mr. Starkle—he let me an' Freda help him feed the rabbits and I held one of the hunting dogs as he fixed its leg." He paused.

Marcus heard clearly the enthusiasm in the boy's voice. "What about your training to become a law clerk? Has Mrs. Knightly not arranged an apprenticeship for you?"

"Yes, she has, I think . . . but I only agreed because she's such a nice lady and all. I'd much rather be apprenticed to Mr. Starkle here at Timberly."

"What about Freda?"

"I haven't said nothing—anything—to her." Charley's shoulders drooped. "She likes books so much—takes to learning like a duck to water."

"And you do not?" Marcus recalled Harriet's saying the boy only "tolerated" his lessons.

"Um . . . not like Freda does. Freda likes it here, though, so maybe if we stayed, she'd like it well enough. I don't want us separated. . . ."

"Maybe she would," Marcus said. "Give me some time to think on this, Charley. I will discuss it with

Starkle and Trenton. And perhaps you should discuss it with Mrs. Knightly as well."

"She ain't—isn't—going to like it."

"Perhaps not, but I feel sure she will agree to what is best for you and Freda."

"Well, of course—if that is your wish" had been Harriet's response to the stammering boy when he told her he wanted to stay on at Timberly.

"You ain't—aren't—angry with me?"

"No, I am not angry. I would ask that you give it some more thought. Life as a gamekeeper is very different from what I had envisioned for you."

"I know," he said glumly. "But I just cannot see me cooped up in an office—I hate the smell of ink!"

She laughed. "Oh, well, then, I suppose that settles it—for you. But what shall we do about Freda?" Harriet could see that he was pleased at her conferring with him as an adult on this matter. And she could also tell that he was genuinely torn about his little sister.

"I'm—I'm still thinking on that, ma'am."

"I should be perfectly happy to keep her with me, but I fear she would be quite lost without you."

"Yes, ma'am. And if the only way we can stay together is in London, then I'll just have to learn to like the smell of ink."

"I should not think it would come to *that*. Something will turn up, I am sure." She tried to sound reassuring, but in truth she had no idea what that "something" might be.

It appeared, however, that Marcus *did* have an idea, for a few days later he invited Harriet and Charley into the library to discuss the Milton children's future. She knew he had been occupied of late with the first of the arriving guests and with estate business, yet he had apparently found time to consider the children's dilemma and consult with others.

"I have met with the Starkles," he announced. "Mr. Starkle would be quite happy to take you as his assistant," he said to Charley. "Says you have a natural gift with animals."

Charley's eyes lighted up at this praise.

Marcus addressed his next comment to Harriet. "The Starkles lost their only child at Waterloo—father and son served in the same regiment."

"Oh, how sad," she murmured.

"Their son was only five or six years older than Charley here when he died. The long and the short of it is Starkle and his wife are already quite fond of Charley and find Freda to be the charmer we know so well."

"Are you saying—?" Harriet started to ask.

"Yes. They are not merely willing to take them in— they are eager to do so."

"Oh, but—but—there are so many questions . . ." she stammered.

"I can provide answers to some of them. But first"— he turned to the boy again—"Charley, you are *not* to feel this is being forced upon you. If you have any objections at all, there is no reason you and Freda cannot continue as you have."

"Thank you, my lord, but I like the Starkles very well. So does Freda. And . . . Mr. Starkle—he don't hold with mantraps."

Struck by the poignancy of that last comment, Harriet was thoughtful for a moment, then she asked of Marcus, "But what about Freda? Are we to condemn that poor child to life as a milkmaid or something?"

She saw a flash of annoyance cross Marcus's face.

"No, madam, we are not. If she eventually *wants* to be a milkmaid, however . . ." He left the idea dangling, then went on. "The Starkles have agreed that Charley will attend school half a day and work with the gamekeeper the other half for a period of apprenticeship. Freda will attend the parish school as long as she can. Then—*if* she wants to go away for further schooling, I shall see that it is done."

"Oh." Her voice was a little squeak. "That—that is very generous of you, Marcus."

Marcus spoke to Charley again. "Now, Milton, you are very young to have such decisions thrust upon you. Are you certain this what you want for you and your sister?"

Charley sat up straighter. "Yes, my lord. Me and Freda"—he glanced at Harriet—"that is, Freda and I—like living in the country. And Joe and Mabel—the Starkles—are good people, I think."

"I think so, too, son." Marcus rose. "Well, if anything ever happens to change your mind about this decision, I expect you to call upon me."

Charley had risen when Marcus stood and took the hand Marcus offered him. "Thank you, my lord. Thank you—for—for everything."

Harriet felt tears springing to her eyes as she, too, rose and gave Charley a hug, which he returned in embarrassed awkwardness.

"Go on, now," she said. "Tell Freda your news."

As Charley left, Marcus gave her a smile of sympathy. "Now we have some idea of what it feels like for parents to send their children off—when the chicks leave the nest."

"Yes, I suppose we do."

"If you would like to meet the Starkles, I will gladly drive you out to visit them tomorrow."

"I should like that very much."

Seventeen

With the arrival of her sister, closely followed by the families of Trevor Jeffries and Melanie Sheffield, Harriet found her time occupied increasingly by her willingness to take some of the duties as hostess off the shoulders of Lady Hermiston. Not surprisingly, Celia accompanied the Berwyns. Annabelle and Celia were immediately inseparable.

When the milliner sent word that Annabelle's new bonnet was finally ready, Harriet and other adult women were busily engaged in preparations for the festival. The two girls were allowed to go to the village more or less alone—which meant they would be accompanied by a groom and a maid as well as the driver of the landaulet. After all, this was the country, Harriet and Charlotte reasoned. What possible harm could come to them in sleepy Ammerton?

Harriet and several other ladies were chatting in the drawing room as they fashioned garlands of greenery into which they would later insert fall flowers for bright spots of color as decorations for the harvest ball. Suddenly, their quiet gaiety was interrupted by loud cries from the entrance.

"Charlotte! Mrs. Knightly! Help!"

"That's Celia!" Charlotte jumped up. Harriet followed close behind as Charlotte hurried down stairs.

"What is it?" Charlotte cried.

Wilma Counts

"What has happened?" Harriet asked. "Where is Annabelle?"

"She—she was grabbed—right off the street!"

"What?" Harriet's voice rose in shocked disbelief, and she felt panicky nausea stab at her innards.

"Abducted?" Charlotte also sounded disbelieving. "In Ammerton?"

Celia was nearly hysterical. "We were just walking along . . . and . . . and"—she sucked in a long breath—"and this carriage stopped next to us and . . . and he just grabbed her. Forced her into the carriage." She ended in a wail.

By then the other ladies had poured from the drawing room and hovered at the top of the stairs. Harriet spoke first to Morris and then to Celia.

"Send for Lord Wyndham immediately," she ordered the butler. "Then bring us some tea—make it strong. Come, Celia."

With Charlotte right behind them, she ushered the girl into the library and directed her to a settee. Harriet sat beside her and put an arm around Celia's shoulder. "Now. Take a deep breath and try to tell us exactly what happened, step by step."

"Oh, it was so aw-w-ful!" Celia cried. "We . . . had gone to the milliner's shop—Annabelle looked so charming in the new bonnet!—and we were looking in another shopwindow—the sweet shop, you know?"

"Yes," Harriet said encouragingly, even though she wanted to scream "get on with it!"

"Suddenly Annabelle screamed. This . . . this —huge, he was—grabbed her and pulled her to-a carriage. There was another man in the car- had a crest. The big man pushed Annabelle looked as though the man inside was pulling e man outside slammed the door and the seat with the driver and they left. Oh, poor, poor Annabelle!"

Morris entered then with a tray. "Cook had just brewed a fresh pot," he said.

Harriet poured a cup and handed it to Celia. "Here. Drink this. Did you recognize either of the men?"

"N-no." She sobbed. "I—we—couldn't help her. It happened so fast!"

"Tell me about the carriage," Harriet said.

"It was dark green—almost black. With silver trim."

"You said it had a crest," Charlotte prompted.

"Yes! It did! The crest showed an eagle carrying a serpent in its claws—"

Harriet and Charlotte drew in sharp breaths simultaneously.

"No!" Charlotte gasped.

"Not even he—" Harriet began to say as Marcus burst into the room followed by Berwyn, Trevor, and Sheffield.

"What has happened?" he demanded.

"Annabelle has been abducted." Harriet tried to keep the panic from her own voice.

"Annabelle has been—what?"

"Abducted. Apparently by Viscount Sefton," she said.

"Sefton? I will kill him," Marcus growled. "When? How?"

Charlotte, with an occasional correction from Celia, explained what had happened.

"Where were the maid and groom who accompanied you?" Berwyn asked his sister.

"They were very near, but it all happened so fast— Jack—the groom—tried to get to her, but . . ."

"Where is Jack now?" Marcus asked.

"He—he said he would get a horse at the smith and try to follow the carriage."

"Good lad," Marcus said.

Marcus stepped out of the room briefly to ba[r]k[or]ders at Morris and a footman. Then he came b[ack to] ask, "How long ago did this happen?"

"I—I am not sure." Celia gave another shuddering sob. "We came right back to tell you."

Harriet hugged Celia to her. "It is all right, Celia. You did precisely what you should have done."

"I—I hope so."

Marcus looked from his brother to his brother-in-law. "They will have a head start of well over an hour by the time we are organized, but I am going after her. Will you come with me?"

They both nodded firmly.

"I shall join you." Berwyn jerked a thumb at Trevor. "I cannot allow the captain to go off on a sortie without his lieutenant."

"Thank you," Marcus said.

Harriet stood up. "I am coming as well."

"Oh, no, you are not," Marcus said. "This could prove dangerous."

Even as he spoke, the butler and footman came in bearing assorted firearms for the men.

Harriet put her hands on her hips and tried to keep her voice even. "You will have to take a carriage—to—to bring her home. Annabelle will need a woman. And she is *my* ward, too!"

Marcus apparently knew when he had been defeated, for he did not argue further. Harriet went to fetch a bonnet and cloak. And in no time at all, it seemed, she was seated in a light, fast carriage with Marcus driving. The other three men—now heavily ⟨arm⟩ed—followed on horseback.

"⟨W⟩hy?" Marcus asked. "Why would he do such a ⟨thi⟩nd where can he be taking her?"

"He undoubtedly learned of Annabelle's for-⟨tune. M⟩y conjecture that he plans to force her ⟨to marri⟩e. Gretna Green?"

"⟨If m⟩arriage is what he has in mind—he ⟨can't do i⟩t there—with her underage and ⟨without per⟩mission. I swear, Harriet, if that fatheaded popinjay has so much as *touched* her, I will kill him."

"He will want to marry her—young as she is. He is desperate for money." She gave a heavy sigh that caught on a sob. "I am just sorry I did not realize how desperate he is."

Unable to take a hand from the reins, he gave her a brief penetrating look. "You have no cause to blame yourself, my dear. You were not there. And even had you been, I doubt your presence would have deterred him."

The endearment and his reassurance sent a pleasant glow through her despite the perilous journey they were on. The road was rough, often jostling them against each other, and Harriet was intensely aware of the firm body next to her own.

When they had been on the road about an hour, they met the groom who had accompanied Annabelle and Celia earlier. He informed them of the direction the fleeing coach had taken. A native of the area, he also pointed out a shortcut that would put them closer to their quarry.

"I hope your groom is right," Sheffield said.

"He is," Trevor assured them. "We used to race that course, did we not, Marcus?"

"Not *we*. You and that scapegrace twin of yours," Marcus replied, but his tone was only mildly accusing. He flicked the reins to start his team again.

It was very late in the afternoon when Marcus said, "There they are."

Harriet caught a glimpse of the dark green coach far ahead of them. The road was very crooked, so they periodically lost sight of the other vehicle. Soon it became clear that the culprits ahead realized they were being followed, for the other driver whipped his team up to a furious pace.

Harriet had never in her life experienced such but at the same time she felt instinctively that rescue mission would be successful. Somehow she felt at one with Marcus as they pursued the same unselfish goal. The actual events of the rescue happened so fast that Harriet was later able to piece them together only when she had heard Annabelle's version of the entire fiasco.

Marcus had steadily gained on his quarry. When they were within hailing distance, Trevor and Berwyn rushed ahead. As Berwyn turned a pistol on the two on the driver's seat, Trevor sought to curb the Sefton team. The sight of a pistol aimed directly at them quickly effected a change of heart in Sefton's hirelings.

"Here now—we didn't bargain for no dealings with poppers!" shouted the man seated next to the driver.

The coach was stopped abruptly and Sheffield, pistol in hand, leaped to open the door as Marcus brought his own vehicle to a stop. Marcus leaped from his seat and helped Harriet. The two of them were right behind Sheffield. The scene that greeted them might have been laughable under other circumstances.

There on the floor of his own coach lay Viscount Sefton curled into the fetal position and moaning incoherently. Annabelle had scrunched herself as far into one corner as she possibly could.

"Oh, thank goodness," she said on seeing first Sheffield, then Marcus and Harriet.

"Is he armed?" Sheffield asked the trembling Annabelle as he held his weapon on the still-moaning ___on.

"___hink not."

___s dashed around to other side of the coach ___e ___e door nearest Annabelle. "Can you stand?"

___her hands still tied, she maneuvered ___toward him and then literally fell ___us carried her away from the coach ___her feet next to Harriet. He made quick work of the rope tying her hands, and Annabelle fell sobbing into Harriet's arms.

Harriet, too, was quietly crying—with relief. "Shhh. You are safe now," she crooned. "We have you. No one will harm you."

Gradually, Annabelle's sobs subsided, and she wiped her eyes in a childish gesture that tugged at Harriet's heart.

Trevor, Berwyn, and Sheffield searched the three captives and Sefton's coach, then bundled them into it. Trevor tied his horse at the rear and climbed into the driver's seat. Sheffield and Berwyn would ride on either side back to Ammerton, where the two hirelings would be locked in a shed that passed as the village jail. Sefton was to be placed under "house arrest" with the sternest admonitions not to stir from his own lodging.

Then the whole story unfolded as Annabelle, seated between Harriet and Marcus, told them what had happened.

As soon as his henchman had shoved Annabelle into Sefton's coach, the viscount tied the stunned girl's hands behind her. He dumped her on the opposite seat and then assumed a relaxed pose on the other seat.

"He was after my fortune," Annabelle explained. "He said I would be glad to marry him once he was through with me this night. Oh, Harry, I was so afraid!"

"I know, dear." Harriet hugged the girl to her.

"Then he just sat there, leering at me. And saying things about . . . about my . . . m-my body . . . and what he would do to me once we got to the inn. It was so *very* disgusting!"

Harriet saw Marcus's jaw clench at this. She patted Annabelle's hand. "He did not . . . uh . . . harm you, did he?"

"No. No, he did not really touch me. He just talking in that revolting manner. I . . . I think enjoyed seeing me squirm." She heaved a sigh was very much at his ease—just lolling back on the seat until he discovered we were being pursued."

"And then what did he do?"

"It was not so much what he did as what *I* did." Marcus turned to look at her briefly.

"When *I* knew there was a friend behind us, I—I kicked him. He did not tie my feet, you see. So I kicked him—hard—right . . . right where it is likely to hurt a man the most." Even in the dim light of a rapidly approaching twilight, Harriet could see Annabelle's blush.

"And then," Annabelle went on, "when the carriage stopped so suddenly, he fell on the floor and hit his head on the opposite seat. And that is where he was when you came up."

Marcus guffawed. "Annabelle, you are a marvel." He looked over at Harriet, and she saw his eyes twinkling merrily.

She hugged Annabelle and said, "We are *so* proud of you."

"That we are," Marcus agreed.

Annabelle then asked about Celia, and they informed her of what had happened after the abduction. They passed the remainder of the journey on more general topics.

The next day Marcus went to see the magistrate to ke the case against the two scoundrels who had Sefton. He wanted the matter handled as dis-
as possible to protect Annabelle. There was lit-
that the two would either be transported or
several years of their lives on prison hulks
al river of England.

Lord Sefton?" Squire Davies, acting
"He's as guilty as these fellows—or

"I have given that some thought," Marcus replied. "He must be pockets-to-let to have taken such a desperate course of action."

"I have heard that he is. Owes the local innkeeper a prodigious amount. And some tradesmen have even come from London to deliver their duns."

"Perhaps, then—with proper incentive—he will be amenable to simply going away, if things are all that bad for him."

Davies raised his brows. "Proper incentive?"

"I will gladly pay him off to get him out of here. He could live frugally on the Continent—or in Canada—on, say, a hundred pounds per annum?"

"What if he refuses?"

"I will personally buy up all his obligations and see him imprisoned for debt." Marcus was coldly adamant.

"That ought to be mightily persuasive," Davies said.

The next day, Davies called unexpectedly at Timberly and requested a private interview with Lord Wyndham.

"I went out to the manor yesterday to tell Sefton what his options were. He seemed at the time to accept them well enough."

"At the time?" Marcus had caught something in Davies's tone.

"I went out again early this morning to make sure he was following through and found the manor all to sixes and sevens. Sefton shot himself."

"What?"

Davies nodded. "Dead. Shot himself. He apparently called for brandy as soon as I left yesterday and drank steadily all day long. Started ranting and raving—no unusual for him. At times like that, the servants most! just tried to avoid him. But this time he located pistol and was waving it about. Scared them somethi' fierce."

"I should not be surprised."

"They were afraid to answer when he pull: bell. A couple of footmen hovered in the h;

heard him ranting one moment and blubbering tears the next. They said it got real quiet. Then they heard a shot."

"Did no one investigate?"

"At first they were afraid to. Then someone opened the door for a peep and saw him slumped over the desk, blood running across it."

"A sordid end to a sordid life," Marcus said, and thanking Davies, he ushered the squire to the door. He found it impossible to be sorry about the loss of a man willing to cause others so much pain. His immediate thought was to summon Harriet. The man had, after all, been related to her—however remotely—and this news was probably already making its way along those mysterious lines of communication among servants.

He broke the news to her gently, but he was not surprised when her reaction echoed his own.

"Such a sad, shocking waste of a life," she said. "I suppose—quite without intending to do so—he has spared many people an inordinate amount of grief."

"Perhaps he has at that."

They sat in silence for several moments, but it was a *shared* quietness. Then Harriet rose from the chair she had taken. "I must go and tell Charlotte."

Nearly an hour later, she and Charlotte and Charlotte's husband returned to the library to speak with Lord Wyndham.

"Marcus, we have been considering this tragedy and [wha]t it might mean for the people—who were once [te]nants—at Sefton Manor," Harriet said.

"[Tha]t will be up to the heir," Marcus said. "Do you [know] that is?"

"[That] is—there is no heir."

"[What do yo]u mean, no heir? *Someone* will inherit."

"[After o]ur father's death," Charlotte said, "[the solicito]rs did a thorough search for acces-[sion to the] title. There truly is no male heir. The title died out when George Glasser took his own life last night."

"Then—" Marcus started, thoughtful.

"Yes," Harriet said. "The title—and more to the point—the *property* reverts to the crown."

"And given the fact that Prinny is always so hard pressed for the ready," Berwyn said, "the manor will almost certainly be sold immediately to the highest bidder."

"So which of you will bid on it?" Marcus looked from Harriet to Berwyn.

"Neither of us," Berwyn answered. "I am far from pockets-to-let myself, but I could not see my way to the kind of funds that would take."

"Nor can I," Harriet added. "My ventures are rather tied up in shipping right now."

"So what are you proposing? That *I* bid for it?"

Harriet smiled. "Precisely. Your property runs parallel with the manor on the north. And you would surely take care of the people."

He grinned at her. "Was that a compliment I just heard?" His grin broadened as she actually blushed, and Berwyn chuckled.

"Will you at least consider it, my lord?" Charlotte asked.

"Yes, I will consider it—but who is to say my bid would be accepted?"

"Oh, come now, Wyndham," Berwyn admonished. "Doing it too brown. Everyone knows Prinny would be most unlikely to refuse *you*."

"But his price—and I do not speak of money— might be too high."

"So long as you offer a fair amount . . ." Har spoke slowly. "It would mean so much to people the Twomeys."

Marcus had no idea who the Twomeys were, supposed he was in a fair way of finding out.

* * *

In view of Sefton's behavior and the ill favor with which he was regarded in the district, it did not come as a surprise to Harriet that there was no prolonged mourning for the man. Because he was a suicide, there was only the briefest of funeral services, and, of course, he had to be buried outside the churchyard proper.

The incident did dim the festivities for a few days, but soon the remaining guests began to fill Timberly's bedchambers, and there were any number of provisions and diversions to be planned for such a disparate gathering.

The most recent arrivals included Lord and Lady Hanford. They brought with them several copies of the latest edition of *The London Review.* Gadfly's attack on political corruption quickly became a burning topic in the drawing room.

"I think the fellow has fairly done it this time," drawled Lord Meritson, a tall, spare man with a shock of white hair that gave him a distinguished look. The gentlemen had just rejoined the ladies after the evening meal.

"Bixby is beside himself," said another man, who Harriet knew held a seat in Parliament. "Says if he has to bribe every printer in London, he will uncover this Gadfly's identity."

"Fair means or foul—eh?" another man asked.

Harriet noticed that it was mostly men who were commenting on the essay, but then Marcus's sister

"it extremely curious," Melanie said into one of those silences that occasionally mesmerize "that so much discussion centers on ——and so very little on the serious

——eone said, but Harriet did not

quite literally erupted into several of them rather heated. Harriet noticed that Marcus did not say much on the topic, and he wore a rather worried frown. She had a sudden urge to kiss it away, but she merely smiled at him and saw his expression clear, temporarily at least.

Finally, Aunt Gertrude managed to restore some order and decorum by ringing for tea and asking one of the ladies, an accomplished musician, to play the pianoforte for them.

Eighteen

Among the houseguests was a certain Mr. John Murray, who was the current publisher of such novels as *Sense and Sensibility* and *Emma*. The author's identity was, as Harriet knew, now very much an open secret in literary and court circles. Mr. Murray also published the works of another novelist writing anonymously, this one apparently a Scotsman, for the stories often dealt with Scottish themes.

Harriet knew Annabelle had devoured the lady writer's works and had lately been sent into transports by the Scotsman's Highland adventures. Annabelle was undoubtedly hounding poor Mr. Murray for interesting bits of information. Trust Annabelle to want to know *everything*, she thought indulgently.

Annabelle's decision to return to school had been welcome news to Celia, Harriet surmised from snatches of conversation between the two girls. Harriet was glad for the presence of not only Celia, but Andrew's ward, Ned, and a few other youths of an age with Annabelle. She knew they had all helped Annabelle put the incident with Sefton long behind her.

One drizzly afternoon, the guests were confined to indoor activities. Some played billiards or card games. Some wrote letters or read. Others merely sat around in amiable conversation. Timberly's formal drawing room was a large, elongated room. Annabelle, Celia, Ned, and another young lady and young man sat at one end of the room, chatting and laughing. Some distance away, Harriet conversed with Lady Hanford and with Dexter Taverner, who had ridden over to call upon Harriet.

Mr. Murray came into the room with a packet of papers in his hand. He caught Annabelle's attention and motioned her to a table with two chairs. Murray tapped the papers and nodded in what—to the watching Harriet—seemed an approving manner. She saw Annabelle's expression take on a glow of pleasure. Was he sharing some as yet unpublished work with Annabelle?

Just what was Murray's interest in Annabelle? Why, the man was old enough to be her father! Surely a man of his stature in the literary world would not risk his reputation in pursuit of a young girl not yet out of the schoolroom!

After a while, Murray arose and left the room, leaving the papers with Annabelle, who now rejoined her younger friends. There was some animated conversation among them, then Celia gave Annabelle a hug.

"How positively, absolutely delightful!" Her little squeal of pleasure was clearly audible to others in the room.

"Famous!" Ned gave Annabelle a look of approval.

Annabelle then rushed from the room, clutching the packet of papers to her bosom. Harriet shrugged and shook her head, wondering at the enthusiasms of youth.

A few minutes later, a footman came in, waited politely to catch her attention, then told her that Lord Wyndham would like to see her in the library. She found Marcus talking with Mr. Murray, Lady Hermiston, and Annabelle. The gentlemen rose until she had seated herself in a chair that had obviously been left for her. She wondered at that.

"I sense something brewing here." Harriet kept her voice light.

"Oh, Mrs. Knightly, you will never guess!" Annabelle's eyes were shining brightly.

"Well, then, you had better tell me," she replied calmly.

"Mr. Murray wants to buy my book!"

"Buy your book," Harriet repeated in a neutral voice. "What book would that be?"

"My . . . my novel." Annabelle's voice wavered, and her eyes had lost some of their eagerness.

"You have written a *novel?*" Totally surprised, Harriet was also miffed at learning this fact only now.

"She has," Mr. Murray said. "And a very fine work it is, too."

Harriet looked directly at Marcus and Aunt Gertrude. "Did you two know about this—and not tell me?"

Marcus returned her gaze with a slight warning shake of his head. "I learned of it only a half hour ago when Murray here approached me about allowing Annabelle to sell the manuscript. I told him we needed to consult with you as well."

Aunt Gertrude looked slightly uncomfortable. "I must confess that I suspected something was afoot because Annabelle spends so much time in her chamber. But it was not my place to pry into her private affairs."

"And you, Annabelle? Why did you not mention you were doing this?" Harriet tried to keep the hurt out of her voice.

Annabelle's eyes now shimmered with unshed tears. "I—I—because I knew you would not approve and I did not know if my work had any merit and I wanted to be sure it did and Mr. Murray says it is publishable." She finally took a deep breath.

"Eminently publishable," Mr. Murray put in.

Annabelle had not taken her eyes from Harriet. "I am sorry, Harry. I *have* to tell stories—can you not see? I am not proficient with the essay, as are Mr. Hazlitt and Mr. Lamb. Please say you understand."

"But you do so *well* with historical and literary themes."

"I am much better at fiction—at presenting ideas through characters and events. Well . . . at least I *enjoy* that more."

"I see . . ."

"Miss Richardson really is a fine writer," Mr. Murray said persuasively. "She has a fresh voice and a good eye for telling details."

"I—I am not surprised at *that*," Harriet said. "I am merely taken aback that I had no idea this was going on. I need a moment to digest it all, you see."

"Of course," the publisher murmured.

Everyone was silent for what seemed a long while but was in reality only a few moments. Then Harriet said, "I shall make no objection to her work being published. In fact, I think it quite remarkable that one so young is turning out publishable material."

"Oh, thank you, Harriet!" Annabelle's enthusiasm obviously caused her to forget to use the more formal "Mrs. Knightly" in the presence of company.

Harriet held up her hand and looked at Marcus. "However, I do *not* think she should publish under her own name. I doubt the high sticklers of the *ton* would look favorably on a 'lady scribbler' in their midst when she makes her come-out." This comment sounded slightly more caustic than she intended.

"Mr. Murray and I have already thought of that," Annabelle said, her eagerness returning full force with Harriet's approval. "My nom de plume will be Miss Emma Bennet." She waited expectantly.

"Emma Bennet? Am I supposed to recognize that name? Do you?" Harriet directed the last question to Marcus and Lady Hermiston.

Marcus shrugged and shook his head. Lady Hermiston looked mystified.

"It is a combination of the names of the heroines

of *Pride and Prejudice* and *Emma*—Emma Woodhouse and Elizabeth Bennet. Emma Bennet!"

"Will that be acceptable?" Marcus asked Murray.

"I see no problem with it."

"Well! It appears we have an author in our midst," Harriet said brightly.

"Truly? You approve?" Annabelle asked.

"If Lord Wyndham has sanctioned this venture, I shall certainly not stand in the way. Actually, I am proud of your achievement, Annabelle."

"Famous!" Annabelle said, then, apparently seeing both Harriet and Aunt Gertrude raise their brows at this use of a cant phrase, she added, "I mean, how wonderful!"

Everyone laughed at this. Mr. Murray then offered his terms, and there was some discreet haggling before Marcus and Harriet, on Annabelle's behalf, reached agreement with him.

Later, Harriet took a long, solitary walk. The air was still damp, but the drizzle had stopped. She carried an umbrella merely as a precaution.

Actually, she thought morosely, the gray overcast sky suited her mood. She felt such a failure. First, she had allowed the potential danger from Gadfly to encompass Marcus. If he suffered because of that, he might never forgive her—nor would she forgive herself.

Then, she had been so terribly *wrong* about Charley and Annabelle. She had happily—and blindly— planned their lives for them with little regard for *their* interests and abilities. Had the two youngsters been less assertive people, she might very well have severely damaged—if not ruined—their lives!

In Charley's case, she should certainly have recognized that he was willing to sacrifice himself to give his sister a better life. Perhaps such a sublimation of *self* had been necessary for the young Harriet Glasser, but that did not make it the right thing for this young man.

She had projected her own interests on Annabelle—just assuming that, because Annabelle wrote well and *enjoyed* doing so, she should write the same sorts of academic tracts that Harriet had long produced. What an utterly narrow—and arrogant!—view to take.

Still, the person on whose life she may have wrought the most havoc was Marcus. Marcus, whom she had consistently misjudged. Marcus, who had such a way of quietly making things right. Marcus, whose very touch set her afire, whose teasing humor she treasured, whose generosity of spirit was unparalleled. Marcus, whom she loved more than life itself. She had kept producing those Gadfly treatises after she *knew* they were a threat to anyone remotely associated with them.

Moreover, it was time she reevaluated the essays themselves. What—truly—had all those statements of outrageous opinions achieved? Yes, she had brought some major issues to the public's attention. Yes, she had been faithful to the facts in dealing with those issues. But—perhaps a less abrasive approach would have been more effective. Making people in power angry and vindictive might be counter to the very reforms she had hoped to see. Melanie had put it very well—*Gadfly,* not the necessary reforms, had become the focus of attention.

Now it truly was only a matter of time until someone found out Gadfly—or, at the very least, associated *her* with the elusive writer. Now that Annabelle was returning to school and Freda and Charley were settled, there was no longer any reason—or excuse—for her to remain a part of the Earl of Wyndham's household.

With so many focusing on identifying Gadfly—ironic now that "he" was officially dead—she would leave for the Continent as soon as this Harvest Festival was over. She had already hinted as much to Charlotte.

As she started back, it began to rain in earnest. Wonderful! Harriet thought. Mother Nature weeps on the outside as I weep on the inside. She knew she had to present a carefree front, though, until she left Timberly.

The origins of the Harvest Festival were buried in antiquity, but Marcus knew it had begun as a religious festival of thanksgiving for bountiful crops. He surmised it had begun as a pagan celebration—possibly druid—and then been assimilated into Christian tradition. In any event, it now started with a church service in which farmers brought ritual offerings that were then distributed to the poor.

A market fair followed that lasted for three days. Here farmers sold their produce and livestock. Here, too, servants and laborers "sold" themselves—those who sought to change jobs would carry symbols of their particular calling and thus make themselves available to prospective employers. The fair included various sideshow entertainments, and organized games and races—and a great deal of dancing. Many a village romance began at the Harvest Festival.

For the common people, the festival ended with the fair spilling over into the street with a final dance and feast provided by the women of the parish. It was accompanied by a generous flow of drink. For the gentry, it culminated in a formal ball held in Timberly's Great Hall, which had once been the very heart of the castle.

The guest list for the ball included a vast number of local people, many of whom—like Thornton and Nichols—brought their outsider guests to add to those already at Timberly. Marcus knew the ladies had been working for days on decorations and food for the event. He was confident that this would be a most memorable harvest ball.

Later that idea would come back to haunt him.

The ball began well enough with a family receiving line to greet guests. Standing with Melanie and Andrew, and Trevor and Caitlyn, Marcus was happy to see many familiar faces, though he did suffer a twinge of jealousy when Dexter Taverner appeared with Captain and Mrs. Nichols and then appropriated Harriet's company while Marcus was trapped in the receiving line.

He shrugged off his jealousy. After all, Harriet had promised him two dances, one of which was a waltz. He looked forward with eager anticipation to having her in his arms again. He had hoped to have more time with her than he had so far managed since the return to Timberly. Perhaps when the festival was over . . .

Among the guests were not only the Thorntons but also their daughter Cynthia, Lady Teasler, and their houseguest, the Earl of Lynwood. Marcus had watched Lady Teasler and Lord Lynwood as they danced earlier. When he himself became her partner, he could not resist teasing her.

"There seems to be a certain aroma of April and May about you and Lynwood."

She laughed. "I did tell you—did I not?—that once I got him in the country . . ."

"So you did. I wish you both every happiness."

"Thank you, Marcus. But not quite yet. We will announce our happy news after Lynwood has a chance to inform his children."

"A ready-made family. That should be interesting for you."

"Yes." A worried frown appeared to mar the otherwise flawless beauty. "Can you see me as the wicked stepmother?"

"Wicked? Hardly, my dear. You will do well, I am sure."

"I do hope so."

Later, when he went to claim Harriet for their waltz, he found her chatting with Taverner and the Nichols couple. He knew—for he had kept tabs—that Taverner had called on her previously and that she had already danced twice tonight with Taverner. What *was* it with those two? Taverner was a good man—Marcus knew his reputation as a rake was deliberately cultivated and grossly exaggerated. However, Marcus Jeffries was not about to quit the field. He was inordinately pleased when she seemed as eager for their dance as he was. She quickly excused herself and simply glided into his arms.

Harriet was breathtakingly beautiful this night. She wore a gown of eggshell-colored silk, trimmed with just a scattering of appliquéd leaves in autumn shades. Her jewelry was simple antique gold. Her hair had been done in an elaborate twist atop her head with wispy curls allowed to trail on the sides.

What he *wanted* to do was waltz her out to the terrace and kiss her silly. He envisioned himself removing the pins holding up that glorious crown of hair and letting it drift through his fingers. What he *did* was engage in polite chitchat.

"You are looking in rare form this evening."

"Thank you. One might say the same of you, my lord. 'Tis a pity so few peers show to such advantage in evening wear."

"No. No," he said in mock sternness. "You are not doing this correctly. I am supposed to regale you with paeans to your beauty."

"Paeans? Oh, I do like that idea. Go ahead. I shall listen with eager anticipation, my lord."

"Now, what *have* I told you about 'my-lording' me?"

"Marcus."

"Very well. Here goes—

'She walks in beauty, like the night
Of cloudless climes and starry skies;
And all that's best of dark and bright
Meet in her aspect and her eyes . . .' "

She laughed, her eyes twinkling with warm pleasure. "Byron. I love that poem."

He gave an exaggerated groan. "Could you not at least *pretend* to believe the lines were my own?"

"Oh, I am *sooo* sorry. Did I ruin the effect?"

He grinned. "Of course you did. But never mind." His tone sobered. "The lines are Byron's, but the sentiment of them is mine."

She drew in a deep breath and held his gaze for what seemed an eternity. It was then that the normally staid and seemly former diplomat, peer of the realm, and proper gentleman, Lord Wyndham, threw caution to the winds. He waltzed her closer and closer to—and then through—the doors to the terrace.

She did not say a word as he nudged her into a secluded corner, pulled her into a tight embrace, and lowered his mouth to hers. There was no hesitation, no pretension in her response. Raw passion ruled both of them.

"My God! Harriet—"

"Oh, Marcus."

In the dim light tumbling from the windows, he could see tears shimmering in her eyes. Then he became aware that the music had stopped and other couples were spilling onto the terrace.

"We must talk," he said. "But not here and not now."

She nodded and readily allowed him to return her

to the Great Hall, where his duties as host of this grand affair claimed him and her next partner claimed her.

Somewhat later, Marcus stood on the sidelines with Melanie and Trevor and the spouses of his sister and brother. They all agreed that as harvest balls went, this one was a spectacular success. Marcus became aware of his butler trying to get his attention.

Morris held a salver on which lay calling cards. "There are two gentlemen here, my lord. They said they have come on official business."

Former diplomat that he was, Marcus was instantly alert. He glanced at Trevor, a former soldier, and Andrew, also a former diplomat, and saw that their reactions mirrored his own.

"Boney *cannot* have escaped again!" Trevor said.

"Surely not from St. Helena," Melanie agreed.

Marcus picked up the cards. "Bixby," he said. "And Montrose."

"Bixby? What can he want so far from Whitehall?" Andrew asked. "It must be something of import to drag Montrose away from his London club."

"I have an idea what it is," Marcus said, an ugly monster of apprehension grabbing at his gut. "I may need your support."

Excusing themselves to their wives, Trevor and Andrew accompanied Marcus to the entrance. There they found four men in travel clothes looking rather weary. Two were obviously "Quality" from their dress, and the other two appeared to Marcus to be Bow Street Runners.

"In here, gentlemen." He showed them to the library and closed the door. "Now—what is it that could not possibly wait until morning?"

Bixby, portly and pompous, looked inordinately smug. "We have come to arrest Mrs. Knightly."

Nineteen

"What? Have you gone mad?" Marcus asked. He could see that Trevor and Andrew were shocked by the bomb Bixby had lobbed into their midst.

"Well, we need to question her about this Gadfly person. We *know* she is associated with him and we are here to find the full extent of her involvement. If she refuses to cooperate, we shall arrest *her* for seditious behavior and take her to London to stand trial."

Marcus tried to control his fury and think. Apparently, Bixby had not yet concluded that Harriet and Gadfly were one.

Andrew addressed himself to Bixby. "Let me see if I understand you, my lord. You plan to arrest a *woman*—a gently bred one at that—for sedition because she *may* know something of a writer whom you cannot identify. Is that the right of it?"

Bixby seemed to squirm a bit at this. He turned red in the face and ran a finger around his apparently too-tight neckcloth. "We know that she knows who he is, and if she refuses to cooperate, we shall be taking her into custody."

There was steely calm in Lord Wyndham's voice. "Bixby, let me remind you that you are—at least at the moment—a guest on my estate. *I* am the authority in this district. You will not be seizing any of my guests and carrying them anywhere."

"Are you telling me, Wyndham, that you will protect

a traitor to the crown? That you will harbor a criminal? That you condone such blatant attacks on our great nation?" Bixby's voice rose with his blustering.

"I think we can do without the melodramatic bombast. And *my* credentials as a patriot are not under discussion." Marcus did not try to hide his contempt for the man. "I shall bring Mrs. Knightly here and you may ask your questions. But know this—and know it well—she will *not* be leaving Timberly in your company." He turned to his brother. "Trevor, offer our 'guests' a glass of wine, please, as I seek out Mrs. Knightly."

As he reentered the Great Hall, he spotted Melanie and Caitlyn first and went toward them.

"Bad news, I assume from your expression, big brother," Melanie said.

"Yes. Have you seen Harriet—Mrs. Knightly?" He knew Melanie would have noticed immediately his use of Harriet's given name.

"She was standing with Aunt Gertrude over near that jungle of potted trees a moment ago." Melanie gestured to an opposite corner of the hall.

"Can we help?" Caitlyn asked, apparently sensing his stress.

"Yes. I am sure she will welcome your presence during the coming interview. I—we—shall meet you in the library." He started to leave them, then turned back. "And find Charlotte and Berwyn. She will need them there, too."

"Of course, Marcus." He could see that Melanie and Caitlyn were mystified. "I cannot explain now. But—Mel? Caitlyn?"

"Yes?" they said nearly in unison.

"Do not be shocked at anything you hear. Anything."

"Very well." Melanie was even more puzzled now, he thought, but he trusted her to do as he had requested.

Marcus finally found Harriet in conversation with

Aunt Gertrude and several other guests. He wedged himself near his aunt and murmured, "Divert the attention of others while I remove Harriet from this gathering. Please."

To her credit, his aunt did not blink an eye, and at a lull in the conversation, she said, "I say, Lady Carstairs, did you not attend that grand banquet the Prince had at Brighton some weeks ago? I have been dying to hear about it."

Trust Aunt Gertrude, Marcus thought. Everyone knew how very much Lady Carstairs loved being able to brag about her associations with *ton* notables. He maneuvered himself next to Harriet and whispered, "Come with me."

Harriet was startled by the urgency in his voice, but she quickly excused herself from the group even as he did the same. Out in the hallway, he directed her to an anteroom off the main entrance.

"What is it, Marcus?"

"Bixby is here. He wants to question you about the Gadfly."

"G-Gadfly?" She was shocked into incoherence by the bluntness of his statement. She had been half expecting just this turn of events, but now she could not think straight.

"We have not much time, Harriet. Bixby does not seem to know who Gadfly is, so be very careful of what you say to him."

"Do you? Know, that is?"

"Yes, my love. I have known for some while."

"Oh." Her eyes searched his gaze and found only caring concern there. "I am so very sorry, Marcus. I should have told you—should never have involved you . . ." How could she bear the anguish of hurting him so? Of leaving him?

He pulled her close and held her tightly. "Never mind. We shall sort it all out later. Right now, however, the situation is rather dangerous. Bixby came to arrest you."

"Well, I shall go quietly. I promise not to embarrass you further, Marcus."

He grasped her shoulders and shook her gently. "Listen to me! And trust me."

"Yes, my lord—Marcus."

He smiled ever so briefly. "Whatever I say, you will offer no objection. Do you understand? No objection. None."

"I—very well." She was confused, but she knew she trusted him implicitly.

When they entered the library, Harriet was glad to see Melanie and Caitlyn there, too. She suspected Marcus had seen to that. The men rose until she was seated. Introductions were effected. The two Runners hovered in the background, and Lord Montrose seemed content to sit on the sidelines. Not so Lord Bixby.

Bixby was, she saw, a short, rotund man. Her immediate impression was of a man very conscious of his own consequence. She knew him to be fiercely conservative—even reactionary—in his politics. She feared he was, indeed, a danger to be reckoned with. He stood in front of the fireplace, ready to pass judgment. She sat in a round, barrel-type chair. Marcus remained standing just behind her.

"Ah, Mrs. Knightly. How nice that you could join us." There was a false note to Bixby's courtesy.

Just then the library door opened and Charlotte and Berwyn came in.

"What is it, Harriet? What is happening?" Charlotte was clearly alarmed.

"Just a misunderstanding, I think," Harriet answered.

Bixby gave Marcus a sour look. "I would have preferred a less public gathering for the questions I have to pose." His gaze swept over the others in the room.

"We view this as a family matter," Marcus said.

Harriet wondered at this, but had she not agreed she would offer no objections? She glanced at Trevor and Melanie and saw them regard their brother with a certain degree of curiosity. Charlotte seemed ready to leap to her defense no matter what. She noticed Berwyn's steadying hand on Charlotte's arm.

"Yes, well . . ." Bixby sputtered. "Now, Mrs. Knightly, it would appear that you are involved in some quite nefarious activities."

"I am not certain I understand you, my lord."

"Oh, come now. Do not pretend ignorance with *me*. I am sure his lordship told you of our mission on behalf of His Majesty's government."

"Yes, he told me you are searching for a writer known as the Gadfly."

"And did he also tell you we have reason to believe *you* are intimately connected to that scoundrel?"

Charlotte gasped.

"I? You believe me to be—"

Bixby made an impatient, dismissive gesture. "Cut line, woman. You were seen in the company of that editor, Watson."

"I *am* acquainted with Mr. Watson," she admitted. "We belong to the same literary society."

"And you have met with him privately on at least two occasions that we know of—in bookshops. He was followed by one of our men." Bixby waved at the Bow Street Runners.

"I may have done so. But I fail to see why a chance meeting in a bookshop—of two people who love books—would be of interest to you."

"Actually, we, too, had dismissed those as 'chance' meetings—until we searched Watson's office and desk." He paused dramatically.

Harriet refused to give him the satisfaction of a response, but she experienced a moment of sheer panic. What *could* they have found? She felt Marcus give her a comforting squeeze of her shoulder.

"Well, madam. What do you suppose we found?"

"I am sure I have no idea."

"We found records of payments for articles written by the Gadfly. They carried notations that indicated the payments were made to you." Bixby's tone had taken on a triumphant note.

Andrew Sheffield had been attending all this with an expression of disbelief. "Are you seriously suggesting a *woman* is the Gadfly?"

"Well, now, she *could* be," Bixby said defensively. "What *is* apparent is that Mrs. Knightly knows his identity and has been acting as a conduit for his particular brand of treason."

"This is preposterous," Charlotte said.

Bixby ignored her and addressed Harriet again. "You are—at the very least—guilty of helping to promote sedition, madam. However, your association with Wyndham here makes this a rather delicate matter."

"Just what do you mean by that?" Marcus demanded.

"The Prime Minister prefers to avoid having any taint of scandal associated with members of his party. That includes you, Wyndham. Therefore, we are prepared to be lenient with Mrs. Knightly. *If* she gives up the identity of the Gadfly, she will be allowed to go into—shall we say—voluntary exile. Otherwise, she will be tried for sedition."

"Nooo. No. No!" Charlotte wailed.

Bixby gave Charlotte a scathing look. "I did say this interview should have been more private."

"This 'interview' has gone quite far enough," Marcus said, giving Harriet's shoulder a reassuring pat. "Mrs. Knightly cannot give you the Gadfly's identity. And that is that."

"Are you telling me she does not know the man? We have evidence to the contrary."

"She cannot—with honor—give up information she has promised to withhold. Besides, the matter is irrelevant, for Gadfly is no longer in England and has no plans to return."

"Are you sure of that, my lord?" Bixby's eyes narrowed suspiciously. "How can you be sure of that?"

"I have Mrs. Knightly's word on it."

"I am afraid that will not be good enough for the rest of us in the government, Lord Wyndham." Bixby was being insufferably condescending and smug, Harriet thought. And to Marcus!

Again Marcus placed his hand on her shoulder. "I am sorry, my dear," he said in a private aside to her that was clearly audible to all the others. "I think we must tell them."

Thoroughly confused at his tone and the open endearment, she looked up at him. "If you think—"

He squeezed her shoulder firmly. She felt the warning he conveyed and fell silent.

"Mrs. Knightly's word may not be good enough for some of you," Marcus said. "However, I think the word of the Countess of Wyndham will be accepted even in Carlton House."

There was a long, pregnant pause, then the room erupted in squeals of delight from the other women in the room and approving comments from the men.

"Marcus—" Harriet started to say.

"I know we said we would wait until the end of the ball to make the announcement, my love," Marcus said. "But you can see that Bixby has forced my hand. You have rather ruined our surprise, Bixby," he added, seemingly annoyed. "I am not best pleased at that."

Bixby turned blustery again. "I am sure you understand the extraordinary nature of our mission . . ."

"Yes. And now it is over. I doubt there will be any who care to accuse *my wife* of treasonable offenses."

His tone left it clear that one might do so only at the greatest peril for his own skin.

Bixby knew when he had been defeated. He bowed stiffly and motioned his three companions to accompany him out of the room. When they were gone, the voices rose again in pleased congratulations and good wishes and comments of "you sly devil" or "you clever puss." Finally, Harriet rose and was able to make herself heard.

"My Lord Wyndham! Might I have a private word with you?"

"Of course, my love."

"Not a word of this in the hall," she admonished the others.

They immediately sobered, looking from Marcus to Harriet, but other than nodding their agreement, no one said anything as they, too, left the room. When the door had clicked shut, Marcus and Harriet were left to stand and stare at each other.

"Oh, Marcus, what *have* you done? How can we untangle this mess?"

"What is there to untangle? We shall simply marry, and there's an end of it."

"You cannot be serious."

"I was never more serious in my life."

"I do thank you most sincerely for your protection. You have, I think, bought me some time. I had intended to travel on the Continent as soon as the Harvest Festival is over."

"Splendid. It will be our honeymoon journey."

"Marcus! I will not have you thinking you must go through with this charade. I have had one marriage of convenience. As such marriages go, mine was a success, but you must marry someone you can love—someone like . . . like Lady Teasler."

"I am trying to do exactly that," he said with a great show of patience. "Besides, Cynthia is marrying Lynwood."

"Oh. You cannot have the woman you want, so you will take me—is that it?" She turned her back to him.

"Harriet, try not to be such a peagoose. I love you. I want to marry you because I love you." He took a step closer and wrapped his arms around her. He nuzzled her neck. "What is more, I believe you love me, too."

She turned in his arms and hid her face against his chest. "Oh, Marcus. I do love you. I have loved you forever. Ever since you rescued that kitten for me. But I cannot marry you."

"Why? You are not promised to someone else, are you?"

"N-no." She bit her lip. "But I cannot give you an heir."

He lifted her chin and held her gaze. "Do you know that for a certainty?"

She nodded and felt unshed tears in her eyes. "I—I think so. I was married for over ten years . . ."

"That may not mean you are incapable of having a child. . . . I admit that I should like to have children of my own, but, Harriet, my own love, I *have* an heir. And Trevor has two sons. I want to marry *you*."

He kissed her eyes, her nose, the corners of her mouth, and finally settled his lips on hers, willing her to respond. And just as she had on the terrace earlier, she became lost in the wonder of the moment.

"Does this mean you *will* marry me?" he finally murmured in a husky voice.

"Only if you ask me properly," she said.

He stepped back and gently pushed her into the chair she had vacated moments before. He sank to one knee and held up his hand in a gesture of supplication. "My darling Harriet, *will* you marry me?"

She put her finger to her cheek in a pretense of thinking it over, then threw her arms around his neck and between kisses said, "Yes! Yes! Yes!"

"Tonight?" he asked, rising and pulling her up against him, holding her tightly.

"Tonight! You must be mad." She laughed. "One cannot marry just like that." She snapped her fingers.

He grinned. "One can if one has a special license."

"But we—"

"Have such a document. And among our guests in the Great Hall is a qualified vicar."

"But why—? How—?"

"I meant it to be a means of protecting you if it proved necessary. I feared they might really discover the Gadfly, you see."

"And you—?

"And I could not risk losing you."

"Oh, Marcus." She pulled his head down for another long, deep kiss.

"Tonight?" he repeated.

"Why not?"

And thus it was that the harvest ball at Timberly that year—a memorable event, indeed—ended as a wedding celebration.

Epilogue

Autumn 1819

The Countess of Wyndham sat at a table in the library of the Earl of Wyndham's London town house, writing out invitations for the house party and the grand ball that would be a part of the Harvest Festival at Timberly this year. Her husband sat at his desk, trying—without much liking for the task, she thought—to make sense of yet another parliamentary proposal for dealing with worker unrest in the midlands.

"What is it, darling? Something with which I might help you?" she asked when he had heaved a heavy sigh and seemed to be staring off into space more than writing.

"I swear, Harriet, sometimes I think we should just go to Timberly and hide ourselves away until this country comes to its senses." He gestured at the paper on his desk. "The Toriest of Tories have struck again! Their method of dealing with workers is yet more repression. Do they not see how futile that route is?"

"Oooh. Careful, my dear. You are beginning to sound like a reformist."

"Perhaps *I* should resurrect the Gadfly and let him deal with some of their idiotic ideas." His grin told her this was far from a serious idea.

She gave him an arch look. "Is this coming from the man who convinced me that it was far more effective, if not quite so expedient, to try to bring about reform from *within* the government?"

He came from behind the desk to bend over her and trail kisses along her neck. "Still, does the idea not appeal to you?" he murmured.

"That you should start writing as the Gadfly? Good heavens, no. Besides, it is not your style."

"No. I meant hiding away at Timberly." He brought his lips to hers and teased her into a quick response that was about to get out of hand.

"Marcus." She laughed. "I must finish these invitations—and I believe you have other matters to attend as well."

"None so pressing that they cannot wait," he said, "but very well, if you must refuse me my husbandly rights, so be it. But know this, madam—you will pay and pay and pay later."

"Promise?"

"Promise." He allowed his hand to caress her cheek before turning back to his task.

Just then there was a rap on the door. "Come," he called, and Annabelle swept into the room. It occurred to Harriet that Annabelle never did anything at a totally sedate pace.

"I have just come from the nursery," she announced. "That child is the most beautiful babe in the world. And he is sooo smart! I think he will be a writer! I am sure he is already learning his letters. You should see him with those blocks that have letters and numbers."

Harriet laughed. "Annabelle! He is only a year old! Stop planning our son's life for him already."

Annabelle lifted her chin in a look of sham hurt. "But I thought that was what godmothers were supposed to do—wave magic wands and make everything turn out right."

"No, no." Marcus said. "That is what *novelists* do.

And, you, my dear, did that very well with the newest venture. I liked it even better than the first one."

"Did you really?" she asked eagerly. "I do believe my skills are improving. I am longing to attempt satire, but I have not yet come up with a proper subject."

"How will you find the time?" Harriet wondered. "You have been out nearly every night for the past month. Since your come-out this house has rivaled Bethlehem Hospital as a madhouse."

"I know. Is it not just too ridiculous? Letty and I have taken vows never to marry."

Marcus gave a derisive snort at this. "I have already fended off three would-be suitors for your hand when you would have none of them. I doubt you will be able to hold out forever."

"Why would you vow never to marry?" Harriet asked. "I can vouch for its being a most enjoyable institution." She gave Marcus one of her secret smiles.

Annabelle sighed. "If one could be sure of marrying for love—as you have. But Letty is pursued for her title and connections and I because the word is out that my father left me a great fortune. It is so very lowering to know that one is not pursued for herself alone."

"You will be. In time," Harriet assured her. "In the meantime, I could use some help planning the Harvest Festival. We need to come up with something special for this year's ball."

Annabelle laughed. "It will be rather difficult to top your wedding of the year before and last year's christening of my favorite godchild! But let me consider . . . perhaps I can come up with something. . . ."

ABOUT THE AUTHOR

Wilma Counts lives in Nevada. She is currently working on her sixth Zebra Regency romance, *Miss Richardson Comes of Age*, which will be published in November 2001. Wilma loves hearing from readers, and you may write to her c/o Zebra Books. Please include a self-addressed stamped envelope if you wish a response, or e-mail her at <u>wilma@ableweb.net</u>.

More Zebra Regency Romances

Put a Little Romance in Your Life With
Betina Krahn

BOOK YOUR PLACE ON OUR WEBSITE AND MAKE THE READING CONNECTION!

We've created a customized website just for our very special readers, where you can get the inside scoop on everything that's going on with Zebra, Pinnacle and Kensington books.

When you come online, you'll have the exciting opportunity to:

- View covers of upcoming books

- Read sample chapters

- Learn about our future publishing schedule (listed by publication month *and author*)

- Find out when your favorite authors will be visiting a city near you

- Search for and order backlist books from our online catalog

- Check out author bios and background information

- Send e-mail to your favorite authors

- Meet the Kensington staff online

- Join us in weekly chats with authors, readers and other guests

- Get writing guidelines

- AND MUCH MORE!

Visit our website at http://www.zebrabooks.com